Witch Rising

BY PAIGE MCKENZIE AND NANCY OHLIN

B*Witch

Witch Rising

Witch Rising

A B*Witch Novel

PAIGE MCKENZIE
AND NANCY OHLIN

LITTLE, BROWN AND COMPANY

New York Boston

Copyright © 2021 by Paige McKenzie and Nancy Ohlin
Cover art copyright © 2021 by Sweeney Boo
Cover copyright © 2021 by Hachette Book Group, Inc.

Little, Brown and Company
Hachette Book Group
1290 Avenue of the Americas, New York, NY 10104
Visit us at LBYR.com

First Edition: September 2021

Little, Brown and Company is a division of Hachette Book Group, Inc.
The Little, Brown name and logo are trademarks
of Hachette Book Group, Inc.

The publisher is not responsible for websites (or their content)
that are not owned by the publisher.

Library of Congress Cataloging-in-Publication Data
Names: McKenzie, Paige, author. Ohlin, Nancy, author.
Title: Witch rising : a B*witch novel / Paige McKenzie and Nancy Ohlin.
Description: First edition. | New York : Little, Brown and Company, 2021. |
Series: B*witch ; book 2 | Audience: Ages 12 & up. | Summary: "In this sequel,
the two covens work together, and harder than ever, to fight against the New Order,
a rising anti-magic group that's sprung up in their hometown"— Provided by publisher.
Identifiers: 2020056048 | ISBN 9780759557697 (hardcover) |
ISBN 9780759557673 (ebook) | ISBN 9780759557680 (ebook other)
Subjects: Witchcraft—Fiction. | High schools—Fiction. | Schools—Fiction.
Classification: PZ7.M19863214 Wit 2021 | DDC [Fic]—dc23
LC record available at https://lccn.loc.gov/2020056048

ISBNs: 978-0-7595-5769-7 (hardcover), 978-0-7595-5767-3 (ebook)

Printed in the United States of America

LSC-C

Printing 1, 2021

To Jens. You fill my life with love and light and magic every day.

—NEO

*To all the inspiring witches who came before…
Sally and Gillian Owens, Kiki, the Sanderson sisters,
Glinda, Minerva, Lamia, Elphaba, and last but
not least, Howl. May your magic live on.*

—PM

We grow accustomed to the Dark—
When Light is put away—

—EMILY DICKINSON

THE TEA WITH T

Hey, listeners! Thanks for joining me on the podcast premiere of *The Tea with T*. That's *tea* as in the drink, and the letter *T* as in my initial. I'll be coming to you each week with the hot tea on all things magical, mystical, and mundane...and of course, my favorite tea recipes!

Today, I'll be talking to you about Callixta Crowe's Descendant. That's *Descendant* with a capital *D*...because there must be many Callixta descendants out there, and it's important to keep *the* Descendant separate from the rest.

So I've been trying to solve the mystery of the Descendant's identity for a while now. Here's what I have so far, and bear with me because it's complicated:

FACTS:

She—I will use *she/her/hers* pronouns for now, although the Descendant could also be male-identifying or have another gender-expansive identity—first made herself known on March 12, 2016. She wrote and posted a letter on several deepsites, like w/witchworld and other hidden locations, and basically blew up everything we thought we knew about witches and witchcraft.

What we knew, pre-Descendant, was that some portion of the population identified as witches and practiced witchcraft throughout history. It was a generally accepted thing until 1877, when the government passed an anti-witchcraft law called Title 6, Section 129, and the Great Witch Purge happened. Hundreds—no, thousands—of witches were hunted down and executed, including Callixta herself. Since then, witches have mostly practiced in total secrecy, including me. Over time, the authorities became less strict about enforcing 6-129. Until now.

The Descendant came forward and warned us in her letter that things are changing. In addition to stricter enforcement of 6-129, there are new anti-witch forces at work, mainly in the government and through a hate movement that seems to be growing more aggressive and violent every day.

The Descendant's letter wasn't all bad news, though. She also shared Callixta's previously unknown theories and scientific findings regarding witches, which are very illuminating. Plus, she posted a link to a partial manual by Callixta called *The Good Book of Magic and Mentalism*. That was the first time I—and I'm sure many other witches—learned about spells and potions, about the fact we aren't alone in the world, and that there is a secret community of witches out there practicing in private.

The Descendant's letter and link to Callixta's book disappeared after twenty-four hours, but not before they presumably went viral.

RUMOR & SPECULATION:

There have been names tossed around on deepsites about who the Descendant might be. A biologist at MIT. A high school technology teacher in Atlanta. A flower-shop owner in Cleveland. Also some famous people, like the gamer Xandri. The artist Ekon Uba, who died last year—although people say he didn't actually die but is in hiding. And even the US president's oldest daughter, Karine Ingraham.

MY PERSONAL THEORIES:

I've tried a number of advanced identity spells, some from Callixta's book and some that I developed on my own, but they haven't resulted in anything solid. I've also tried some of my divination tea blends, but no luck there, either.

Lately, I've been leaning toward the Karine Ingraham theory. I suspect the death of Elsa, her younger sister and an alleged witch, turned their dad into a ragingly anti-witch politician, and those events could have motivated her to post that letter and link. But I don't have any proof, and neither does anyone else, as far as I know. Of course, the White House has publicly denied that anyone in the Ingraham family has anything to do with witches or witchcraft.

WHERE TO GO FROM HERE:

Recently, I've been experimenting with some old-school methods to solve the mystery of the Descendant's identity. Like codes—I've tried bifid and Amsco and some other ciphers, but nothing. I will continue along these lines, though, and maybe create more divination tea blends. I will be sure to report on further developments.

In the meantime...things are bad for witches, here in my new hometown and everywhere else. But it's important not to lose hope. As Callixta says, "It's when things seem darkest that we must find the dying flame within us and breathe it back to life."

Keep breathing, fellow witches. Don't give up.

And someday soon, when all is safe and well, I can tell you what the letter *T* in *The Tea with T* stands for.

Now for today's tea recipe...

PROLOGUE

She was supposed to be dead.

She remembered dying as clearly as if it had happened yesterday. Although to be honest, concepts like "yesterday" had little meaning for her anymore.

How could she describe what she'd been doing this past...whatever? Taking a nap. Dreaming. Floating in the sea. Riding her favorite horse into an endless sunset.

Honestly, it wasn't that different from living. Just fuzzier. More solitary. Also, no Internet.

Something new was happening, though. The creature—the *thing*—wanted her awake again, alive and earthbound. She'd been resisting, but her resistance was starting to dissipate. Was the creature growing stronger, or was she growing weaker? Or was she missing the big picture? Was the life-death dichotomy not a dichotomy at all? Should she trust the darkness and jump into the void again?

She would research this online once she returned, *if* she returned, and maybe vlog about it, too.

But for now...whatever "now" was...she would go back to her lovely nap and dream about love. And light.

PART 1

DARKNESS FALLING

Does Nature provide a way to destroy evil
without resorting to destruction? Is there
such a thing as a beneficent poison?

(FROM THE GRIMOIRE OF GRETA YSABEL NAVARRO)

1

ENEMY TERRITORY

A sign can appear in many forms.
Your intuition will yield the
most authentic interpretation.

(FROM *THE GOOD BOOK OF MAGIC AND MENTALISM*
BY CALLIXTA CROWE)

The forest air was cool and damp as Ridley stepped carefully along the trail, keeping a distance behind the others. Her polished brown loafers sank into the loamy earth, and mud peppered her new khakis. Why hadn't she worn hiking boots and jeans? But she'd rushed out of the house this morning, not remembering that the Kai Rain Forest field trip was today.

She used to be more organized than this. Laying out outfits the night before, keeping elaborate color-coded to-do lists, constantly updating her electronic calendar. The stress of the past month had been getting to her, obviously. If only she could deploy *cessabit* to center herself and maybe *tersus* to clean up a bit. *Yeah, dream on.*

Also, *stress* wasn't the exact right word. *Upheaval* would be more accurate. Or *trauma*. Or *calamity*. Or how about *end-of-the-world disaster of epic proportions*?

Up front, Mr. Terada was walking backward, tour-guide-style, and lecturing to the students off a pile of index cards.

"So, the main theater of the American Civil War was in the East and South. That's 'theater' as in a military theater where battles take place, not a movie theater," he said with a grin. "But there were other theaters besides the eastern and southern ones. In fact, regiments were stationed in the Pacific Northwest, including right here in the Kai Rain Forest, in case the Confederates attempted a sneak attack by sea."

Ridley knew a lot about rain forests—last year, she'd written a research paper for freshman bio about regeneration strategies, and she'd turned in three times the minimum two thousand words—but she hadn't known there were rain forests in Washington. Looking around, she marveled at the tall, curved trees that were covered entirely with lush green moss and were strangely human-looking. At times, they seemed to close in on the trail like a Hansel-and-Gretel ecosystem on steroids. At other times, the trail was more open, flanked by small fields of grass, ferns, and wildflowers. Ridley found it fascinating that this surreal and eerily beautiful landscape had a military backstory.

"We're going to connect up with another trail soon. That trail will take us to the ruins of a fortress where Union troops were garrisoned," Mr. Terada explained.

Mr. Terada, with his man bun and flannel shirt and faded denim jacket tied around his waist, looked barely older than the students. He was already sub number four in US history this year, and it was only October. Ms. Hua, their regular history teacher, was out on maternity leave. The first sub, Ms. O'Shea, had left in September because of a family emergency. Sub number two, Mr. Eggars, had broken his arm in a boating accident in Puget Sound.

Sub number three, Ms. Gillespie, had been fired last week for wearing a pentagram amulet. She'd claimed it was just a cheap piece of Halloween jewelry from the mall, but Principal Sparkleman had refused to hear her out. Presumably, he couldn't take the chance that a Sorrow Point High employee, even a temporary one, might be in violation of Title 6 of the US Comprehensive Code, Section 129. Might be a witch.

"Here's an interesting piece of pre–Civil War trivia. Did you guys know there were territorial disputes in this area between the British and the Americans? Have any of you ever heard of the Pig War of 1859?" Mr. Terada asked.

"Bored out of your mind yet?"

Ridley whirled around to see who had spoken to her. Boxer braids, black leather jacket. Aysha Rodriguez.

"I-I didn't know anyone was behind me," Ridley stammered. She'd made a point of hanging back so she could be alone.

"Well, I can be very super-sneaky," Aysha replied without smiling. She rarely smiled.

"What do you want?"

"That's nice. Hello to you, too."

Ridley furrowed her brow. Seriously, why on earth was Aysha talking to her? She was technically a rival, i.e., a member of Div Florescu's coven.

Although Ridley's best friend, Binx, was now a member of that coven, too, so maybe she should be thinking less . . . divisively?

"I guess you're in one of Ms. Hua's other history sections?" Ridley asked politely.

"Yup. Fourth period. Have you heard when she's coming back?"

"I heard January or maybe later."

"Huh. So what happened to the first sub? O'Shea, right? Did she really have a quote-unquote 'family emergency' or—"

"Oh my gosh, look at that adorable squirrel!" Ridley said loudly. "*Calumnia*," she whispered into the collar of her white oxford shirt, trying to move her lips as little as possible. With a *calumnia* spell, anyone listening would think that she and Aysha were discussing hairstyles or homecoming or some other equally banal topic.

Of course, Ridley shouldn't be using *any* magic in public, but Aysha had forced her hand. What had the girl been *thinking*?

"What squirrel? And why did you do *calumnia*?" Aysha asked, frowning.

"I'm sure there's a squirrel around here somewhere. And why didn't *you* do *calumnia*?"

"Because our bossy overlords, I mean our beloved coven leaders, said we're not allowed to? Besides, people can't hear us back here, and no one cares about some rando sub."

Bossy overlords? *Interesting.* Ridley had never heard Aysha describe Div that way, although it was 100 percent accurate. Greta, not so much, although she *could* be bossy when the mood struck her. Mostly, she was like a nervous mother hen.

"Ms. O'Shea is a *witch*," Ridley reminded Aysha. "If anyone here is aware of that fact, and they thought we were connected to her..."

Her voice trailed off as she glanced worriedly at the pack up ahead, at the three dozen or so sophomores trailing behind Mr. Terada. She wished her coven-mates were here—she always felt better, felt stronger, in their presence—but Greta and Iris had Mr. Lemire for history. So did Binx.

Ridley's other ex-coven-mate—or, more accurately, her ex-*almost*-coven-mate—wasn't here, either. Penelope Hart. A transfer student from Ojala Heights, she used to be in Ridley's history section at the very beginning of the year. Used to be, until she died...was murdered for being a witch. The police had ruled it a suicide, but the two covens, Greta's and Div's, knew better. They were in the process of figuring out who the killer was so they could be brought to justice. Which wouldn't be easy, given that the entire country seemed to be consumed by an anti-magic fever.

Penelope. Ridley's chest tightened at the thought of her. They'd been just starting to become friends before she died. And they might have become more than friends, or at least that's what Ridley had wanted....

Aysha's voice cut into her thoughts.

"Do you guys have a theory about what happened to O'Shea?"

"*Calumnia*," Ridley repeated, to make doubly sure that they were safe, even though *calumnia* didn't really work that way. "We don't know if Ms. O'Shea really had a family emergency or not. Greta and Iris and I've been trying to locate her, but she never gave us her contact info, and none of the usual scrying spells have helped."

"Huh." Aysha seemed to consider this. "The laptop witch mentioned O'Shea at our last coven meeting, which is why I was thinking about her."

The laptop witch? "Is that what you call Binx?"

"Yeah. You know, if the name fits..."

Ridley's BFF happened to be a cyber-witch who was skilled at inter-facing computer code with magic spells. Binx kept her grimoire on her phone, and her wand, Kricketune, was permanently disguised as a gaming console. But...*laptop witch*? Ridley wondered if Aysha had a funny-not-funny nickname for her, too.

"How's she doing, anyway? I mean, is she happy in your coven, or..."

"Dunno," Aysha said, shrugging. "If it were up to me, I'd send her back to your coven ASAP. She's a bad fit. You guys are into your cute l'il healing potions and world-peace spells and all that crap. Our coven is into much more hardcore stuff. *Real* magic. But I'm not the leader; I don't make those decisions." She added, "Besides, don't you and the laptop witch hang out? Ask her yourself."

"Yeah…"

That was another piece of Ridley's recent stress, upheaval, etc. Binx's coven switching hadn't been an easy, amicable transition. Rather, it had been triggered by a drama-filled falling out with Greta. Binx had wanted their coven to be more aggressive against the radical anti-magic groups—the Antima, not to be confused with Antifa, which stood for "antifascist"—that were proliferating across the country. Binx had suggested to Greta that their coven join forces with a secret witches' rights organization called Libertas, which she'd apparently learned about from an online gamer friend named ShadowKnight. In response, Greta had read Binx the riot act, saying they couldn't trust some random Internet stranger who might or might not be who he claimed to be. They'd argued, and Binx had stormed off, saying that if Greta wouldn't support her in her quest against the Antima, she knew a coven leader who would.…

It was so bizarre. Binx had always disliked, even despised, Div. Not to mention, she'd had a not-so-playful prank war going with Aysha and with Div's other underling, Mira Jahani, since forever. Although, it wasn't like Binx had a lot of options. As far as they knew, Div's and Greta's were the only covens at their school…and in all of Sorrow Point.

Mostly, Ridley just really, really missed Binx, who'd been her closest friend since beginning of freshman year. Sure, they saw each other at school, and they still texted lots and exchanged goofy memes and GIFs. But soon after Penelope's death, Div had upped the frequency of her coven meetings to practically daily. So between those meetings and everything else in her life, Binx always seemed to be too busy for shopping, sleepovers, and their other beloved rituals.

Aysha was jabbing Ridley with her elbow.

"See him?" Aysha jutted her chin in the direction of a red-haired guy who was standing near Mr. Terada. Francisco something. "He's wearing that ugly camo hoodie now, but, this morning—he's in my homeroom—I noticed he had an Antima patch on his T-shirt. There." She touched a spot on her left shoulder. "I'm pretty sure he didn't have a patch on his clothes last week. Might be a new recruit?"

"*Another* one?"

"Right? It seems like there's another new recruit at our school every day. Soon, it'll be the entire student body."

Ridley shuddered.

"I think those two girls are new recruits, too," Aysha said with another chin jut. "Valerie Yeargan and that girl with the ponytail who's talking to the blond dude. Sylvia...no, Siobhan. I saw them with Orion Kong yesterday, and as we all know, he's basically the Antima poster boy of Sorrow Point High." She sniffed. "I could have predicted Valerie. She's a jerk and a racist. It makes sense she's anti-magic, too."

"This is why we need to be using *calumnia* right now, okay? Even though we're not supposed to," Ridley said in a tense voice. "That's three possible, probable, Antima members on this field trip. At least. If they figure out we're witches, they'll turn us in to the authorities in a heartbeat."

Just then, Mr. Terada caught Ridley's eye and gave her a small wave. Ridley smiled uncertainly and rainbow-waved back. What did he want? Was he signaling to her—and Aysha, too—that they should stop chatting and pay more attention to his index-card commentary about pig wars and such? Or was he simply being friendly? Or...

They'd reached a fork in the trail. *Oh, so maybe that's why he was waving. Because we're stopping.* Mr. Terada turned to consult a worn wooden sign at the intersection of the two paths. The students bunched up in a semicircle behind him, waiting. Ridley and Aysha joined them at the rear.

"All right, the Union garrison is this way," Mr. Terada said, pointing. He untied his denim jacket from his waist and shrugged it on.

That's when Ridley saw it. Mr. Terada's jacket was decorated with patches and enamel pins. Wedged between a *Super Mario* Princess Peach pin and a *Star Trek* United Federation of Planets pin was a patch with a cage suspended over a bonfire.

An Antima patch.

Aysha elbowed her again, harder this time. She must have seen it, too. Ridley responded with an almost imperceptible nod. Up until now, they'd been aware only of Antima *students* at their school. There were Antima *teachers*, too?

Aysha, who usually exuded total fearlessness, showed a glimmer of fear as she pivoted toward Ridley.

"Soooo. Are you going to the Homecoming Dance?" she asked casually.

It was not a *calumnia*-scrambled question. With this new revelation about Mr. Terada, Aysha had apparently abandoned any attempt at magic talk, *calumnia* or no. Ridley was right there with her.

"Um, maybe? How about you?"

"Yeah, I kind of have to. I'm on the organizing committee."

"Excuse me, what?" Ridley couldn't picture that. "*You're* on the organizing committee?"

"Yeah. Long story. Div's on it, too, and Mira and Binx just joined. Anyway, you should go. It's gonna be lit."

"Um . . . okay?"

As the two girls continued fake-discussing homecoming, Ridley side-eyed Mr. Terada and wondered how many other adults at Sorrow Point High wanted to see witches rounded up and arrested...

...or eliminated. Like poor, sweet Penelope.

The afternoon sky, or what Ridley could see of it through the dense canopy of moss-covered hemlocks and cedars, had turned an ominous dark gray. An approaching storm. The air felt thick and charged with electricity, and mist blanketed their feet. Ridley wondered if they would make it back to the school vans in the parking lot before the rain started.

Aysha was up ahead, snapping photos of birds and insects with her phone. The other students were scattered about, taking pictures or just talking. Ridley and Aysha had decided that it might look suspicious for them to be huddling and whispering during the entire field trip, even with *calumnia* obscuring the true nature of their conversations, and so they'd split up before lunch and barely spoken to each other since.

Now, in hindsight, Ridley wished she hadn't deployed *calumnia* at all. Just recently, Greta had made the executive decision that their coven shouldn't use witchcraft in public unless it was an emergency, and Div had declared the same for her coven. The two covens had always used magic surreptitiously because of 6-129, but now, they had to restrict themselves even more. After what had happened to Penelope, and with the ever-increasing Antima presence, they couldn't afford to be discovered.

You have to be more careful, Ridley chided herself.

A shimmering haze through the trees caught her attention. She blinked.

Is that...?

No, it can't be.

But it is.

Tucked away in the middle of the Hansel-and-Gretel rain forest was a house. Not an ordinary house—a mansion. Gothic-style, with a steeply pitched roof and gables.

And Ridley wasn't seeing just the outside of the mansion. She could see the interior, too, as though the walls were invisible. A roaring fire in the grate. A velvet settee. A round mahogany table.

Ridley gritted her teeth to stifle any emotion, any reaction, lest she call attention to herself. There couldn't possibly be a mansion in the middle of the rain forest. Or *any* structure...granted, there was the Union garrison that Mr. Terada had shown them earlier, but that had been just a pile of ruins, the crumbling remains of a stone wall. Surely, this "mansion" had to be an optical illusion? An alchemy of mist and Ridley's own agitated mood?

She blinked again.

On top of the round mahogany table, thirteen unlit candles suddenly materialized, encircled by a ring of gems and herbs.

"*Aysha!*" Ridley burst out before she could stop herself.

Aysha was a few yards away, photographing a cluster of dark purple mushrooms. She rose to her feet and scowled at Ridley. "Yeah? What?"

Ridley noticed that Valerie and Siobhan and Francisco had stopped midconversation and were looking with interest at her and Aysha. Mr. Terada was, too.

Quick, make something up.

Ridley pointed in the direction of the mansion. "Um...could you take a picture of those cool trees? My phone's out of battery."

Aysha cocked her head. "Sure, because I'm your personal photographer?"

"Please?"

Aysha sighed and snapped a few quick photos. By her bland demeanor, it was clear to Ridley that she couldn't see the mansion.

"I'll text them to you when we have service," Aysha said.

"Thanks."

"You're not welcome."

Ridley turned her attention back to the mansion. Someone—or something?—had lit the candles on the mahogany table. Thirteen tiny flames flickered, illuminating the gems and herbs—black onyx, bloodstone, mugwort, wolfsbane....

What. The. Hex.

A second later, the sky flashed silver, and it began to rain—huge, pelting drops.

"This way!" Mr. Terada shouted as the students covered their heads with their backpacks and began running in the direction of the parking lot.

As Ridley turned to go, she swiped the rain out of her eyes and glanced at the mansion one last time.

It had vanished.

2

KRUSHING

Feelings are a potent weapon.

(FROM *THE GOOD BOOK OF MAGIC AND MENTALISM*
BY CALLIXTA CROWE)

Alone in the girls' bathroom, Iris peered into the mirror and smiled. She tried a smile *with* teeth, then without teeth, then with teeth again. *Definitely with teeth.*

"Oh, hey, Greta! Fancy meeting you here!" Iris said to her reflection.

Sounds forced.

"Oh, hey, Greta! Long time no see!"

Same.

"Sup, Greta?"

Ugh. No.

"Hi, Greta!" *Better.* Iris added a hair flip. "So, yeah…what are you doing on November eleventh? Oh, is that the Homecoming Dance? Gosh, I totally forgot! Well…uh…so, since we're on the subject, do you want to go? You know, as friends? We could invite Ridley and Binx to come with us. Except, oops, I forgot, Binx is our mortal enemy now. You're right, maybe 'mortal enemy' is a bit harsh. How about just plain old 'enemy'? It's a dilemma either way, or *quel dilemme*, as we say in Madame Moutillet's French class. Anyhoo, so, maybe we could just go, the three of us? You and me and Ridley? Or it could be just the two of us, you and me, and…and…and…"

Iris's voice was rising in a semihysterical crescendo. *Breathe, relax*, she told herself.

"…no, it wouldn't be a date, exactly," she continued in a lower, slower voice. "Unless you want it to be a date. Do *you* want it to be a date? Because if you want it to be a date, well, I'd be down with that. I've never been to a Homecoming Dance with a date. Actually, I've never been to a Homecoming Dance. Actually, I've never been on a date with another person, I mean, I've never been on a date *not* with another person, either, since by definition dates are with other people, and…*argh*!"

She stopped and face-palmed and shook her head. In the mirror, her doppelgänger was blushing—not an attractive blush but a splotchy, beet-red, ugly blush. The homecoming thing was a bad idea. An awful, terrible, *horrible* idea. What was she thinking? Greta didn't like her in a romantic way. She liked her in a friendly, witch-sister way.

Things used to be so much easier when Iris had liked Greta in a friendly, witch-sister way, too. When had her feelings morphed into this messy mess? Could she unmorph them somehow?

Iris sighed and returned her shoulder-flipped hair to its original position, then peeled a strand that had gotten stuck to her Red Any Good Books Lately? lip gloss, which she'd seen on a "Brown Girl Mini-Makeover" tutorial. She needed to give up and move on, maybe ask someone else to the dance. But how? She wanted only Greta. Kind, smart, pretty Greta, who talked to animals and who smelled like lavender.

Lately, Iris had been experiencing crush symptoms every time Greta was around, like sweaty palms and a racing heart and major awkwardness. She knew they were crush symptoms because that's what the Internet said. Of course, sweaty palms and a racing heart and major awkwardness could also be symptoms of Iris's generalized anxiety disorder and sensory processing disorder.

Maybe she should ask the Internet how to tell the difference. And also how to get Greta to romantic-like her back.

A toilet flushed.

Iris made a choking sound in her throat. Someone had been in the bathroom the entire time? Listening to her make a fool of herself about . . .

Noooooo!

Thinking quickly, she began reciting a memory-erase incantation, *praetereo.* Then stopped and faked a coughing fit. Greta had forbid their coven to use witchcraft in public.

Greta. Swoon.

A stall door opened, and a girl walked out, pushing her backpack onto her shoulder. She glanced at Iris with a bored expression as she headed for an open sink.

"Oh, hey!" Iris called out nervously. "I was just . . . uh . . . practicing lines for drama club"—she searched her memory for a play, any play— "yeah, that was from *The Crucible* by Arthur Miller." *No, not that one.* "Actually, they made a musical out of *The Crucible* and combined it with *Mamma Mia!* and—"

"You should just text her," the girl cut in.

"Excuse me?"

"It would be a lot easier than whatever you were doing."

"Um . . ." Iris dropped her gaze and frowned at her feet.

"Or, if you need a date for homecoming, you should just look on Krush."

"Krush?"

"It's a dating app for teens. Krush with a *K*. That's how I met my"—she counted on her fingers—"last six boyfriends. People use it for prom dates and stuff, too."

"Oh!"

The girl finished washing her hands and left the bathroom. *I guess she didn't buy my story about drama club.* Iris pulled her phone out of her jeans pocket and searched for Krush. She was directed to a hot-pink web page with lots of *X*'s and *O*'s and the headline FOR ALL YOUR SHIPPING NEEDS. Cute.

Conversation, laughter, and other hallway noises seeped in, reminding Iris that lunch period would be over soon. She checked her reflection one last time, straightened her glasses, and headed out the door. Her Greta scheming and plotting would have to wait.

Really, though...maybe she should stop daydreaming about Greta and homecoming altogether, not just because there was zero hope on that front but because there were way more important priorities. Like solving Penelope Hart's murder. Like dealing with the growing Antima presence in Sorrow Point—and across the entire country. According to the Internet, witch arrests were higher than they'd been in decades. And on October twenty-eighth, the president of the United States planned to roll out a new-and-improved 6-129 law to increase the penalties for practicing witchcraft and beef up enforcement nationwide. Which meant things were bound to get much worse.

There was another matter, too. A few weeks ago, Iris had inadvertently touched Greta's velvet scarf, and scary images had flooded her brain....

"Come to our meeting?"

In the hallway, a guy thrust a flyer at her. He had dark hair with blue streaks, and his brown eyes were earnest bordering on uncomfortably intense as they laser-focused on her.

It was *him*. Orion Kong. He was Antima—not just Antima, but one of the most active and vocal members at Sorrow Point High. On the first day of school, when Iris had been trying to get her bearings as the new girl from New York City, he'd bumped into her—deliberately?—and treated her like a pariah, making her worry that he'd somehow sussed out her witch identity. Later, he and his Antima buddies Brandon Fiske and Axel Ngata had drunkenly cornered her on the street and tried to intimidate her.

Did Orion remember that she was that same girl? She *had* gotten new glasses, so maybe he was confused? Or had Greta done a memory-erase on him? She had, hadn't she?

"Um..." Iris took the flyer from him with a trembling hand. For a brief second, she shuttered her eyelids to try to glean information from the piece of paper. Nothing.

She opened her eyes. The flyer said:

If we don't put an end to **THEIR** *way,*
They'll put an end to **OUR** *way.*
Join us this Saturday at 1 p.m.
Community Center, Main Street.

At the top of the page was a picture of a cage suspended over a bonfire. The Antima symbol, just like the one on Orion's shoulder patch. It was how they used to execute witches 140 years ago, during the Great Witch Purge.

Iris bit her lip so hard that she could taste blood. What should she do? Run? Scream? Hide? Kick Orion in the shins? But she knew that the only way to stay safe, to keep Greta and her other witch sisters safe, was to pretend to go along.

"Wow! Thanks! This is...just so cool, and you guys are so cool, and wow! I'll definitely try to be there. Tomorrow afternoon, right? That is, if my grandma doesn't need me to work the lunch shift at her restaurant, or my mom doesn't need me to watch my little brother and sister. But hey, we all have to make sacrifices for the cause, amiright? This very, very supercool cause? Go, Antima! Woo-hoo!" Iris pumped her fist in the air.

Orion stared curiously at her. "Sure. Yeah. Feel free to bring your family and friends. Here." He offered her some extra flyers.

"Thanks, you, I mean, *thank* you, I have to run now, 'k, bye!"

Iris grabbed the flyers from him, turned on her heels, and began speed-walking in the other direction. She felt rattled, dazed, queasy, having been in such close physical proximity to Orion and also having had to lie so, so outrageously. She was a witch. She was proud of being a witch. That she couldn't say those things openly—on top of which that she'd had to pretend to be pro-Antima just now—was enough to make her want to projectile vomit her PB&J and baby carrots.

She reached up to touch her smiley-faced moonstone pendant, to settle her nerves, but it wasn't there. *Oh, right.* Greta had instructed her and Ridley to stop wearing their magical talismans until further notice because of what had happened to that US history sub lady with her pentagram necklace.

Turning the corner, Iris spotted Div and Binx in a secluded alcove, their heads bent close in conversation. She speed-walked over to them.

"*Youwouldn'tbelievewhatjusthappened!*" she blurted out on a rush of breath.

Div turned and regarded her coldly. For a moment, Iris wondered if her albino boa constrictor—Prada—was coiled around her shoulders, hidden from view by an advanced invisibility spell. Probably not, because of the "no magic in public" thing, but on the other hand, did Div follow her own rules, especially when it came to her familiar? Just to be

safe—because who wanted to be bitten by an invisible boa constrictor?—
Iris took a couple of steps back and prepared to cast *repellere* if necessary.

"Hello, Iris," Div said in her usual soft, silky voice, which belied how
incredibly scary she could be.

"Yeah. Hey." Binx pulled her phone out of her pocket and began
scrolling busily through it. Iris wondered if she was still feeling awkward
about switching sides.

"Is that a Klink?" Iris asked, pointing to Binx's phone case. Binx's
phone cases always featured a Pokémon character.

Binx's face lit up. "Actually, it's a Klang, which is the second evolution.
Klinks have two interlocking gears with six teeth each, and Klangs have
one six-tooth gear and one eight-tooth gear."

"Interesting!"

"Yes. Fascinating. Iris, can we help you with something?" Div asked.

Iris opened her mouth and then shut it again. Why, exactly, had
she wanted to speak to Div and Binx about her upsetting Orion Kong
encounter? They weren't her friends—well, actually, Binx was, or at least
she used to be before she'd joined Div's coven. Of course, the two sides
did talk to each other when it came to matters of mutual interest, like
catching Penelope's killer. But they didn't have casual conversations about
everyday stuff. Still, an Antima meeting at the community center wasn't
exactly "everyday stuff," and in fact, it might be related to Penelope's murder. Their current working theory was that Penelope had been killed by
some angry, violent Antima member. Although...was there such a thing
as a not-angry, not-violent Antima member?

Iris peered around to make sure there were no eavesdroppers nearby.
There weren't.

"Orion Kong just invited me to an Antima meeting tomorrow," she
whispered. She held up one of the flyers.

Binx and Div studied the flyer.

"Jerks," Binx muttered.

"Why would he think you'd be interested in attending?" Div asked Iris.

"No idea. I think he's just passing out flyers to everyone. See, I was rushing out of the bathroom"—the memory of that girl overhearing Iris's Greta monologue made her blush again—"and, uh, he was right there in the hallway, and he was like, 'Please come to our meeting!' I couldn't say no or flip him off or whatever, because then he might get suspicious, right? Like, he might think I was a w-w-wi"—she didn't feel safe saying *witch* even in the secluded alcove—"*wildebeest.*"

"Wildebeest, ha," Binx repeated, cracking up.

"May I keep this?" Div took one of the flyers. "I should send one or two of my girls to the meeting, for information-gathering purposes. Maybe you, Binx."

"Oh, please don't," Binx groaned.

"You could go with Aysha."

"*Please* don't."

Iris's gaze bounced back and forth between Div and Binx. She was about to say something when her Spidey-sense told her to look to her right.

Down the hallway on the other side, Greta was standing underneath a HOMECOMING 2017 CATCH THE SPIRIT! poster and watching Iris with a confused frown on her face. Next to her was a guy with curly dark blond hair and wire-rimmed glasses. With his salmon-colored khakis and sky-blue button-down shirt, he looked like a major prepster.

Their arms were linked, and their shoulders were touching.

Iris's Greta-crush energy whooshed out of her. She didn't know which was worse... Greta being upset with her, presumably for hanging with their rival coven, or Greta engaging in PDA with... who *was* he?

A new boyfriend? Or maybe that was PPDA—*platonic* public display of affection.

"Greta!" Iris called out, hating the anxious crack in her voice. "Hey! Hi!"

Greta replied, but Iris couldn't hear her because all of a sudden, shouts were breaking out from somewhere nearby. The commotion seemed to be coming from room 159. Iris, Binx, and Div—and Greta and the guy—all turned in that direction. More shouts, and then two Sorrow Point police officers bustled through the doorway, escorting someone between them. It was Mr. Dalrymple, the English teacher.

He was in handcuffs.

"I am *not* a witch!" he was protesting loudly. "This is a travesty of justice! I wish to speak to my solicitor *immediately*!"

"Mr. *D*?" Binx gasped. She leaned over and whispered something in Div's ear. In response, Div clenched her fists angrily and whispered something back.

Iris opened her mouth to speak, but nothing came out. Her heart was hammering against her rib cage, her stomach hurt, and her skin prickled with cold sweat. She didn't need the Internet to tell her that she was having a panic attack.

There were police *inside* their school now? Arresting suspected witches? This had never happened before. Was this to be the new normal?

The officers led Mr. Dalrymple past Greta and the guy. Greta stumbled a little as she backed up against the lockers and gazed helplessly at Mr. Dalrymple, and then at Iris. She looked terrified.

It's okay, Greta, Iris wanted to say. But it wasn't okay. It was the polar opposite of okay.

We are so doomed.

3

MOONLIGHT AND MAGIC

Pretense can be achieved by magic or
by malice—or both.

(FROM *THE GOOD BOOK OF MAGIC AND MENTALISM*
BY CALLIXTA CROWE)

"All righty, people! Happy Friday! We're going to get started with the Homecoming Committee meeting in just one minute," Hannah Ballinger announced. "But first, we want to welcome our newest members, Mira Jahani and Beatrix Kato. Div and Aysha brought them on board, so thank you, Div and Aysha!"

In the art room, two dozen heads swiveled toward Mira and Binx with a chorus of hellos and welcomes. Mira beamed and fluttered her fingers. Binx fake-smiled and stifled a swear.

The swear was because of the way Hannah had introduced her. She'd pronounced Kato *cat-toe* instead of *kah-toe*, which was the proper Japanese pronunciation, or *KAY-toe*, first syllable stressed, which was the more common American mispronunciation and which Binx normally tolerated.

What Binx couldn't tolerate, however, was the "Beatrix." No one was allowed to call her that awful, old-lady name, which she'd been cursed with thanks to her father's childhood obsession with the Peter Rabbit books.

To be honest, Binx's uncooperative mood was also due to just *being* here at this soul-crushing assemblage. Binx didn't *do* meetings. Okay, coven meetings, sure...but she definitely didn't do committee meetings of any kind, especially those for school-spirit-related events like homecoming.

And was Div seriously considering sending her to an *Antima* meeting?

Get me the hex out of here, Binx thought irritably. If only she could do an *aegresco* spell to make herself sick so she'd have an excuse to leave...or better yet, make everyone else in the room sick so that the meeting would be canceled altogether.

"A little enthusiasm, please," Div hissed in her ear, as though reading her thoughts.

"*Fine*," Binx hissed back. She quirked her mouth in a way that she hoped would pass for a socially acceptable smile and queen-of-England-waved to the room.

Hannah raised her perfectly groomed eyebrows at Binx. With her fussy pink dress and high-pitched voice, she resembled a teen version of Dolores Umbridge from the *Harry Potter* series. Mean disguised as prim and proper.

Hannah directed her attention back to the room. "All righty, then! I'll turn this over to my committee cochair, Hannah W., to go over the countdown until November eleventh!"

Hannah Wojcik, who was perched on the edge of the art teacher's desk, jumped to her feet and consulted her clipboard. If Hannah B. was Dolores Umbridge, Hannah W. was Professor McGonagall, all efficient and orderly.

Of course, neither Hannah practiced the craft like those *Harry Potter* characters. In fact, that was why Div had insisted their coven join this very annoying committee—so they could blend in with the basic humans of Sorrow Point High and make sure no one thought they were different, that they were witches.

Granted, this might not be the *worst* idea, after what had gone down with Mr. D this afternoon. Binx wondered if he was okay. She had him for first-period English, and she hadn't had a clue that he was a witch. That is, *if* he was a witch...it was entirely possible that the police had made a mistake. Or that the evil Orion Kong and/or some other evil Antima member had narced on Mr. D in error.

"Yes! Hello! So it's four weeks until the big day, and we still have many to-do list items to tackle. First, let's get a status report from all the sub-committee chairs, and we can go from there...." Hannah W. began.

Binx sat on a high stool between Div and Aysha and tried to resist the urge to pull out her phone and play a quick round of the new *Witchworld* video game, pocket edition. Or reorganize her grimoire; she'd recently developed a spell that disguised it as a cooking app. But...*nah*, those were probably bad ideas for many reasons, including unleashing Div's wrath.

Instead, Binx made herself seem super-interested as the subcommittee chairs gave their status reports. DJs, *blah, blah, blah*. Fundraising, *blah, blah, blah*. Concessions, *blah, blah, blah*. Decorations, *blah, blah, blah*.

"...and since our theme will be 'Moonlight and Magic,' we're thinking about putting moon-shaped glitter and little fairy wands on every table," the decorations subcommittee person—Agnes?—was saying. "Depending on our budget, we can buy the wands or make them ourselves. I found some adorable DIY stuff on Pinterest!"

Some guy raised his hand.

"Um, excuse me? I wasn't here when the committee voted on the theme, but...do we think that's wise? 'Moonlight and *Magic*'? Won't we get into trouble because of...you know...I mean, it's illegal. We might as well call it 'Moonlight and Armed Robbery,' or 'Moonlight and Murder,' or..."

Binx inhaled sharply. *Okay, that dude* really *deserves an* aegresco *spell. The advanced version, with pus-filled boils and diarrhea.*

"I think everyone understands we're talking about made-up magic, like in 'Cinderella' or 'Sleeping Beauty.' Not the real kind," Hannah W. explained.

The guy shrugged. An uncomfortable silence settled over the room.

Mira raised her hand. "I'm really good with crafts. I could help with the wands!" she said cheerfully.

"Great! Thank you, Mira!" Hannah W. scribbled on her clipboard.

Div nodded approvingly at Mira, then turned to Binx. "You should volunteer for a subcommittee as well," she whispered.

"Why?" Binx whispered back.

Div narrowed her eyes. Binx sighed and raised her hand, too. "I can do wands, too," she told Hannah W.

"Wonderful! Thank you, Beatrix!"

That's it, girl, you're getting aegresco'd, too. With extra boils.

At four o'clock, when the meeting was *finally* over, Binx headed out to the parking lot with Div, Mira, and Aysha. It had rained earlier, so the asphalt was pocked with puddles. The sky was just beginning to break with faint pre-twilight streaks of lavender and gold.

Div did a 360-sweep of the half-empty parking lot. "We seem to be alone. So . . . that guy who made the comment about magic being illegal. Does anyone know if he's Antima?"

"I didn't see a patch," Mira replied.

"Well, if he *is* Antima, I think we fooled him into thinking we're 'normal,'" Binx said with air quotes. "But maybe we could do more to enhance our regular-people rep? I know! How about inviting the Hannahs for a spa day? We could all get mani-pedis!" she joked.

Mira held out her hands palms down, displaying ten purple ombré nails. "What do you have against mani-pedis?" she asked in a hurt voice.

Binx held out her hands, too, displaying bright yellow nails with Pika-chus on them. "Nothing. Not a thing. But I do object to the Hannahs. And homecoming."

"Can we please focus?" Div said impatiently. "What happened today with Mr. Dalrymple? *Not good.* Police at our school...we have to do something about this."

"Can we just cast a big *muto* spell and morph all the police officers into cute little pets?" Mira said with a grin. "JK! Or maybe not."

"Yeah, that won't call attention to our witch identities *at all*," Aysha remarked. "Listen, guys. I have something to report."

Div turned to Aysha. "Yes?"

"There was a history field trip today, to a Civil War site in the Kai Rain Forest. On the trip, we noticed maybe three new Antima members. Valerie Yeargan, Francisco—I don't know his last name—and Siobhan— I don't know her last name, either. Plus, Mr. Terada; he was wearing an Antima patch on his jacket." Aysha added, "He's our sub for the next few months until Ms. Hua comes back from maternity leave. Unless he disap-pears, too, and we get *another* new sub."

"An Antima *teacher*?" Div shook her head. "He's the first one, that we know of. This is very bad."

"What do you mean, 'unless he disappears, too'? And who's 'we'?" Binx asked Aysha.

"I just meant, he's the fourth sub we've had since the beginning of the year. Although, Ms. O'Shea *did* kind of disappear, right? As in, none of us knows where she went or how to contact her, and is that 'family emer-gency' story for real? And by 'we,' I meant me and your bud Ridley. She was on the field trip, too."

"Oh."

Binx reached down and plucked at the rainbow-colored macramé bracelet that Ridley had made for her last Christmas. Guilt tugged at her brain. She'd been too busy to hang with her best friend lately, ever since leaving Greta's coven and joining Div's.

Binx was making a cool Christmas present for Ridley this year—hand-knit fingerless gloves, dove gray and decorated with silver musical-note charms because Ridley played the violin. Binx had also started to knit gloves for Greta and Iris, back when they were coven-mates, although she wasn't sure she *wanted* to finish Greta's. Not after she'd been so...well, *Greta-ish* about the whole ShadowKnight/Libertas matter. Stubborn, shortsighted, my-way-or-the-highway.

At least Div, who wasn't exactly easygoing and flexible, either, had supported Binx's view that the Antima were a major, major threat to the freedom, to the very existence, of witches. And that witches everywhere needed to take the threat seriously and figure out a solution, *fast*.

Still, Binx had noticed the horrified expression on Greta's face when the police dragged Mr. D away in handcuffs. *Maybe she's finally getting it. Maybe she's realizing just how dire and dangerous the situation's become.*

As for Ridley, Binx made a mental note to call her BFF ASAP. They could have a nice, long chat and catch up about everything, even make a date to go to Starbucks or the mall.

"—and Francisco and Siobhan are in my chem class," Mira was saying to the others. "Francisco's kind of hot, and Siobhan has really cute taste in clothes."

"Really, Mira? They're *Antima*," Div pointed out.

Mira flushed. "I know, I know. But Antima people can be hot and stylish, too. They're only evil on the inside."

"Says the girl who's dating a certain hot, stylish Antima member named Colter Jessup," Aysha teased her.

"I am *not* dating him, Aysh. Not for real! And we don't know for a hundred percent sure that he's Antima," Mira protested.

Aysha cocked her head. "Yeah, uh-huh. He and his brother and their dad just say horrible things about witches because hashtag-stopwitchcraft and hashtag-antimaforever are trending and they don't want to feel left out. Not to mention—"

"Enough," Div cut in irritably. "Speaking of the Jessups—Mira, you and I need to go home and get ready for Dr. Jessup's birthday dinner tonight. Six o'clock at the country club. Aysha and Binx, I want you to go to that Antima meeting at the community center tomorrow."

Binx groaned.

"Seriously?" Aysha complained.

"Yes. Keep a low profile and report back. Mira, perhaps you should go with them, too."

"Of course."

Div's gaze scanned all three witches. "Okay, so, no coven meeting tonight, but we'll have one tomorrow night at my house. Bring your grimoires; we have a lot of work to do." She turned to Binx and added, "I'll also want an update on Libertas."

Binx nodded. *She* wanted an update on Libertas, too. It had been a few days since ShadowKnight had been in touch. Pulling out her phone, she went to her DMagic app, disguised to look like a gaming icon, and sent another encrypted and coded message to him via their secret server: *CAN WE PLZ TALK ABOUT THE UPCOMING POKÉBATTLE?*

Half an hour later, when Binx got home, the small dirt-colored puppy raced up to her the second she walked through the front door. His little legs splayed this way and that as he skated and skidded across the gleaming wood floor, yipping with joy.

"Hey, guy!" Binx squatted down to greet him. He propelled himself onto her lap and licked her face.

"*Ew.* Okay, thanks for the free facial. Who needs a spa day with you around? It's nice to see you, too."

The puppy continued licking. He made a happy crooning noise.

Binx stood up and set her backpack on the front hall table. Aside from the puppy soundtrack, the house was silent. She knew that her mother was still at the university, at a faculty meeting. Binx was glad to have the house to herself for a while. For one thing, she could practice her spells—*finally!* It was so hard not being able to use any magic whatsoever at school or elsewhere in public. In the privacy of her room, though, she could cast away. On top of which, she never looked forward to the obligatory end-of-the-day questions from her mom: *How was school? Did you finish your homework? Don't you think you've had enough screen time for today? What are those strange cartoony things on your nails?*

The puppy, at least, was never annoying and judgy like that.

"You probably need to go outside, don't you? Let's go outside."

He wagged his tail and panted, so Binx opened the front door again and led him around to the backyard. The property was pristinely landscaped and also loaded with fancy extras she hardly ever used: an infinity pool, two Jacuzzis, a tennis court, and a Japanese Zen garden with a meditation hut. At the edge of the yard, a hiking trail led down to a private beach.

Behind the garage was the basketball hoop that Binx's father had installed for her years ago. They used to play one-on-one, but not so much anymore, now that he lived in Palo Alto full-time with his new wife, Sloane, and their new spawn, Lucas, who was fairly useless except in the crying, eating, and pooping departments. Binx's dad had made his fortune as the founder and president of Skyy Media, *Skyy* being a mash-up of his name, Stephen Kato, and her mom's name, Yoko Yamada, from back when they were together and didn't hate each other's guts. *Witchworld*, currently one of the most popular video games in the world, was the crown jewel of the Skyy Media empire.

That wasn't why Binx was a *Witchworld* fan, though. She liked *Witchworld* because it was a legit awesome game and also the one place it was legal to practice witchcraft, even if it wasn't IRL. In the fictional universe of *Witchworld*, witches ruled, and everyone else, humans included, were considered beneath them. Sometimes, when the threat of the Antima became too much, Binx wondered how it would feel to live in a universe like that.

The puppy ran to his favorite place to do his business, under a madrona tree. As he hunkered down on a carpet of dried-up red berries and leaves and got to it, Binx's phone rang. The custom ringtone was the first line of the *Witchworld* theme song, which she'd recently assigned to one person and one person only—and it wasn't her absentee dad.

She hit the talk button eagerly.

"Hey, ShadowKnight4811!"

"Hey, Pokedragon2946!"

Binx sat down on a nearby stone bench and shifted the phone from one ear to the other. She was glad he'd gotten her message . . . messages, plural. "What's up? What's going on? It's been a while." She picked up a small rock and began doodling with it on the bench.

"Sorry for the radio silence," ShadowKnight apologized. "Haven't slept much. A lot's been happening."

"What do you mean, specifically?"

"Specifically? For starters, I just got off the phone with one of our Libertas members. She's been keeping track of nationwide arrests. She reported that two weeks ago, there were two hundred ninety-five arrests. Last week, there were seven hundred thirteen more arrests. That's over a thousand arrests in fourteen days, which is more than we've had in the past hundred forty years since the Great Witch Purge."

"*What?* Over a thousand . . . *gah*! I didn't realize it was that many." Binx scratched out a surprise-face emoji on the bench.

"Yeah. Unfortunately. We've been keeping track of assaults, too. Twenty-nine across the country in the past month. None of the assailants was charged."

"Oh my god! Were they Antima?"

"Yeah, we think so."

Binx eyed the puppy nervously. "What about familiars? I heard there've been some mysterious pet disappearances?"

"We've heard that, too. There's no proven connection to the Antima yet, although I wouldn't put it past them. Your new puppy's okay, right?"

The puppy had moved over to the bazillion-dollar Japanese crane sculpture—a long-ago wedding anniversary gift from Binx's dad to her mom—and was peeing on it, hydrant-style. Binx frowned and mouthed, *No!* He blinked innocently at her and continued peeing.

"Have you named him yet?" ShadowKnight was asking.

"What? Nope, not yet. I can't decide between Lillipup and Growlithe. Or Herdier or Stoutland, which are Lillipup's evolutions. Or Arcanine, which is Growlithe's evolution when exposed to a Fire Stone."

"Lillipup, definitely."

"You think so?"

"I *know* so."

"Hmm." *Lillipup*, she scribbled on the bench, then nodded.

"So have you guys found who killed your friend?" ShadowKnight asked.

"No, not yet. Did I tell you? Mira and Div—those are my new

coven-mates—are fake-dating Penelope's ex and the ex's older brother, who may be Antima, to try to find out if they or someone else in their family might be connected to Penelope's murder. The police are still ruling it a suicide, which is beyond bogus."

"The police aren't going to do anything to catch her killer. She was a witch."

Witches > Humans, Binx doodled. "That's why we have to solve this case on our own. Soon, I hope."

The puppy was digging now, scooping and scattering dirt everywhere. *Mom is gonna be so pissed*, Binx thought, pleased. "What's happening with Libertas? Will I ever get to meet the members? Will I ever get to meet *you*?" she asked. She'd only ever communicated with ShadowKnight online, by phone, and by video chat. Neither of them knew each other's real names or even where the other lived, although he *had* mentioned once that it was somewhere in the Pacific Northwest, and she'd told him she lived in the Pacific Northwest, too.

"Funny you should mention that. Do you know about the Witch-WorldCon in Seattle? Day after tomorrow?"

Binx hadn't told ShadowKnight that her dad was the creator of *Witchworld*. Too much identifying personal information, plus, to be honest, she'd never told *anyone* about her dad, because she didn't want people to think of her as some tech mogul's rich, spoiled daughter. ShadowKnight *was* aware of her *Witchworld* obsession, though, and her gaming obsession in general. In fact, they'd first met on the *Witchworld* Sub9 discussion board.

"Yeah, I know about it," she said after a moment.

"Are you going, by any chance?"

"Actually, yeah. Wait, are *you* going, too?"

"Yup. A bunch of other Libertas members will be there, too. We're using it in part as a cover to meet up and strategize in person."

"Really? That's *awesome*."

"Hey…if you're going to be there, we should definitely get together. How about at the cosplaying competition? You signed up, right? At one thirty? I'll be dressing up as Dargon. Who are you dressing up as?"

Dargon. The half-human, half-witch former prince who'd been exiled from the kingdom of Vandervallis for attempting to assassinate the entire Low Council. Brilliant, unpredictable, ruthless, and seriously O.P. *It fits him.*

"Um…I hadn't really planned on…" Binx hesitated. Cosplaying was not her thing; it involved way too much IRL social interaction. But this was official Libertas business. "Yeah, okay, I could do that. I'll come up with a costume ASAP. I do have some crafting skills."

"Let me know. It's a date, then."

A date?

"Wh-who else will be there?" Binx stammered. "From Libertas, I mean?"

"At least a dozen members, maybe more. I promise you'll meet them all."

"Okay, yeah, cool."

They said goodbye after promising to talk again soon. Binx stood up, pocketed her phone and also her rock—maybe it was lucky?—and started inside. She had a costume to design.

"Come on, Lillipup," she called out to the puppy.

He bounded up to her, his tail wagging. Obviously, the new name worked.

Binx felt inexplicably happy for the first time in days. If only she didn't have to go to an Antima meeting tomorrow. With Aysha and Mira. *Blurg.*

4

THE UNFINISHED CIRCLE

A lone witch has powers. A coven
has a multitude more.
But sometimes, there is a cost.

(FROM *THE GOOD BOOK OF MAGIC AND MENTALISM*
BY CALLIXTA CROWE)

Greta's familiar, Gofflesby, sat Sphinx-like on top of her mandala-print comforter as she set up for the coven meeting. His emerald-green eyes followed her every move, and his whiskers twitched occasionally. Otherwise, he was perfectly still.

"Iris and Ridley will be here any minute," Greta told him as she laid out a circle of candles, gemstones, and herbs on the rug. "Our new witch might be a little late, though."

Gofflesby blinked.

"I was thinking of using amber today. Or should I go with alexandrite?

They're both good for protection. And maybe I'll add amethyst, for scrying."

Gofflesby shifted slightly and meowed. Greta reached over to stroke his ears, and he began purring.

It was such a relief. He seemed like he was back to his old self. For a long time, he'd had a serious respiratory illness that the vet couldn't seem to cure or even diagnose—this, despite all the office visits and state-of-the-art tests that Greta's parents were still paying off in installments—and despite an array of advanced healing spells and potions, many of them from Callixta's book, which Greta had tirelessly tweaked and retweaked.

And then Gofflesby had disappeared. Run away... or possibly been taken? Greta, Iris, Ridley, and Binx had found him the following day, lying next to Penelope's dead body at a nearby construction site. Fortunately, he'd recovered soon after... more than recovered, actually, because his respiratory illness, the perpetual cough and raspy breathing, was totally gone. Although he'd acted bizarrely for weeks after that. Wild, out of control, scratching and damaging Greta's grimoire and crystals and other magical items. But that, too, had passed. Now he was the same quiet, contemplative, well-behaved Gofflesby that he used to be.

Why had he been at that construction site with Penelope, though? Greta had tried to read his mind multiple times, but with no success. Even Iris, who possessed powerful psychic abilities, had been unable to glean any answers.

Still. Greta felt like the universe, and the Goddess, were trying to communicate important clues to her about that day. Filaments of memory kept flitting through her brain, gossamer and ghostlike. A red chair. A cup of tea. A woman's voice. Fire. Were these things connected to Gofflesby's disappearance and to Penelope's murder? Or were they just random visions?

A soft knock. "Honey? Are you in there?"

"I'm here!"

The door opened a crack, and her mother, Ysabel, peeked in. She had the same auburn curls as Greta, except that hers were bunched up in a loose bun with a pair of antique chopsticks. Today, she was wearing a brown linen dress, an Irish wool cardigan, and clogs.

"Hello, my love!" Ysabel said in a happy, breathless voice. "I'm taking Teo to his OT appointment; then we have to stop by the pharmacy and maybe pick up dinner at Taste of Thai. You don't mind carryout two nights in a row, do you? Oh, and your dad might be a little late. He's dealing with a ceiling leak at the store. It's in the biography section... I guess the karma gods don't like biographies." She smiled. "Kidding! He said no water damage to the books themselves, which is a big relief. Just a wet, messy floor."

"Does he need help?" Greta asked. "My friends are coming over soon, but I'll be free in an hour or so."

"Oh, that's very thoughtful of you. I think he'll be okay, but I'll tell him to text you if that changes." Ysabel's gaze dropped to the circle of candles, gems, and herbs on the floor. Her smile wavered. "Are you having a meeting?"

"Yup."

"You girls are being very careful, right?"

"Of course, Mama."

"Because the other day when I was dropping off a new batch of oatmeal soaps at Organic Bliss, Sparrow told me that Brianna next door was arrested for suspected witch activity. Brianna, that sweet young woman who works three jobs and takes care of her father who's got Alzheimer's! Things are getting very bad around here."

Greta had met Brianna a couple of times. She hadn't picked up a witch vibe off her, but one never knew. *Poor Brianna*, she thought, and made a note to cast a protection spell for her during the coven meeting. The same for poor Mr. Dalrymple. Greta winced as she recalled the terrible scene at school this morning, the police officers dragging him away in handcuffs.

"This is why my coven and I have to keep meeting, Mama. We're trying to figure out how to help stop the hate."

"How on earth do you girls hope to stop it? Maybe in three years when we have a new president, *if* we have a new president. But right now, he's . . . it's . . . well, the whole country is turning against witches. It's insane, and it's scary. Your dad and I"—Ysabel's voice shook—"we worry about you all the time, mijita."

"I know. We'll be careful. I promise."

"Yes, please be *extra* careful. I'm locking the front door and the back door, too. Text me if you need anything. Teo and I will be home around six. With vegan pad thai, extra peanuts and bean sprouts, the way you like it."

"Thanks, Mama."

"Back soon, sweetie. Stay safe."

After Ysabel left, Greta turned her attention back to the circle. She lit the candles and watched the flames glow. Her parents had known about her being a witch ever since her discovery moment at age eleven when she'd willed a dead zinnia in the garden to come back to life, and its wilted brown petals had immediately, spontaneously burst into fresh, glorious color. Ysabel and Tomas supported her magical life completely—they believed passionately in free rights for all, including witches—but they also feared constantly for her safety.

Her brother, Teo, on the other hand, was in the dark. Ysabel and Tomas didn't want him to have to lie or keep secrets from his friends and teachers at the middle school.

Greta was fully aware of how lucky she was that her parents accepted her witch identity when so many parents didn't feel the same about their children, *or* their children didn't trust them enough to be open with them. Ridley kept her identity a secret from her family, and ditto Iris. In Div's coven, only Aysha's family was aware—and supportive—of her identity. Greta wasn't sure about her new witch's family situation.

A new witch to take Binx's place... at least things are moving forward in that department.

A sudden chilly breeze blew in from the window and extinguished one of the candles. Greta got up to close the window... except, it was already closed. Confused, she glanced around. Where had the breeze come from? The house *was* old and could be drafty sometimes. *Yes, that must be it.*

On the bed, Gofflesby sprang up and hissed at the window.

"What is it, my love?" Greta asked, alarmed.

She parted the curtains and peered outside. It looked the same as always. There was her garden, nicknamed Bloomsbury, flush with her special herbs and flowers... Teo's cocoon swing hanging from the sycamore tree, *Platanus occidentalis*... the row of English laurel hedges, *Prunus laurocerasus*, that separated their house from Mrs. Mianowski's next door... the garage, which was mostly an overflow space for her father's used books and storage for her and Teo's old toys....

But no one was there. And nothing was out of place.

Still, Gofflesby continued hissing.

Gofflesby had finally managed to calm down by the time Iris and Ridley arrived at the house. *Maybe he saw one of the neighbor dogs*, Greta thought. Ridley texted that they were on the front porch, and Greta let them in using an *apertano* spell. "Open," she added, and visualized the lock unlocking. Even though incantations and such were important, magic was ultimately about intention.

As soon as the girls walked into Greta's room, Iris thrust a paper bag at Greta. "Hello! Greetings! I brought snacks!" she announced. "I mean, I know you didn't ask me to, but I thought it would be useful, so I stopped by my grandma's café, and she gave me some of her famous kitchen-sink cookies. Don't worry, though... they're not called that because they have little pieces of kitchen sink in them. They're called that because of that expression, you know, 'everything but the kitchen sink'? And even that's not accurate because, well, they don't have everything but the kitchen sink in them. Just"—she began ticking off the ingredients on her fingers—"peanut butter, dark chocolate chips, white chocolate chips, nuts, oats, dates, et cetera. They're vegan *and* gluten-free, if we care about gluten-free. *Do* we care about gluten-free? Anyhoo, speaking of expressions, did you guys know 'et cetera' is a Latin expression that means 'and the rest'?"

Greta grinned. Iris was always so... Iris. In a good way.

"They sound yummy. Thank you."

As she took the paper bag from Iris, she noticed that her friend's cheeks were flushed and that her eyes were brighter than usual. What was *that* about?

On an impulse, Greta mentally evoked a *modus* spell, trying to glean Iris's mood. Her field of vision filled with a soft, shimmery scarlet haze.

Wait. Was Iris... in *love*? Or at least crushing on somebody? But she hadn't mentioned anyone to Greta. Maybe the *modus* spell wasn't working properly? Also, Greta's intuitive powers weren't perfect; she was still working to grow and improve them.

"Hi, Greta." Ridley sat down on the rug and crossed her legs. She picked up a sprig of lavender, studied it, and put it back down again. She flicked away a piece of invisible lint from her khakis.

Greta sensed anxiety and agitation. "Hey, are you okay?"

"Yes. No. Maybe." Ridley threw up her hands. "Oh, I don't know."

"That's *exactly* how I always feel pretty much all the time!" Iris exclaimed. "Sorry, sorry. This is about you, not me."

"What's the matter?" Greta asked Ridley.

Ridley uncrossed and crossed her legs the other way. "Okay, so...my history class went on a field trip today. To the Kai Rain Forest. The sub, Mr. Terada...well, he was wearing the patch. The Antima patch."

"What?" Greta gasped.

"No way!" Iris cried out at the same time.

"Exactly! I think he's the first adult at the high school who's Antima—that we know of, anyway."

"FWIW...or is it FIWI?...*fee-wee,* that's funny...or maybe it's *fye-wye?*...so I've been wondering about the cafeteria lady because she's really mean, although 'mean' isn't the same thing as 'Antima,' obviously, so..." Iris's chin dropped to her chest.

"Second of all, I saw this house in the middle of the forest. A mansion," Ridley went on. "Except, it wasn't really there. Or it *was* there, and it seemed to be invisible to everyone but me."

Greta frowned. If there *was* a mansion in that spot, had some witch cast an invisibility spell on it? How, then, had Ridley managed to perceive it? "Can you describe it?" she asked Ridley.

"It was big and old—Gothic-looking—with a pointy roof and big windows. The thing was, I could see inside. Not just through the windows, but through the walls, as though the walls had disappeared or become transparent or whatever. I saw a whole entire room, with a fireplace and an antique table."

"Wow! Do you have Superman X-ray-vision superpowers?" Iris exclaimed.

"Not that I know of. Anyway—and guys, this gets even weirder—thirteen candles, like, suddenly appeared on the table. They were unlit at first, but then they just spontaneously lit up. There were gems and herbs on the table, too, in a circle around the candles. I recognized them."

Greta reached for her grimoire. "What were they?"

"I'm pretty sure it was black onyx and bloodstone. Plus mugwort and wolfsbane."

"Oh!"

Greta furrowed her brow and began flipping busily through the pages of her grimoire, which was full of her pencil drawings and handwritten spells and potion recipes. A dried lily of the valley sprig fell out, emitting a faint, sweet fragrance even after all these years; she carefully replaced it on the page with the happiness spell she and Div had created together when they were a coven of two.

She already knew what Ridley's gems and herbs represented, but she wanted to make absolutely sure. *Black onyx, page 24. Bloodstone, page 25. Mugwort, page 51. Wolfsbane, page 119.*

Iris peered over Greta's shoulder. "What does your super-smart grimoire say?"

"Um...it says that these items, especially in combination, are commonly used in necromancy spells," Greta said slowly.

Iris's eyes grew huge. "Necromancy? As in, bringing-dead-people-back-to-life magic?"

"Yes, although necromancy is a little broader than that. Generally speaking, it's about communicating with the dead. To get information from them, maybe see into the future," Greta replied.

"As in precognition," Ridley added.

"Exactly. An ability you seem to possess, Iris."

"Sort of. Kind of. I mean...sometimes my brain tells me that I'm going to have a mango Popsicle soon, but that's just because I'm hungry for mango Popsicles. Other times, though…well…my dreams and my visions *do* feel real. And some of that stuff does actually come true."

"Did you see anyone in the mansion? Or sense anyone, even?" Greta asked Ridley.

Ridley shook her head. "No and no. I asked Aysha to take photos of it with her phone. I wanted to find out if the mansion was visible to her without asking her directly, since there were tons of other people around. But I could tell from her reaction that it *wasn't* visible to her, and I didn't get a chance to talk to her about it after the field trip."

"*Aysha* was there?" Greta asked.

"Uh-huh."

"Anyone else from their coven?"

"No."

"Did Aysha text you the photos she took?"

"She did." Ridley pulled her phone out of her pocket and began scrolling. She held up the screen for Greta and Iris. "These."

Greta studied the images. There were three in all, showing tall trees covered with bright green moss. She recognized the species: western hemlock, *Tsuga heterophylla*, and western red cedar, *Thuja plicata*. And in the far background, Sitka spruce, *Picea sitchensis*, and Douglas fir, *Pseudotsuga menziesii*.

She spidered her fingers across the screen to enhance the first photo, then the second, then the third. No mansion. No candles. Nothing out of place.

Except…

"What's this?" Greta pointed to a pinprick of bluish light at the corner of the third photo.

Ridley squinted at the screen. "Hmm. I'm not sure. It might just be a lighting glitch?"

"Maybe we could send these pix to Binx and have her play around with them on her computer, and maybe cast some of her supercool cyber-magic spells?" Iris suggested.

Ridley turned to Greta. "What do you think? Can we ask Binx to help us with this stuff, now that she's...um..."

"Not in our coven?" Greta stirred uncomfortably. "I guess so? I mean, the two covens are working together on—" She stopped, not wanting to say Penelope's name out loud; she and Ridley had been close, and even now, Greta could sense a deep, palpable wave of grief radiating from Ridley. "Anyway, these photos aren't related to the case we're trying to solve, but they're still worth checking out," she finished.

A phone vibrated with an incoming text.

"Not mine!" Iris said, raising her hand again.

"Not mine, either," Ridley added.

"Must be mine, then." Greta reached for her phone, which was lying on her bed next to Gofflesby. There was a message from an unfamiliar number:

I'M HERE.

"Oh!" Greta fired off a quick text with instructions. "*Apertano*," she murmured under her breath, and once again pictured the lock unlocking.

Iris pushed her glasses up the bridge of her nose. "Greta? Why are you opening things?"

"Because our guest's here."

"*Guest?* What do you mean, *guest?*" Ridley asked nervously.

Greta hesitated. She probably should have discussed it with her witch sisters first. This was how she'd invited Iris to join her coven, too...on the spur of the moment, acting on pure instinct, without clearing it with Binx and Ridley. And they had been unhappy about it initially. Binx especially had been *really* unhappy about it.

But that situation had turned out just fine. Iris had proved to be an incredible witch and a wonderful addition to the coven, not to mention a good friend. And Greta's instincts told her that Torrence would prove to be the same.

She heard his footsteps coming up the stairs, and then a quiet knock.

"*Apertano*," Greta repeated. The door clicked open, and Torrence walked in.

Iris and Ridley stared at him with shocked expressions.

"*You!*" Iris burst out.

Torrence smiled. "Um…hi. You must be Iris. And you must be Ridley."

Ridley rainbow-waved but said nothing.

"Ridley, Iris…this is Torrence. Torrence Innsworth," Greta explained. "He just transferred here from Ojala. I met him last night in front of Mrs. Poe's store. Starlie—"

"Who's Starlie?" Iris interrupted.

"My new familiar," Torrence replied.

Greta turned to Iris. "Remember the little black kitty who hangs out in front of the store? Well, she turns out to be a stray. I was walking by last night, and I saw Torrence holding her and talking to her. She'd gotten a piece of broken glass stuck in her paw, and she was bleeding and in pain. Torrence got the glass out and healed the wound. Using a *sana* spell. He didn't see me there at first, but when he did, he panicked and started to cast a memory-erase spell on me. But I told him not to because it was okay, because I was a witch, too."

Ridley sat up, her eyes flashing with interest. "You can do *sana*? That's really cool. I should learn it, too. Agent Smith—that's *my* familiar, he's a rabbit—gets these gum injuries sometimes because his teeth grow so fast and so sharp."

"I could teach you," Torrence offered. "I changed up Callixta Crowe's version of the spell, and now it's way easier. Is Agent Smith named after the character in *The Matrix*?"

Ridley grinned. "Absolutely!"

Greta's gaze bounced between Ridley and Torrence. She exhaled with relief. Ridley seemed to accept him.

Her gaze moved to Iris. She, on the other hand, seemed upset. *Really* upset. Greta hadn't expected that of Iris, who was usually so agreeable and go-with-the-flow.

What was *that* about?

5

THE CLUB SCENE

The truth has many layers, and some of them
should be avoided.

(FROM *THE GOOD BOOK OF MAGIC AND MENTALISM*
BY CALLIXTA CROWE)

Div checked her pale pink lipstick in the mirror in the lobby of the Sorrow Point Country Club. *Perfect.* So was her long platinum hair that flowed like silk down her back. So was her winged eyeliner that made her green eyes look even more snakelike than usual—which was a plus, of course.

She'd also chosen her outfit well, a little black dress with a modest sweetheart neckline and black heels. These were not things she would normally wear—her preferred fashion palette was all white, and her overall style was far edgier and more interesting than an LBD and peep-toe pumps—but they were just right for dinner at the country club with the wealthy, conservative family of her Antima boyfriend.

Correction: her *probably* Antima *fake* boyfriend.

Next to her, Mira smoothed bright coral gloss onto her lips and air-kissed the mirror. "*Mwa!* Gorgeous! Now let's go find our men."

"Our men?"

Mira's cheeks flushed. "You know what I mean."

"Do I?"

Sometimes, Div worried that Mira was taking their ruse a little too seriously. They were pretending to date the Jessup brothers, Hunter and Colter, to find out if someone in their family was the leader of a powerful new Antima faction in town, called the New Order. And if one of them may have been responsible for Penelope's death, or at least knew something about it.

Penelope herself had been dating Colter right up to the time of her murder. In fact, Greta's coven had discovered an Antima patch in Penelope's backpack a few days after her death, which had raised the question: Did Penelope find the patch on Colter's person or among his possessions and confront him about it, leading to an angry—maybe deadly—argument? Was *that* when he learned about her witch identity, which she'd kept a secret from him throughout their relationship?

Was Mira able to be objective? She used to date Colter for real a couple of years ago, so they had a history. He was popular, rich, charming, and extremely hot. *He might be Antima*, Div had to warn Mira from time to time. *He might be a murderer.* Mira claimed she was well aware, but sometimes, she seemed so...smitten. In denial. Naively clinging to the idea that Colter could simply be a lost soul in need of saving.

Div's own fake boyfriend, Colter's older brother, Hunter, was likewise popular, rich, charming, and extremely hot. And super-smart—he was only seventeen, but he'd grade-skipped a year and was now a freshman at the university, pre-med. If anything, he seemed even more anti-witch than Colter, at least in the things he said. Although so far, there was no proof that he was definitely Antima, and ditto Colter.

O'Shea, the history-sub-slash-witch, had told Greta's coven about the New Order. O'Shea's own coven, based somewhere in the mountains north of Sorrow Point, had subsequently identified the possible connection between the New Order and the Jessup family. But O'Shea had vanished into thin air, which meant that now, it was up to Div and Greta and their respective covens to figure it out. Ergo the pretend dating.

"*Div!*"

Hunter was striding across the lobby toward her. He wore a navy suit, a crisp white shirt, and a beautiful silk tie that was somewhere between blue and black—Div couldn't tell. The elegant attire made him look even more handsome than usual.

Fortunately, Div was immune.

"Hi, there!" She smiled and walked over to meet him.

"Hey." Hunter wrapped his arms around her and hugged her tightly. He was wearing a new aftershave—what was that fragrance? It was warm and almondy and reminded Div of the scent of meadowsweet. It couldn't be, though. Meadowsweet was an herb that witches liked to use for love potions. She made a mental note to google commercial aftershaves that might have meadowsweet as an ingredient. There was no way her probably Antima boyfriend was indulging in magical concoctions.

Her probably Antima *fake* boyfriend, that was.

Hunter leaned back and scanned her from head to toe. "Wow, you look…*amazing*. Let me take you to our table; my family's all here. Hey, Mira, you look really nice, too."

"Thanks. Is Colter here?"

"Yeah, he's helping Caitlin with her tablet. Some sort of software glitch. Follow me, ladies."

Hunter took Div's hand, and Mira followed close behind. Div's heels sank into the thick beige carpet with each step, making her wobble a little and cling more tightly to Hunter. Annoying, although she guessed he probably liked it. In the short time she'd known him, she'd gleaned that he liked to be chivalrous, to be the strong, capable guy who helped helpless women.

Div was anything *but* helpless, but she knew how to act the part.

"Are you sure it's okay for Mira and me to be here?" she asked Hunter. "This is a big birthday for your mom. Don't you guys want it to be family only?"

"Dad insisted that we invite the two of you," Hunter replied.

"Oh. That's sweet."

Div peered over her shoulder at Mira and arched an eyebrow. Mira shrugged. Was Mr. Jessup keeping tabs on them? He didn't suspect they were witches...did he? She was very glad she'd imposed the no-magic-in-public rule on her girls. Still, she and Mira had to be extra careful tonight. They couldn't raise even the slightest red flag.

"This way."

Hunter pushed open a set of double doors; on the other side was a large, circular dining room. Classical music played over invisible speakers. Some servers in black hurried about with trays of cocktails, while others presided over silver chafing dishes at a long buffet station. A massive picture window overlooked a lush, rolling golf course that seemed too brightly green to be real.

This was her first time at the country club. She knew Mira's family had recently joined, even though they weren't particularly rich. Mr. Jahani, a councilman, apparently needed to mingle with the Sorrow Point elite since he was running for mayor, and he still had a lot of fundraising to do before the election next month.

The Jessup family was sitting by the window: Mr. Jessup, Dr. Jessup, Colter, and the tween identical twins, Cassie and Caitlin. Eight place settings rimmed the elegant white-cloth-covered table. Each of the white china plates bore the initials SPCC, in gold.

"Yay, you're here!" Cassie jumped to her feet and waved madly at Div and Mira.

Colter handed Caitlin her iPad, stood up, and gestured to the empty chair on the other side of him. "Mira, I saved you a seat."

Greetings were exchanged. Mr. Jessup kissed both girls on the cheek, like he always did. Dr. Jessup offered a polite smile and handshakes.

The twins flung their arms around Div and Mira.

"We got a cool new game! It's called *Witchworld*! Have you heard of it?" Caitlin asked them excitedly.

"I've never played. Do you want to teach me?" Mira replied.

"Yes! Sit next to me!" Caitlin exclaimed.

"No, sit next to *me*! I'm already on Level Three!" Cassie said, pointing to her own tablet.

"*Witch* world? As in, *W-I-T-C-H* world?" Mr. Jessup picked up his martini glass and took a long sip. "I don't believe I approved this purchase, Janie," he said to his wife.

"It's the funnest game, Daddy! It's about a fantasy realm where there's good witches and evil witches and lots of other good and evil characters, too—" Cassie began.

"—and battles and treasures and scrolls written in ancient languages—" Caitlin continued.

"—and lots of supercool side quests—"

"—and even extra-dimensional portals, can you believe it?"

"It's just a silly fantasy game, Jared," Dr. Jessup said, touching her husband's arm. "It's not like some of those other games out there. Like the one with the drug smugglers that's so popular. Or the one about desert combat. Games like that are so inappropriate for young, developing brains. This one, this *Witchworld* game, seems harmless enough."

Dr. Jessup was a pediatrician, and during the half-dozen occasions Div had spent time with the family, she often brought up kid- and teen-related issues like screen time and sugary sodas and such. The twins usually made unhappy faces whenever their mother gave one of her advice-filled speeches.

"Mom, we're totally old enough for *any* video game," Caitlin complained.

"Yeah, we're not babies," Cassie added in a surly voice.

"Guys? Let's change the subject, okay? We're here to celebrate Mom's big day," Hunter said, raising his drink.

"Yeah. Happy birthday, Mom!" Colter joined in.

Everyone clinked glasses.

After several toasts, they all got up from their seats to head over to the buffet table. Div fell into step beside Cassie.

"Soooo. The last time I saw you, you were studying for a math test. How did you do?" Div asked her.

"Oh, that. I got an eighty-nine," Cassie replied.

"Eighty-nine is good!"

"I guess? Why do we even have to take math, though, when everyone has calculators?"

"Excellent point!"

Div was sympathetic on this issue, more than Cassie knew. She and Mira and Aysha used to employ magic to alter their grades from B's and C's to A's, and to complete their homework, not just in math but in all their subjects. Nowadays they couldn't take the risk, which meant they'd been forced to pay attention in class and do their homework on their own. All of this was beyond tedious, especially when they had other, more important matters to tend to. Like bringing down the Antima and the New Order. Like catching Penelope Hart's killer. Like protecting themselves.

And also protecting Cassie? Div was 99 percent sure that Cassie was a witch but didn't know it. When they'd first met, Cassie had made a casual remark about wanting more rainbow highlights, and her hair had spontaneously changed colors before shimmering back to normal. That was the one and only time Div had witnessed Cassie's maybe-magical abilities.

Being a witch was complicated. According to Callixta Crowe's illegal magic manual, it was hereditary, although it could skip generations. A witch's powers usually manifested at puberty, although they could also manifest earlier or later. Also, some witches might go through their entire lives without realizing they were witches.

Crowe was reputed to be the most powerful witch in history. Before her death, she'd left behind one copy of her manual, although it had disappeared into the void. Then, about a year and a half ago, excerpts had been mysteriously posted online and deleted twenty-four hours later by someone claiming to be her descendant. Div and her girls, and Greta's girls, too, had learned vital information about witches and witchcraft and also dozens of new spells and potion recipes from those pages. She could only assume— could only hope—that scores of other witches had benefited in the same way, although she couldn't be sure because of the necessary secrecy.

Cassie, though. In the buffet line, Div watched the girl as she heaped about fifty croutons and no salad onto a salad plate. If she really *was* a witch, she was in danger living with such an anti-witch family. Especially if they were Antima—or worse, the force behind the New Order, which O'Shea had represented as being a particularly virulent upgrade.

Unfortunately, Div and Mira hadn't made much progress on this front. They still didn't know if the Jessups were New Order specifically, Antima generally, or neither. They hadn't gleaned any further information about the New Order, including if it actually existed. All they knew for sure was that the Jessups—or at least the Jessup men, Jared, Hunter, and Colter—despised witches and considered them to be criminals. They'd never heard Dr. Jessup or the twins express an opinion on the subject, though.

After everyone had sat down again, the conversation turned to the upcoming local election.

"How's your dad doing, Mira, honey? Hanging in there? Political campaigns are no picnic," Mr. Jessup said as he cut into his steak.

"He's hardly ever home, that's for sure. He's usually at his campaign headquarters or going door-to-door in the neighborhoods, shaking hands and stuff," Mira replied.

"Well, darlin', his hard work will pay off, because he's definitely going to win. I've seen the poll numbers. Our current mayor, you know, 'Ms. Witches-Are-People-Too' "—Mr. Jessup chuckled and shook his head— "she doesn't stand a chance against your dad. The citizens of this town have been very unhappy with her because she's way too weak on enforcement of 6-129."

Div saw the color drain from Mira's face.

"You're absolutely right, Mr. Jessup!" Div jumped in.

Mira nodded and didn't say anything.

"Can we not talk about politics *again*? It's booooring," Cassie complained.

"Yeah. Why do adults talk about such booooring stuff?" Caitlin added.

"Politics isn't boring. Politics is essential. The leaders who run our government, whether it's local or statewide or national, keep this country safe for all of us," Hunter told his sisters.

Cassie leaned over and whispered something in Caitlin's ear. The two girls giggled.

Div glanced over at Mira, who was picking at her salad with an unhappy expression. Div knew that Mira's family was unaware of her witch identity.

But this was the first time Div had heard the suggestion that Mr. Jahani might be explicitly *anti*-witch; was it Mira's first time, too? Just now, Mr. Jessup had seemed confident that Mr. Jahani would oust Mayor Lovejoy, who wasn't pro-witch, exactly—that would be too dangerous—but *was* openly anti-Antima. Lovejoy was an avowed pacifist and had publicly denounced the group's aggressive, sometimes violent tactics. Div herself could care less about her own family's support or lack of support about her being a witch. Aunt Marta and Uncle Paul, with whom she lived, had no idea who or what she really was. Her mother, Daniela, a witch herself, lived in Barcelona, Spain, with her boyfriend-of-the-week. Her father, Andrei, lived in Bucharest, Romania, and she hadn't spoken to him in years.

But Mira was different. She was close to her family, or as close as she could be while also keeping her true identity a secret from them. If her father turned out to be anti-witch, or at least willing to act that way in order to get elected... well, what did that mean for poor Mira?

After dinner, Hunter drew Div aside as they walked out to the parking lot. Colter and Mira were up ahead, as were Cassie and Caitlin and their parents.

Hunter put his hands on Div's shoulders. "Did I already tell you how amazing you are?"

"Yes, but you can tell me again," Div flirted back.

Hunger grinned. "You're amazing. And I don't just mean the fact that you're smart and fun and gorgeous. You really seem to get it."

"Get...what?"

"The threat. The thing that could destroy our society as we know it."

Div didn't flinch. She looked him straight in the eye and nodded. "Of course, I get it. What sane person wouldn't? But I'm not scared of it, either. We're stronger than them, and we *will* prevail."

"Exactly. Okay, I have to say it one more time. You're *amazing*."

He pulled her into his arms and kissed her on the lips. He was a good kisser. *Too* good. Div felt her cheeks flush and her heart race as he cupped her face with his hands and kissed her deeply, probingly.

Stop it. He's the enemy.

After a moment, he leaned away. She caught her breath.

"So there's something I have to tell you," he said.

"Yes?" Div blinked, trying to regain her composure. She noticed traces of her pale pink lipstick on his mouth.

"You know about the Antima, right?"

Div stared at him and stood a little straighter. *Something's happening.* "Sure."

"How do you feel about them?"

She didn't miss a beat. "I completely understand their cause. I wish they didn't have to resort to violence, because, well . . . violence is bad, no matter who uses it and for what reason. But I get what they're trying to do, that they're just trying to enforce the law."

Hunter nodded. "Exactly! I *knew* you'd understand. The thing is— and you may already be aware of this—but they aren't very well organized. Up until now, it's been a bunch of randoms here and there who hear about the Antima movement online or wherever and decide to join, maybe form a local group and give themselves a cool-sounding name. The Sons of Maximus, the Truth Bearers . . ."

"I've heard that."

"Well, we're trying to change all that. Make things more centralized, have just one leader."

Div's heart began racing again, for an entirely different reason. Hunter was about to reveal vitally crucial intel.

"That's a great idea. So you're involved in that? Good for you!" Div told him.

"Me and some of my family, yeah."

Who in your family, exactly? But Div didn't want to push.

"So I was thinking—" Hunter hesitated, then nodded to himself. "I think you're ready, and please keep this confidential. Here goes—I want you to be in this with me."

What is he saying? "Of course."

"Good. That's excellent. What are you doing tomorrow afternoon, two thirty?"

Her girls were coming over, but not until evening. "I'm all yours. Why?"

"We're having a meeting at the house. I'd like you to be there."

Div inhaled deeply to steady herself. This was *huge.*

"You mean...like an Antima meeting?"

"Not just an Antima meeting. It's more of a VIP leadership meeting. It's all the people who are trying to centralize the effort."

"Yes! I'd be honored. So this is kind of like the Antima 2.0."

"Kind of. Except we're giving ourselves a new name. We're giving the whole national movement a new name. The New Order...what do you think?"

Div smiled to herself. O'Shea and her witches had been right all along. The New Order *did* exist, and the Jessups *were* behind it...*some* of them, anyway.

"The New Order...it's perfect," she told Hunter.

As they walked out of the country club arm in arm, Div's mind swirled with satisfaction. And strategies. And rage.

Got you, Hunter. Got you, Jessups. The New Order is about to become history.

6

DISSIMULATION

There is a fine line between enemies and allies.

(FROM *THE GOOD BOOK OF MAGIC AND MENTALISM*
BY CALLIXTA CROWE)

After the coven meeting, Ridley left Greta's house and began walking briskly down Junipero Serra Drive. The sky was dark, with a smattering of stars, and the air was cool and damp. Way below, the lights of downtown Sorrow Point twinkled faintly against the black, invisible bay as a veil of evening fog rolled in. From somewhere in the neighborhood, a dog began barking; a second dog joined in, and then they were still.

A new witch in their coven. That was big, and also unexpected. Greta hadn't mentioned Torrence Innsworth to them before today, or even that she was thinking about replacing Binx.

Of course, just last month, she'd recruited Iris into their coven without giving Binx and Ridley any notice....

Torrence seemed okay so far, just as Iris had turned out to be okay—in her case, more than okay. Greta had a good instinct about people as well as a kind heart. Although Iris, who was usually so cheerful and animated, had acted sullen and unhappy during much of today's coven meeting. What was up with that?

Ridley glanced at her watch. It would be dinnertime when she got home—Momma had texted earlier that she was making her famous pot roast with the little potatoes and carrots. It was nice to see Momma back to her old self, or almost back to her old self, anyway. She'd even started working again, as the head of communications in the mayor's office at City Hall, which was similar to the job she'd had back in Cleveland. Ridley and her father were both terrible cooks, and with his crazy-busy shifts as a paramedic, they'd been living mostly on Taco Bell, pizza, and other carryout foods this past year while Momma healed from her depression.

Ridley turned the corner onto Hazelnut. She was about ten minutes from home—fifteen, including her usual stop. As she walked, she made a mental checklist of tasks she should knock off after dinner, because honestly, she missed being an organized person. She'd promised Harmony she would play Candy Land, so there was that. She'd also promised to help Momma box up everyone's summer clothes, bring them up to the attic, and bring down the winter ones. And she could combine hanging-out-with-Daddy time with homework time by studying for her French test while he watched TV.

Later, she would practice her violin—Kreisler's "Liebesfreud," with the light, graceful pulse and the carefree Viennese-waltz vibe that should have been easy to execute but were actually really challenging. She'd end the day by cleaning out Agent Smith's cage, changing his litter box, and feeding him fresh timothy hay and kale.

Good. This was progress. Like Momma, Ridley could—she *would*—morph back to her former multitasking, super-efficient self.

At the end of the block, she hesitated for a moment, then turned right and headed in the general direction of her house. This way took longer than the route through the new development, Seabreeze, but she'd pretty much avoided that shortcut ever since...

No, don't think about that.

The other advantage of her old route through Seabreeze had been all the vacant building lots and unfinished houses where she could hide and do her awful *muto* ritual. Lately, she'd been making do in the non-Seabreeze neighborhoods, trying to pick random safe, or safe-*ish*, spots like behind trees and bushes and people's garages. The twice-a-day *muto* was her only defiance of Greta's ban on public magic...well, that, plus the *calumnia* she'd had to employ this morning during the field trip, thanks to Aysha's indiscretion.

The *calumnia* might not have been totally necessary, but the *muto* most definitely was. Ridley still hadn't told her parents that she was a trans girl, and they knew her only by her untrue identity. She'd been trying to teach herself a couple of very advanced spells to solve her dilemma for good—*vertero*, to transform her anatomy and physical appearance permanently without surgery or medicines, and *dissimulatio*, to make her parents perceive her as a male-seeming version of herself...also permanently, or at least until she was ready to come out to them.

But when would that be? Would Daddy and Momma ever be capable of hearing the truth? The family had moved to Sorrow Point last fall to make a fresh start after Ridley's brother Daniel's unexpected death. The horrible diving accident. Ridley had decided to make an additional fresh start in their new town by using *muto* and a few other spells to live as her true self at school and around Sorrow Point...everywhere but at home. The aftermath of Daniel's death had plunged Momma into a deep depression, and Ridley had been reluctant to add more drama and difficulty to the situation, especially since Daniel and Daddy's last conversation had been a huge fight over the fact that Daniel was dating a boy. If Daddy was anti-gay, surely he was anti-trans as well?

And likely anti-magic, too? No one in the family knew about Ridley's magic except for her aunt Viola, who was also a witch. It was a secret the two of them shared. Aunt Viola was her father's older sister and still lived in Cleveland, running a small neighborhood flower shop where she held gardening classes and herbology lectures in the back room. Aunt Viola was the one who'd discovered Ridley's abilities, when Ridley was ten.

Ridley pulled out her phone and made a note to e-mail her aunt tonight. She'd written to Ridley a couple of days ago, saying that she had a big surprise for her, and Ridley had never written back. *I am a bad niece*, she chided herself.

She pocketed her phone and glanced around. *There.* To the right was a narrow alleyway that snaked between two bungalows. *Seems pretty private.* She turned into it and eventually came upon a large dumpster. She slipped behind it, sighed, and began the unhappy ritual.

It was after ten o'clock when Ridley's phone buzzed with an incoming call. She'd just gotten into her warm, cozy bed, so she decided to ignore it and let it go to voice mail. Besides, who would be calling so late?

Silence…then the phone began buzzing again. Across the room, Agent Smith rattled his metal cage agitatedly.

"It's okay," Ridley murmured to him. She sat up, reached for her phone, and glanced at the screen.

Div?

The girl had never called Ridley, ever. She happened to be in Ridley's contact list only because of an old group text that Greta had sent around to both covens. That, along with the lateness of the hour, could only mean…

Panicked, Ridley pressed talk. "Is everything okay? Did something happen to Binx? Or one of the other girls?" she whispered frantically.

"Everyone's fine. Sorry, I didn't mean to frighten you," Div replied.

"Oh, whew."

Ridley reached over to the nightstand and clicked on her Darth Vader lamp—a long-ago birthday present from her parents that was definitely not her style, despite the excellence of the *Star Wars* movies…*most* of them, anyway. "O-kay. So what's up?" She continued to whisper since her family was likely asleep.

"I wanted to update your coven on some news. Normally I do this with Greta, but she hasn't been returning my calls or texts. Likely she's still nursing a grudge over Binx's defection to my coven. So that left me with either you or Iris, and to be perfectly honest, Iris drives me crazy."

"Why?"

"For one thing, she never seems to shut up."

"She gets nervous."

"Still. Also, why are you whispering?"

"Because I don't want to wake up my parents or my little sister. Why are you *not* whispering?"

"Once my aunt and uncle take their sleeping pills, *nothing* wakes them up. Anyway, I'll get to the point."

"Sure."

Div proceeded to tell Ridley about her new discovery, that some of the Jessups—she wasn't sure which ones, exactly—were indeed the force behind a new Antima group called the New Order, just as Ms. O'Shea and her coven had theorized.

"*Whoa.*"

"Yes, exactly."

Ridley mulled over this revelation. Among other things, did this mean that Sorrow Point was about to become the center, the apex, of the Antima movement?

And did this further implicate Colter in Penelope's death?

"Do you think Penelope found out? Do you think that's why Colter... or maybe someone else in his family...felt they had to...um"—Ridley's voice caught in her throat—"*silence* her?"

"It's possible. So there's going to be a New Order meeting at their house tomorrow afternoon, and Hunter invited me. This is big."

"Are you going to go?"

"Of *course* I'm going to go. I'll basically be getting access to the Antima inner sanctum."

"What if you...I mean, what if they figure out who you are?"

"They won't. Will you please let your coven know about this development?"

"Yeah, of course!"

"There's also a regular Antima meeting tomorrow at one o'clock at the community center. I'm sending Binx and Aysha and Mira. Does anyone from your coven plan to attend?"

Binx at an Antima meeting? "Not that I know of. Will Binx be safe? And Aysha and Mira, too?"

"My girls can take care of themselves."

Ridley wasn't so sure. There hadn't been any confirmed reports of Antima violence in Sorrow Point—Penelope's murder excepted, assuming that Colter or another Antima member had been responsible—but there was always a first time.

"...and last but not least, please tell Greta she should stop acting like a child and start returning my messages," Div was saying. "Otherwise, perhaps she should reconsider her status as coven leader and hand the reins over to you. Anyway, I must go; Prada requires my attention. Good night."

Div hung up. Ridley stared at her phone and then set it aside. What a strange, unsettling conversation. Also, how could Div suggest that Ridley take Greta's place? Greta was a wonderful coven leader. It would be a huge betrayal even to *think* about replacing her.

Although frankly, just speaking to Div without Greta involved felt like a betrayal. The two of them were rivals. They apparently used to be friends and coven-mates, but that was ages ago. According to Binx, they may have had a romantic history, too... but again, that was ages ago.

No matter. Ridley would just tell Greta first thing in the morning about this conversation. Honesty was always the best policy. Or it was *usually* the best policy, anyway.

Her phone rang again. Had Div forgotten to tell her something?

"Hello?"

There was buzzing and crackling, then a blur of different voices.

"Hello? Div?"

Two beeps, then someone muttered, "Holy hemlock! How does this stupid thing work?"

Ridley sat up. "Aunt Viola? Is that you?"

"Oh, good, it's working! Yes, it's me. Hello, darling girl!"

"Are you okay? Where are you?"

"I'm at the airport. In Los Angeles. I think I accidentally packed my cell phone in my checked luggage, so I had to use a pay phone. Although you're probably too young to know what that is."

"Um, why are you in Los Angeles?"

"My connecting flight was delayed, so I'm cooling my heels, as they say. I'm on my third Jamba juice."

Ridley rubbed her eyes. This conversation was very confusing.

"Your connecting flight to where?"

Aunt Viola laughed. "To visit you, of course! If nothing else goes wrong, I should be at your house sometime tomorrow."

7

NEST OF VIPERS

In a situation, never assume you know all,
or that you know nothing.

(FROM *THE GOOD BOOK OF MAGIC AND MENTALISM*
BY CALLIXTA CROWE)

On Saturday afternoon, Binx hurried down Pleasant Street toward the community center. She'd overslept, which was understandable, given that she'd stayed up half the night trying to advance to Level 25 in *Witchworld*—she'd been *this close*—and also researching how to make cosplaying costumes. She liked to knit and crochet and was really good at both, but she didn't own a sewing machine and couldn't imagine making a whole entire outfit from scratch. She also couldn't decide who she wanted to dress up as that wouldn't make her seem *too* geeky. Someone from the Valkyrie Valley High Council? Or from the Dimensional Diamond Lair? Or from some other part of *Witchworld*? Honestly, though... the whole thing seemed silly and way too social and not a worthwhile use of her time.

Except that she'd promised ShadowKnight, and she didn't want to bail on him. Besides, it was a net positive overall. She was finally going to meet him. And some of the other Libertas members, too...but mostly, she was looking forward to meeting *him*. They'd been through so much together, virtually, in the few short months they'd known each other.

As Binx waited for the WALK sign at the next intersection, she wondered if she should just make a U-turn and go home. *Why* did she have to play undercover at an Antima meeting? And with Aysha and Mira, no less? Aysha was so obnoxious and full of herself—and downright mean, when the mood struck her. Mira wasn't much better, and she usually delivered the mean with an irritating *who, me?* smile.

Plus, there was the other thing later, at the Jessups' house, providing security for Div while she mingled with a bunch of Antima/New Order VIPs. Aysha and Mira would be running security with her, too, which meant that Binx was basically stuck with them for the entire day. *Blurg.*

"Hey! Binx Kato!"

Speaking of...on the other side of the street, Aysha was standing in front of the Curious Cat, Greta's dad's used bookstore. She was dressed in a red tank top, jeans, and a black leather jacket, and she was holding a bag from Starbucks. Mira wasn't with her.

Binx lifted her hand in an unenthusiastic wave as she crossed the street on the WALK sign. "What, no 'Beatrix'?" she called out.

"Thought we could have a truce for a day. Figured we should stick together on account of, you know, *that*." Aysha scrunched up her face and nodded in the direction of the community center, which was three doors down.

"Yeah. *That.* Can't we just bail and tell Div we went?"

"LOL. As you probably know by now, Div doesn't react well to insubordination."

"True. So where's Mira?"

"She has her ballet class, so she's meeting us there." Aysha reached into the Starbucks bag, pulled out two bottles of mocha Frappuccino, and offered one to Binx.

Binx quirked an eyebrow at her. "You...bought me a drink?"

"Truce for a day, remember?"

"Huh. Okay, well, thanks."

"Sure."

Binx had skipped breakfast plus lunch due to the oversleeping, so she was actually glad for the unexpected caffeine freebie. As she turned and started toward the community center, she uncapped the bottle and took a sip. "So have you ever...*blech*!"

She spit out the foul-tasting beverage. She held the bottle up to the light.

There were dead insects floating around in the liquid. Were they... *mealworms*?

"Are...you...*SERIOUS*?" Binx yelled at Aysha. She ran to the nearest garbage can and dumped the contents. She tried not to vomit as the mealworms wriggled and writhed in a Frappuccino puddle.

Aysha burst into hysterical laughter and slapped her thighs. "*Yessss!* You fell for it!"

"I thought we were having a truce for a day! Besides, I'm in your cov"—Binx corrected herself quickly; there were people walking by— "*group* now, jerk. I thought we were past the pranking phase." Before Binx had joined Div's crew, she and Aysha used spells to prank each other almost daily. Mira had been involved, too, but Aysha had been particularly, and annoyingly, skilled in that department.

"Who said we were past the pranking phase?" Aysha countered. She was laughing so hard now that tears rolled down her cheeks. "Oh my god, that was excellent! I should have made a TikTok! You should be impressed because I did that without, you know, *shortcuts*."

The girl was obviously talking about magic.

"Well, I know a good *shortcut* to shut your ugly face."

"Good one, Beatrix."

Glaring, Binx dug through her backpack to find water, gum, mints... anything to take the taste of mealworm out of her mouth. Aysha handed Binx the second bottle of Frappuccino.

"This one is mealworm-free. I swear."

"Like I believe you."

"I can prove it. Watch." Aysha uncapped the bottle and took a sip. "See? It's totally normal. You can even do a quick, uh, *confir*...confirmation on it if you want."

She'd almost said *confirmo,* the C-Squared spell to verify that an inanimate object was what it appeared to be. "Why, so you can go running to Div and tell her I broke her little rule?"

Aysha grinned and shrugged. "I would never."

Binx scowled at her. Then she grabbed the Frappuccino bottle, studied it carefully, and took a tiny sip. It tasted fine. She took several larger sips.

"I'm ready. Let's go. And be very, very afraid because I *will* get you back...when you least expect it."

"Looking forward to it, Beatrix."

Binx stifled a swear and continued down the sidewalk toward their destination. Aysha doubled her steps and caught up to her. They headed into the community center in stony silence.

Once inside, Binx stifled *another* swear. The lobby was jam-packed with people, most of them wearing Antima patches. She'd expected a crowd, but not *this* big of a crowd. Where had they all come from? Did sleepy little Sorrow Point really have this many active witch haters?

"Guess we should have come in our Antima costumes," Aysha muttered under her breath.

"Yeah, guess so."

Everyone was slowly funneling into the auditorium. Binx and Aysha followed and found three empty seats on the aisle. Binx did a quick head count; there seemed to be two hundred or so in attendance.

"Mira just texted. She's on her way." Aysha draped her leather jacket over the empty seat between herself and Binx.

"Super looking forward to this fun event," Binx said sarcastically.

"Yeah, me too."

A few minutes later, Orion Kong stepped onto the stage and grabbed the microphone, which elicited clapping and cheering. Binx shifted nervously in her seat. The awful meeting was beginning. For some random reason, she noticed that Orion had switched out his blue highlights for orange ones. She appreciated highlights as much as anyone—currently, she was sporting several different shades of purple—but Orion looked both ridiculous and frightening with his flame-colored buzz cut and all-black outfit complete with not one, not two, but *three* Antima patches.

He raised a hand to silence the crowd. Wait…was that an Antima symbol inked on his right forearm? *Ugh.*

"Hello, welcome! I want to thank you all for giving up part of your Saturday to be here."

Behind him, half a dozen Antima members walked onto the stage and sat down on metal folding chairs. Three of them were also from the high school—Axel Ngata, Brandon Fiske, and Francisco Lopez. Binx didn't recognize the others—two girls and a guy.

"Hey." Mira appeared and slid into the seat between Binx and Aysha as she set her gym bag on the floor. Her long brown hair was scrunched up in a bun, and she wore a fuzzy black sweater, denim cutoffs, and black leg warmers over faded pink tights. "Did I miss anything?" she whispered.

"Just started," Aysha whispered back.

"This is our third meeting as a group," Orion was saying to the crowd. "In those few short weeks, we've gone from a half a dozen folks to this." He swept his arm in a wide arc, and there was more clapping and cheering. "I see a lot of new faces here today. Welcome." His gaze seemed to land briefly on Binx, Aysha, and Mira. *Gross.*

"And today, I want to welcome a very special guest." Orion pointed to a dark-haired man sitting in the front row.

The man stood up, turned, and waved to the audience.

Mira grabbed Aysha's wrist.

"Is that—" Aysha began.

"Ohmigod, that's my dad. What is he doing here?"

Mira's dad? Binx frowned. *Why is he hanging out at a hate-group meeting?*

"This is Councilman Neal Jahani, and, as you probably all know, he's running for mayor. Councilman Jahani, why don't you come up here and say a few words?" Orion called out.

"Thanks. Love to."

Mr. Jahani strolled onto the stage, and Orion handed him the mic. Mira was still death-gripping Aysha's wrist.

"Thanks, Orion. Hey, everyone. I'm Neal Jahani, and I have the privilege of being one of your councilmen. During these past four years, I've been responsible for spearheading many important efforts, including the rec-center expansion, low-interest loans for small businesses, and faster approvals for new construction. But there's so much more that I want to do for our great community, which is why I decided to run for mayor." His expression grew serious. "I think it's safe to say that our current mayor is out of touch with these times. In fact, and some of you may know this already, but she's been working behind the scenes to turn Sorrow Point into a sanctuary city for witches."

Gasps rippled through the crowd. Binx hadn't been aware of the sanctuary city thing.

Good for Mayor Lovejoy. Except that Mr. Jahani—and the Antima horde—would no doubt make sure any such plan was DOA.

"I think I speak for everyone here when I say, witches don't belong here," Mr. Jahani went on, and Mira clapped a hand over her mouth to stifle a cry. "Not in Sorrow Point, not in Washington, not in our country. There are a million reasons for this, but I'll give you just one. Their use of magic gives them an unfair, not to mention unnatural, advantage over the rest of us humans. A witch could use magic to take your job away from you"—Mr. Jahani pointed to a middle-aged man in the front row—"and a witch could use magic to steal your hard-earned money from your bank account"—he pointed to a woman to his left—"and a witch could use magic to cheat off your test at school, the one *you* studied so hard for and they didn't"—he pointed to a couple of high school students. "I say, this must end. *Here. Now.* We must make witches give up their powers and live like the rest of us. And any witches who are unwilling to comply *will* be punished to the fullest extent of the law. I'll make sure of it."

Now Mira was visibly shaking and gritting her teeth to fight back tears. Binx felt sorry for the girl for the first time in, well, ever. She patted Mira's shoulder, not knowing what else to do; she wasn't used to comforting people.

This was bad. *Really* bad. Binx was aware Mr. Jessup and Mr. Jahani were friends—in fact, Mr. Jessup had thrown a big fundraising party for Mr. Jahani's mayoral campaign just last month—and Mr. Jessup was a big ole witch hater, which meant he wouldn't be supporting someone who was explicitly pro-witch. But . . . *this?*

"Thanks, everyone. Please make your voices heard. Please vote for me on November seventh. And if you need a ride to the polls, we have a team of volunteers who would be happy to drive you."

"Thank you, Councilman Jahani." Orion took the mic back and turned his attention back to the audience. "If anyone would like to join Councilman Jahani's campaign, please come see me after the meeting! Right now, we could use more people to go door-to-door, make phone calls, send texts, and distribute lawn signs."

We? So Orion was a member of Mr. Jahani's campaign, then? Him and how many other Antima members?

"I need to get out of here," Mira whispered to Binx and Aysha.

"I know, sweetie, but if we leave now, we might look suspicious," Aysha pointed out.

"I guess." Mira slumped down in her seat. "I'm getting a new dad."

Binx leaned over. "Does he know you're a...um..."

"No! And after this, I will never, ever tell him. *Ever.*"

Mira dug through her bag, extracted a pair of earbuds, and pushed them into her ears. Orion and the others on the stage proceeded to give various updates about Antima business. Kind of like the Homecoming Committee, except this committee was evil whereas the other one was just stupid. Binx ticked through a mental list of items they would report back to Div later. Huge attendance. Young, old, middle. Way too many Antima patches. Orion was the leader, or *a* leader. Brandon, Axel, and Francisco from school were also there. And worst of all, Mira's dad was running on an anti-witch platform and recruiting Antima members to work on his campaign.

"*Now* can we go?" Mira asked Aysha as soon as Orion had called the meeting to a close.

Aysha nodded, and the three girls rose quickly to their feet. But before they could reach the exit, Mr. Jahani sauntered up to them.

"Mira, honey, I didn't know you were coming to this!" he said, reaching over to hug her.

Mira stiffened and pulled away. "Some kids at school mentioned it."

"Excellent, that's great. Nice to see you, Aysha." Mr. Jahani pivoted toward Binx and thrust out his hand. "And you are...?"

"Binx." She shook his hand reluctantly.

"Pleased to meet you, Binx. I must say, it's a terrific surprise seeing you girls at this gathering. It's so wonderful that your generation is getting involved in these important social issues. Gives me hope."

Important social issues. Binx squeezed her fists. She marveled at Mira's ability to not have a meltdown in the aisle, because she herself was *this* close.

Fortunately, Aysha saved the moment. "Sure, uh-huh. 'Our generation is the future' and all that. We have to run now; we're meeting up with some friends at the library for this group project thing that's due on Monday," she fibbed. "Bye, Mr. Jahani!"

"Bye, girls! Mira, I'll see you at home later."

"Yup." Mira pushed her backpack onto her shoulder and made a beeline for the exit. Binx and Aysha rushed after her.

Once on the sidewalk, Mira stopped and turned to the other girls. Tears shimmered in her eyes, and her cheeks were flushed with anger. "I knew he wasn't, like, pro-witch. When Penelope died, he made a stupid remark about teens who make bad choices and break the law or whatever. But *this*?"

The tears were pouring down her face now. Aysha reached over and hugged her tightly. Binx was not the hugging type, but she felt like she should do *something*, and so she patted Mira's shoulder again. Binx's own father might be an absentee dad who'd let her down more than once. And she didn't trust him—or her mom—enough to tell them about her own witch identity. But she knew her parents would never participate in an anti-magic hate movement...or *any* hate movement.

Oh, what the heck. Binx reached over and gave Mira an awkward hug.

"We're gonna fix this," she said fiercely.

She had no idea how. But she meant it.

8

THE INNER SANCTUM

In battle, learn to cloak your emotions, except
when vulnerability can be used to your advantage.

(FROM *THE GOOD BOOK OF MAGIC AND MENTALISM*
BY CALLIXTA CROWE)

Div wasn't sure whether to act excited or nervous about her first New
Order meeting, which was really her first anti-magic meeting of any
kind. As she followed Hunter to the family library—she was early and he
had things to take care of, so she would hang out there for a bit—she tried
to wear both emotions on her face like the eager, supportive girlfriend
she was pretending to be. "Excited" and "nervous" didn't begin to cover
her true feelings, though. Her pulse thrummed and adrenaline coursed
through her veins... honestly, she felt as though she were preparing to go
into battle.

She was ready.

Inside the library, Hunter waved to a dark brown leather chair. "Is this
okay? I'll just be a sec."

Div sat down, crossed her legs, and pulled her phone out of her bag. "No worries, I can occupy myself. What time does the meeting start again?"

"In about ten, fifteen minutes, in the living room. People are beginning to arrive."

"Will Colter be here?"

"As far as I know."

Div knew Mira wouldn't be present, though, because she was stationed outside with Aysha and Binx, and besides, Colter hadn't invited her. Did he not feel comfortable sharing the New Order/Antima part of his life with her? Or was Colter not hugely involved in the group? Although... Hunter said "me and some of my family" last night at the country club. If Div had to guess, that meant either Mr. Jessup, or Colter, or both. Dr. Jessup hadn't expressed any Antima sentiments—not in Div's presence, anyway. She'd also defended the twins' new obsession with the *Witchworld* video game to her husband. If indeed one or both girls had powers, perhaps there was a small chance they could count on their mom to shield them from the bigoted men in their family.

And speaking of bigoted male relatives... Div felt awful for Mira because of what her coven had learned about Mr. Jahani at the community center earlier. She made a note to have a one-on-one with the girl soon, to cheer her up and also to strategize about how best to protect Mira inside her own home. Plus, they needed to brainstorm how to use this new angle to further penetrate and decimate the Antima. Mira might be feeling upset and vulnerable at the moment, but she was a witch first and foremost, and she knew her duty.

Hunter kissed Div on the cheek and left the room. As soon as the door had closed behind him, Div began texting her three witches.

Are you guys in position?

Aysha wrote back:

We're in position.

Binx added:

Taking pix of the people as they get out of their cars. So far, no one we recognize.

Mira joined in, too:

There are police officers guarding the front. Did you know they'd be here?

Div frowned. She was *not* happy to hear this.

No. Obviously don't let them see you.

Binx replied:

Obviously!

Div wrote:

The plan is like we talked about. If anything goes wrong on my end, I'll text CANCEL. Then you guys need to enter the house through the kitchen door and look for me. No enhancements unless absolutely essential.

Enhancements was their new word for *spells*. Mira replied:

Got it. Be careful.

Div wrote:

You too. All of you.

Div deleted the texts—this was their new protocol—then slipped her phone into the inner pocket of her blazer. She hadn't known how to dress for a VIP New Order meeting, so she'd elected for an all-beige outfit: tailored jacket, pencil skirt, and silk tank top. Boring but classic, nothing that would scream "witch," although she wasn't sure what that would be, either. Maybe Greta's thrift-store boho look? Honestly, the girl might as well be wearing a pointy black hat and matching cape.

Div was glad her girls were obeying orders and taking pictures of the incoming guests with their phones. Later, they planned to run the images through a magical photo-recognition program that Binx had recently created.

Binx. Recruiting her had been a brilliant move. Not only did she have unique and impressive skills—Div didn't know any other cyber-witches—but the girl was as determined as Div herself to wipe the Antima off the face of the earth and create a society that accepted witches. Maybe more than just *accepted*. Respected. Revered, even. Div wasn't one of those tedious "equality" types who believed that witches and humans were the same, that neither was inherently better than the other. *Of course* witches were superior. *Of course* they should be at the top of the hierarchy. It was only logical, and it was only a matter of time. Based on their recent conversations, Binx seemed to be coming around to this idea, too.

Div stood up restlessly. The library was an unusual room—a true luxury, because how many families had the space or the money to have a personal library in their homes? Thousands of books filled the floor-to-ceiling shelves—novels in alphabetical order by author, nonfiction books in alphabetical order by title. The furnishings consisted of pricey-looking antiques. Two Tiffany lamps cast a soft glow on the burgundy-and-gold wallpaper.

A strange unease settled over her. All of a sudden, she felt as though she'd been here before, alone, although she couldn't remember when or why. She remembered having been in danger.

Shake it off. You're being paranoid.

Still, she couldn't help it; she needed an ... *enhancement.*

"*Pleukiokus,*" she whispered. A protection spell.

The unease dissipated and was replaced by a shimmery white sensation, like an invisible cloak. *Better.* Div walked around the room, feeling more confident, and ran her fingers along the spines of the books, checking out their titles. *The Art of Knitting.* Boring. *The Art of War.* Hmm, more interesting.

She moved to a large oak desk. An old-fashioned radio sat on top of it, along with a leather-bound notebook and an expensive-looking silver pen. Div glanced around. Yes, she was definitely alone. She inched closer to the desk and regarded the notebook. It had been locked with a small combination lock. Was it a personal diary? Or something else? Who did it belong to? She glanced around again, just to be sure. *Still alone.*

"*Transpicere,*" she whispered. In her mind, she pictured being able to read the contents of the notebook without opening or even touching it.

It worked. Div could see a handwritten list of some sort. But the list was barely legible because words from other pages were superimposed on them.

"*Transpicere*," she repeated.

Three words floated into focus.

Penelope Rue Hart.

And Penelope's name was followed by some random numbers, no, letters, maybe part of a word. *ONEG.*

What the hex?

Div pulled out her phone to text her girls about this. She typed:

I found something that might be a clue.

She hit send, and an alert popped up:

UNABLE TO SEND.

She tried to resend, but the delivery failed again. Her phone seemed to have lost all its bars. Strange...she'd texted with Aysha, Binx, and Mira just a few minutes ago.

Frowning, Div picked up her purse and headed into the hallway, holding up her phone and moving it this way and that. Still no bars. She could hear the low murmur of voices coming from the front of the house, no doubt the guests gathering for the New Order meeting. Maybe she should try the second floor? She wandered down the hallway until she found herself at the bottom of one of the back staircases. Her eyes on her phone, she began to climb. She didn't like not being able to communicate with her witches.

On the second-floor landing, she heard more voices. She followed the sound and realized that it was coming from Cassie's room. She peered inside. Cassie and Caitlin were sitting on the bed watching something on a pink laptop, their heads bopping in unison to electronic beats.

Cassie glanced up and waved. "Hi, Divvy!"

"Are you looking for Hunt? We don't know where he is, plus we're mad at him," Caitlin spoke up.

Div walked into the room and leaned against a dresser. She peered quickly at her phone. *Still* no bars. "Why are you mad at him?"

"He told Mom and Dad that we were watching Xandri videos on You-Tube, and they said we aren't allowed to!" Cassie sighed dramatically.

"Who's Xandri?"

"You don't know *Xandri*?" Caitlin cried out.

"Nope."

"Xandri's nonbinary. They have this cool channel called 'We Heart Magic.' It has like a bazillion subscribers," Cassie explained.

Div stared at the twins. Had she heard correctly? " 'We Heart... *Magic*'?" she repeated.

Caitlin nodded. "Yeah! They're a gamer, and they post videos of themselves playing *Witchworld*. Except, sometimes, they say stuff during their commentary that sounds like they really *do* heart witches."

"IRL witches, not *Witchworld* witches," Cassie added.

"Oh!"

How had Div not heard about this person before? And how was Xandri getting away with saying pro-witch things on YouTube? Why hadn't the police or some other authority shut them down? Also, why did Hunter tell his parents about his sisters watching Xandri videos? Did he suspect Cassie was a witch? And perhaps Caitlin, too? Or was it just his general anti-witch attitude? Div wished she could just come right out and *ask* the twins if they were witches. Although they might not know, either.

The whole thing was so delicate. Maybe it was best to pursue the topic indirectly.

"Do *you* guys think Xandri's a real witch?"

Caitlin shrugged. "I don't know. Maybe? Probably?"

"And if they were, how would you feel about that?" Div pressed on.

Cassie started to answer, then clamped her mouth shut. She and Caitlin were staring at something past Div.

Div twisted around. Dr. Jessup stood there, her arms crossed over her chest.

She seemed angry.

No, not angry . . . *worried*.

Div plastered on a quick smile. "Oh, hi, Dr. Jessup! I was just catching up with the girls," she said lightly.

Dr. Jessup entered the room and glanced around. Her blond hair was pulled back in a tight ponytail, and she smelled like eucalyptus shampoo. "Uh-huh. Is Hunter with you?"

"No. He was, but he said he had to talk to Mr. Jessup," Div improvised. "I was looking for cell reception because I needed to check my voice mail." She held up her phone, which had recovered a couple of bars, *finally*.

Dr. Jessup frowned. "Oh. Well, I'm not sure why Hunter made plans with you. He's busy this afternoon."

"Yes, I know. The meeting. He invited me."

"He did?"

"*There* you are, Div!"

Now Hunter was standing in the doorway. "Come with me. Hey, Mom—Dad was looking for you before. He wanted to know where you keep the smoked almonds. He said Mr. Soto likes them."

Div was glad for Hunter's arrival, since Dr. Jessup wouldn't be able to continue asking her questions. But . . . smoked almonds? Div could see the Instagram post now: *The best snacks for your hate-group meetups!*

"Mr. Soto doesn't like them; your *dad* likes them. I've been hiding them from him because he really needs to cut down on the salty foods, for his blood pressure."

Hunter chuckled. "Yeah, I should have guessed. Let's go, Div."

"*Traitor!*" Caitlin called after him.

"*Double* traitor!" Cassie yelled.

"Honestly, girls," Dr. Jessup said as she closed the door after Div and Hunter. She said something else to the twins, but Div couldn't hear.

"They're pissed at me because I told Mom and Dad they were watching inappropriate content online," Hunter explained to Div.

Inappropriate content. "You're a good big brother. You're just looking out for them."

"I wish they got that."

As Div followed Hunter down the stairs, she wondered why Dr. Jessup had seemed so bothered by the sight of her hanging out with the twins.

Or why she cared that Hunter had invited Div to the New Order meeting.

In the living room, Mr. Jessup was talking to the assembled crowd.

"It's good to see so many familiar faces here today. You know we really appreciate your taking the time from your busy schedules for this important cause," he was saying.

Div paused in the entryway. Okay, so Mr. Jessup was definitely a part of this. Could he even be the New Order leader? Or would that be Hunter? She would learn soon enough.

Pretending to adjust her shoe strap, she surreptitiously scanned the guests. *The inner sanctum.* About three dozen people, mostly Mr. Jessup's age, sat on folding chairs that had been arranged in rows; the majority were men, although there were a few women, too. She recognized some of the guests from a political fundraiser that the Jessups had hosted for Mr. Jahani last month, in this very same room. Three of them were the fathers of Sorrow Point High students whom Div knew to be Antima: Mr. Ngata, who was Axel Ngata's dad; Mr. Fiske, who was Brandon Fiske's; and Mr. Kong, who was Orion Kong's. Colter sat in the front row.

Mr. Jessup was standing in front of the large stone fireplace, his hands stuffed into his pants pockets and an unlit cigar dangling from his mouth. He wore a brown suit, a white shirt, cowboy boots, and a tie with an American flag design. *He looks like a cartoon*, Div thought. *Except, there's nothing funny about what he's doing.*

He pulled out the cigar and set it aside. "I think we're almost ready to start the meeting. We're just waiting on a few folks. But in the meantime, I can share some updates. As some of you already know, we've assembled a database of all the Antima groups across the country, and we've reached out to every single one. We're still waiting on a few, but so far, we've had one hundred percent positive responses. They're eager to come into our tent, so to speak. Our very well-*funded* tent." He grinned. "We should be able to make a big national announcement about the New Order very soon. We have our media folks working on it already."

Everyone began clapping. Div forced herself to clap, too, even though mostly, she just wanted to cast a *praetervolo* spell on Mr. Jessup and the rest of this evil crowd and make them disappear...for good.

Still, this was *it.* This was the physical, tangible proof that she and her girls, and Greta's coven, too, had been after for weeks...or at least an important piece of it. The New Order was an undeniable reality, and Mr. Jessup appeared to be their leader.

And what about that clue she'd found in the library? Did this mean the New Order, and the Jessups specifically, were definitely connected to Penelope's death?

"And speaking of databases…some of us local folks have already started working on another important database," Mr. Jessup continued. "We're talking about a comprehensive list of all known witches in the great state of Washington, starting with Sorrow Point."

Div froze.

"And once we've folded in the Antima groups from everywhere else, those new folks can do the legwork to collect names from *their* states," Mr. Jessup added.

Div couldn't believe what she was hearing. A database of all known witches? *No, no, no,* that absolutely could *not* happen. Plus, what did Mr. Jessup and the New Order plan to do with these names? Turn them over to the police or the FBI? Or would they take a more vigilante approach and go after the witches themselves through intimidation or worse? Div had to get her girls on this ASAP, especially Binx, who might be able to hack into this database and disable it; she also had to alert Greta's coven.

Mr. Fiske raised his hand. "How will this work, Jared? Will the New Order have a top-down hierarchy? Will all those local groups who join us take their orders from us?"

"Yes, sir, that's the plan. We here will be the central committee. And the central committee will be taking orders from *our* leader," Mr. Jessup explained.

Our leader? Div frowned. So Mr. Jessup *wasn't* the leader. Was it Hunter, then?

"Speak of the devil...here she is now. I'll step aside and let her take over with the proceedings. She's a whole lot smarter with words than I am, anyway." Mr. Jessup laughed as he pointed to the back of the room.

Someone passed by Div, leaving a faint cloud of eucalyptus, and took Mr. Jessup's place.

Dr. Jessup.

She was the leader of the New Order?

9

THE HELMET OF INSCRUTABILITY

There is no such thing as a chance encounter.
Magic informs all.

(FROM *THE GOOD BOOK OF MAGIC AND MENTALISM*
BY CALLIXTA CROWE)

"Iris, love, can you fold these for me?"

"Sure thing!"

Iris took the messy pile of napkins from Grandma Roseline. Still warm from the dryer, they were a jumble of colors and patterns: apricot with pale green stripes, turquoise with yellow lemons, indigo with white moons and stars. Nothing in Café Papillon matched, which was part of its charm. The linens, the china, the silverware, and even the tables and chairs were a motley assortment of flea market finds. All the art on the walls was for sale—this month it was paintings of dinosaur-sized robins, jays, and other birds perched atop skyscrapers, by an artist named REwind—and there was a bead shop in the adjoining space. Upstairs was an apartment that Grandma Roseline usually rented to university students, although at the moment, it was unoccupied.

"Do you want swans or regular?" Iris asked her grandmother.

"Swans?"

"Swan napkins. It's a thing. I learned it on YouTube! But never mind, I'll just do regular today."

"All right, chère."

Iris sat down at a table near the kitchen and began folding. She was helping out at the café while her mother, Rachelle, took Nyala and Ephrem to their swimming lessons at the Y. In a few hours, her mom would return for the evening shift while Iris did bedtime at home with the younger kids. Or with Ephrem, anyway. Nyala would no doubt disappear into her room and lock her door, which she seemed to be doing more and more these days.

A steamy sputtering sound...Grandma Roseline was fiddling with the monster espresso machine on the counter. The air smelled like freshly ground coffee beans and also scones; there was a fresh batch in the oven. The café wasn't too crowded right now—just a couple in the corner talking quietly over their cappuccinos, and an older gentleman reading a British newspaper and finishing up his spinach-and-okra soup. They'd all paid their checks and were happily lingering as Ella Fitzgerald sang over the ancient speakers: *"Someone who'll watch over me..."*

Near the top of the napkin pile was a pale blue one with the initials rRl monogrammed on it, the middle letter bigger than the other two, for Roseline and Louis Romain. Iris knew it was one of her grandmother's favorites from when she and Grandpa Louis were first married. Iris murmured a quick prayer under her breath, as she did every time she thought of Grandpa Louis: "May the angels smile upon you. May they have free premium cable in heaven so you can watch all the ESPN stations. May you and Dad stop arguing about politics up there because it is *very annoying*."

Dad. Beau Gooding, aka her favorite person in the whole entire world.

He was the reason why the family lived in Sorrow Point now and not New York City. He'd passed away unexpectedly in May, and after that, Rachelle had struggled to make ends meet and take care of the family on her own, especially with Kedren's expensive tuition at Barnard College. So Grandma Roseline had invited them to move to Sorrow Point and live in her house with her; she'd also given Rachelle and Iris jobs at the café.

"May the angels smile upon you, too, Dad, Daddy-o, Dadster," Iris added softly. "May they have indie folk bands in heaven so you can keep playing your acoustic guitar and singing your songs, even that super-awkward love anthem you wrote for Mom, the one that I used to make fun of. Because, surprise, I secretly liked it, too. Oh, *argh*."

Tears were gathering in her eyes. She reached up and quickly pinched her nose, hard. It was a trick she'd learned from the school social worker to keep from crying.

Although . . . for some reason, she was having a hard time remembering the social worker's name. Mrs. Bird? Mrs. Plume? In any case, Iris hadn't seen her around lately. She reminded herself to stop by her office to say hi, maybe on Monday.

She refolded the RRL napkin neatly and set it aside. "Grandma?"

"Oui, chère?"

"How did you and Grandpa Louis meet?"

"I never told you this story?"

"Nope, negatory."

Grandma Roseline smiled. "We were both seventeen. His family ran a grocery store in Port-au-Prince. He wanted to introduce himself to me, but he was too shy. So one day when I was running errands, he saw my red bicycle parked in front of the store, and he sneaked up and let the air out of one of the tires. A few minutes later, he appeared with one of those little portable air pumps and pretended to rescue me. I knew, though."

"You did? How?"

"I know everything." Grandma Roseline tapped her forehead twice. "By the way, I forgot to ask...how is your school going?"

"I thought you knew everything!"

"Clever girl. I know *almost* everything. You're a hard one to read."

"That's because of my Helmet of Inscrutability."

"Your what, now?"

"It's from *Witchworld*. It's a rare to ultra-rare item made of Draggidian steel. You can acquire it for twenty thousand Firx once you reach Level... never mind. School's okay. Although..."

"Although what?"

Iris held up a finger and glanced over at the three remaining customers. They were all standing up and putting on their jackets.

She waited until they'd left. The front door opened and closed with a clattering of tiny seashells. Then she turned back to her grandmother.

"One of our teachers was arrested. My English teacher, Mr. Dalrymple. The police think he's a witch."

Grandma Roseline pushed her shoulders back. Her mouth twisted with anger. "*Another* arrest? It's absurd. Honestly, what harm did witches ever do to anyone?"

"Right?"

Iris had never told anyone in her family that she was a witch—not that she didn't trust them to keep a secret. Well, maybe she *didn't*, especially when it came to Ephrem, who was too young to understand about secrets, and Nyala, who might blab on Iris just to be an annoying brat.

She'd *almost* revealed her identity to Grandma Roseline on one or two occasions because sometimes, Iris suspected that *she* might be a witch, too. Although maybe that was wishful thinking. Still, what about that time when Grandma Roseline had made Nyala's science-experiment plant from school, the dead one because lazy Nyala had forgotten to take care of it—come back to life overnight? Or the time she'd touched the cut on Ephrem's knee, and it had immediately stopped bleeding?

"—and it's all because of that President Ingraham," Grandma Roseline was saying. "He's only been our president for . . . what? Nine months? And in that short time, he's stirred up a whole lot of witch hatred, anger, prejudice. *Those* things should be crimes, not being a witch! Right, chère?"

Whenever Grandma Roseline got like this, she reminded Iris of Grandpa Louis. Except that Grandpa Louis had been a big fan of President Ingraham back when the president was governor of Washington because he was always cutting taxes. Grandma Roseline had been the opposite of a big fan, though, saying she didn't want to save a few dollars on her tax bill if it meant gutting programs for the poor and needy . . . or if it meant supporting a vocal witch hater. Although at that time, President Ingraham had been more of a vocal witch *disliker*. After his teen daughter had died under mysterious circumstances—she might have been a witch, according to the rumors—his dislike had morphed into rage.

The oven timer buzzed. "Excuse me a sec," Grandma Roseline said, and headed for the kitchen.

Iris continued folding and stacking. She was worried—not that she wasn't always worried, but this was a whole new level. *I've leveled up in the worrying department, ha.* There was too much happening. In part because of President Ingraham, the Antima had leveled up, too. They now possessed more power, and they were engaging in more activities, more attacks—not in a fun, fantasy, *Witchworld* sort of way, but in a dire and dangerous way that was harming witches IRL. Iris wished she could type *NTG*—"need to go"—and walk away and never come back to this terrible, scary game that wasn't a game.

There was the matter of Penelope's killer, too. They had to be caught and brought to justice, sure. But there was another, more urgent concern, which was: Would that person go after another witch?

Maybe me? Or Greta?

The front door opened suddenly with a clattering of seashells. Iris gave a yelp.

"Sorry, I didn't mean to startle you!" a familiar voice called out.

Iris squinted at the silhouette haloed by sunlight.

Not a deranged witch murderer. Greta.

"Oh! Hi! Hello!" Iris stood up abruptly and accidentally knocked over the stack of neatly folded napkins. She'd just been thinking about Greta; did that mean she'd mentally, magically caused her coven-mate-slash-crush to appear? No way. Besides, she kind of thought about Greta a lot, so statistically speaking, her appearance could easily be a coincidence. "*Argh*, I am so...I was just...and here you are...anyway, hi!"

"Hi!" Greta walked over and sat down at Iris's table. She took off her old-fashioned blue wool hat, which had a pretty velvet ribbon and a cluster of silk violets. She set her backpack on the floor, the vegan faux-leather one with the button that said I LOVE ANIMALS, BUT NOT FOR DINNER.

"How are you?" she asked Iris.

"Um..." Iris suddenly wanted to hide, or jump up and down with joy, or both. Greta had come to the café! To see her! "I'm good. I'm great! Are you here to eat? Do you want a menu?" She grabbed a menu from the next table; she turned it upside down and then right side up again, then thrust it at Greta. "So, yeah...the vegan items are marked with a little picture of a carrot...that was my idea, although I had *the* hardest time deciding if it should be a carrot or a tomato. Do you have an opinion on carrots versus tomatoes? Of course, tomatoes are technically fruits, so it's kind of an apples-and-oranges comparison. Although that's confusing, too, since apples and oranges are both fruits. They're not both apples, though. *Argh.*" Iris sat back down and began refolding napkins.

"I'm actually here, well, I wanted to make sure you were okay after..." Greta glanced around. "Good, we're alone. You seemed kind of upset at yesterday's coven meeting. About Torrence."

"What? *Nah!*" Iris waved her hand in a no-biggie gesture.

"I know I should have asked you and Ridley first," Greta went on.

"Nah!"

"It's just that, well...I've been feeling really upset about losing Binx to Div. And Penelope was going to join us, too, until she..." Greta's voice trembled. "Anyway, I really want to grow our group and make it stronger. Especially with what's happening. I got a good vibe off Torrence when I met him in front of Mrs. Poe's store. I didn't, and I still don't, sense any malevolence in him."

Iris furrowed her brow and nodded slowly. This was one of Greta's magical skills that she'd been developing—empathy, trying to intuit people's moods and emotions and even intentions.

But wait. Did that mean Greta could pick up on Iris's feelings for *her*? And the fact that she, Iris, was upset about the possibility of Torrence liking Greta, and worse, Greta liking him back?

I really, really need that Helmet of Inscrutability now.

"It's totally fine! Torrence is fine! Do you want some tea?" Iris burst out shrilly.

"Yes, that would be nice. Do you have mint tea? Today seems like a mint tea sort of day."

"Would you like lavender mint tea, Moroccan mint tea, or regular old mint tea? Or peach-ginger mint tea? Or is it ginger-peach? Does the order make a difference? Is peach-ginger more peachy, and ginger-peach more gingery? Sorry, I'm rambling."

Greta laughed. "You're fine. I'd like regular old mint tea, please."

"Okeydokey, coming right up."

Iris went to the kitchen to prepare the tea. Grandma Roseline was on the phone, talking to one of the local farmers about a particular kind of turnip she would need for tomorrow night's casserole special.

A few minutes later, Iris returned to Greta's table with a tray: a pot of mint tea, Iris's favorite mug with the pink roses on it, a pitcher of oat milk, and a plate of Grandma Roseline's scones, fresh out of the oven. "This one's cranberry-orange, this one's coconut-almond, and this one's lemon-poppy-seed. All vegan," she explained.

"I love scones. Thank you!"

Greta picked up the lemon-poppy-seed scone, split it in two, and offered half to Iris. "So do you have any thoughts about what Ridley told us? About the mansion in the rain forest?"

"No! That was so bizarre. Although I've been thinking..."

"Yes?"

"We talked about precognition at the meeting. The ability to see into the future. What if Ridley was experiencing *retro*cognition instead?"

"The ability to see into the past. Yes! We should research if there were ever any mansions at that site. There must be old deeds in City Hall?" Greta sighed. "I wish Binx were still with us. She's so good with all that computer stuff."

"I know. I wish she'd come back."

Greta's phone began to vibrate. She peered at the screen and frowned.

"What is it?" Iris asked.

"It's Div. It's a text for Ridley and me."

"Oh. But not me? Weird. What does it say?"

Green slanted her phone toward Iris. Div had written:

Emergency meeting NOW. All of us. We need a private place though. Any ideas?

"W-what emergency?" Iris stammered nervously.

"I don't know. But if Div says it's an emergency, it's an emergency. She's not one to overreact." Greta steepled her hands under her chin. "Let's see... we can't use my house, because my dad has a friend visiting. We can't use Ridley's house, either, because... well, I'm not sure, exactly. But she never wants us to meet there. How about your house? Is your family home?"

"IDK, but I have an even better place!"

"Where?"

Just then, Grandma Roseline bustled out of the kitchen with an armful of menus. She regarded Iris, then Greta.

"Well, hello there! You must be Greta Navarro. Iris has told me so much about you!"

"I have?" Iris didn't remember ever mentioning Greta to her grandmother. Or had she? "So, yup, this is *the* Greta. Greta, this is my grandma Roseline. *The* Grandma Roseline."

Greta waved. "Hi! It's really nice to—"

"Can we use your upstairs apartment? It's empty, right?" Iris cut in.

Grandma Roseline raised her eyebrows, then chuckled. "I understand. You girls want privacy. Well, who am I to say no to young love? I remember back when your grandfather and I were first dating—"

"*NO!* It's not *THAT*!" Iris practically shouted. "Greta and I need to... I mean, we need a place to meet with some friends to... um... do this *thing*. An important school thing. Right now. And it has to be up there versus down here because we need... we don't want to bother your customers... not that you have any right this second, but you will because it'll be dinner soon, and... argh!"

Grandma Roseline waved her hand. "Of course, chère. Not to worry. Here, let me get you the key."

Iris's face was so hot that it felt as though it might start melting. She couldn't make herself look at Greta. This was the most mortifying, most embarrassing experience of her life, bar none, which was saying a lot because mortifying, embarrassing experiences were kind of her brand.

Greta touched her arm. "Your grandma's so sweet. And thank you for thinking of this. I'll text Div right away and tell her coven to meet us here...and Ridley and Torrence, too."

Torrence.

"Can I ask you a nosy question? Do you like him?" Iris blurted out before she could stop herself.

"Of course. He's..." Greta stopped and stared at Iris. "Oh! You mean *like*, as in...*like*...." Her voice trailed off.

Iris finally managed to look up at her.

Now *Greta* was blushing.

Iris's heart sank all the way down to the floor.

10

THE SCIONS OF CALLIXTA

Existence is never final.

(FROM *THE GOOD BOOK OF MAGIC AND MENTALISM*
BY CALLIXTA CROWE)

n the empty studio apartment upstairs from Iris's grandmother's café, Greta and the other witches sat around in a circle on the bare wooden floor. The only furniture in the space was a twin bed with no sheets, a teal dresser with a faded Sorrow Point University bumper sticker on it, and a reading lamp with no light bulb. Venetian blinds half-covered a couple of windows that overlooked downtown Sorrow Point.

Greta smoothed her gray wool skirt over her knees and gazed around at all the faces. Everyone exuded major stress and unhappiness—including Mira, who'd arrived at the café without her usual bubbly hellos; Binx, who seemed both flustered and annoyed; and Iris, who'd been quiet and moody ever since their conversation earlier, or at least the Torrence portion of the conversation, anyway.

And there was Div, who was having a minor temper tantrum. Also about Torrence.

"Seriously, Greta. Tell me again why you brought a total stranger to our gathering? And tell me again why I shouldn't cast *praetereo* on him immediately?"

Greta's ex-coven-mate and ex-crush wasn't dressed in one of her usual sexy, stylish white outfits, but in a preppy jacket, skirt, and silk blouse. Of course, she was so stunning that she would likely pull off *any* look. Greta closed her eyes and took a deep, centering breath. Why was Div being so unreasonable...so *Div*? When Greta had texted Div about meeting here, she'd added that Torrence was a new coven member and that he would be joining them. So it wasn't as though she'd left Div out of the loop. Besides, Greta was in charge of her own coven, not Div. Div had no authority to tell Greta who could and couldn't be a member.

Not to mention, if Div hadn't stolen Binx away, Greta might not have been so eager to find a new fourth witch.

When Greta opened her eyes, she saw that Div was giving her one of her cold, unrelenting death stares.

Greta took another deep breath.

Don't fight with her; that never works.

"Div—" she began in a conciliatory voice.

"Honestly, it's okay," Torrence said, rising to his feet. "I don't want to cause a problem. I can just leave."

"Don't go!" Greta fluttered her fingers toward him, then turned her attention back to Div. "Let him stay. I can vouch for him."

Binx peered at her watch. "Can we *puh-lease* get on with this? I've been nonstop all day, and I have to go home and let the puppy out."

"Oh, right, your new familiar! How's he doing?" Ridley asked Binx.

"He's awesome. You should come over sometime and—"

"I have an excellent idea," Aysha cut in. "Let the hot newb stay, and if we're not convinced that he's legit by the end of the meeting, we can do a massive group *praetereo* spell on him. That should pretty much wipe out his entire memory bank."

Torrence smiled nervously. "Um...thanks?"

"Fine. Let's proceed. We're wasting time," Div snapped.

Torrence sat back down. Everyone fell silent as Div's gaze swept around the circle.

"We have a lot to discuss, but first, there's an urgent matter that requires our immediate attention. *Several* urgent matters." Div paused and steepled her hands. "Most of you are aware that I just now left a New Order meeting at the Jessups' house. I was there at Hunter Jessup's invitation. During the meeting, I learned that the leader of the New Order isn't Mr. Jessup. Or Hunter. Or Colter. It's the mother, Dr. Jessup."

Mira gasped. "Colter's *mom*? *She's* Antima, too? Weren't we thinking it was just the guys?"

"It seems to be all four of them. And they're not just Antima. They're the leadership behind the New Order—or, *she* is, anyway," Div amended.

"Colter's *mom*," Mira repeated. She looked shell-shocked.

Greta had never met Dr. Jessup, who was a pediatrician. It was scary, thinking that a person who'd devoted her life to healing children was a cold-blooded witch hater. Did that mean she'd have no qualms about rounding up and punishing young witches? And what did this mean for the Jessup girls, the twins?

"There's something else. The New Order is apparently compiling a database of all known witches," Div went on.

Ridley leaned forward. "Wait, what? A database of witches?"

"I'm afraid so. They're starting with Sorrow Point and then extending the database to the rest of the state, then the rest of the country. No doubt they'll use this information to report us all to the police or the federal authorities, or take matters in their own hands and harass us, hurt us. Needless to say, we have to stop this madness."

Binx held up her phone, which today had a case with a pink, round, sleepy-looking Pokémon character on it. "Already on it! Once I find this database, which will be soon, I hope, I can use this new hacking spell I've been developing."

Torrence grinned. "You can cast hacking spells? That's awesome!"

"Thanks. You must be my replacement. I'm Binx Kato," she said, waving.

"Torrence Innsworth," he said, waving back.

"Let's wrap up the socializing, shall we? There's more," Div interjected. "Before the New Order meeting started, I happened to be in the Jessups' library, and I came across a leather notebook, like a diary or a journal. It was locked, so I used *transpicere* to try to peek inside, and I saw a list of names. I was only able to make out one of them. Penelope Rue Hart."

Ridley clamped a hand over her mouth. Greta sensed fear in her, and also fury.

"There was some sort of code or part of a word after her name, too. The letters *O-N-E-G*," Div added.

Iris jumped to her feet. "Hello, everyone? Fellow witches? I have an important announcement to make!" she cried out.

"What is it?" Greta asked her gently. Iris seemed unusually agitated.

Iris pushed her glasses up the bridge of her nose. "Some of you already know this, but I get these visions. Sometimes in my dreams. Sometimes *not* in my dreams, like when I touch stuff and it can trigger images. I can't really control when they happen; they sort of come and go, even during super-inconvenient times, like last week in the middle of my algebra quiz when the quadratic formula on my paper turned into an army of pigs, and I had to be excused because of my hyperventilating and other panic attack-y symptoms. *Anyhoo…*" She stopped and twisted her hands. "You mentioned Penelope just now, Div…and when you said her name, I had this vision. About kitty-cats. And fire. I think it might be connected to this *other* vision I had when I touched your scarf, Greta."

"When you touched my scarf? Which scarf? When?" Greta asked, startled.

"A few weeks ago, you and I were sitting in the courtyard at lunchtime, remember? And I was eating a banana muffin from my grandma's café, or was it blueberry? And you were upset because"—Iris cast a quick glance at Binx—"yeah, and I hugged you. Not like a romant…not like a—" She cleared her throat. "It was a friendly *comfort* hug, and I accidentally made contact with your scarf, and suddenly, this vision came to me. I kind of suppressed it—or is the word *repressed*? I can never keep them straight. Either way, I hoped the vision wasn't based on reality, because it was kind of upsetting. Anyhoo, I had that vision again just now, or part of it. Like two seconds ago while you were talking about Penelope, Div, and I wasn't touching *anyone's* scarf."

Iris stopped and folded her arms across her chest.

"So what else was in your vision, or visions, or whatever?" Binx asked her.

"Well…" Iris was now gazing at Greta with a worried expression. "So there was this gray house, and it was on fire."

Gray, not peach like my *house.* Greta exhaled. "Did you recognize the place?"

"Yes and no. I mean, it looked familiar, but I don't know why. There was other stuff in my vision, too. There was this kitty-cat with one eye. And a lady with grayish-blond hair. And..." Iris hesitated. "Mr. Gofflesby. He was in my vision, too."

"*Gofflesby?*" Greta burst out. "What was he doing in your vision? Was he hurt?"

"I don't think so. But I'm not totally sure."

Greta spun around, grabbed her backpack, and reached into the front pocket for her phone. She believed Iris *was* truly psychic, which meant that this particular vision might be significant, be real. If so, Gofflesby could be missing or in danger...*again.*

Heart racing, Greta typed a message to her mother.

> Can you check on Gofflesby? Is he there? Is he okay?

She hit send, and a moment later, Ysabel wrote back:

> He's right here on the kitchen counter trying to steal my crackers and almond butter. Why?

Greta exhaled with relief. Then she remembered Iris's detail about the one-eyed cat.

> Can you check his eyes? Are they okay?

Her mother replied:

> His eyes are fine. Why do you ask? Is everything all right?

Oh, thank Goddess.

Yes. Thank you, Mama, I'll see you at dinner.

"He's fine," Greta announced to the group as she put her phone away.

"Yay, Mr. Gofflesby!" Iris cheered.

"Could I make a suggestion?" Torrence spoke up. "Greta, do you have that scarf with you, by any chance?"

"I do." Greta dug through her backpack and pulled out a velvety red wrap.

"Could I see it?"

"Sure." Greta handed it to Torrence. She wondered what he had in mind.

He held the scarf for a moment, then set it on the floor in the middle of the circle. "Do you guys know *agnitionis*?"

"*Agni*-what? How do you spell that?" Binx began scrolling through the grimoire on her phone.

"*A-G-N-I-T-I-O-N-I-S*. It's an advanced scrying spell. I have my own version of it, which involves using three pieces of azurite."

Azurite was one of Greta's favorite gemstones; she was aware of its power to seek the truth. "That sounds really cool. Except . . . we don't have any azurite with us. Div and I made a rule for our covens, that we can't carry magical items around in public."

"Makes sense. Wait a sec."

Torrence reached into his pants pocket and pulled out three coins. He curled his fist around them and closed his eyes. "*Morpho*," he whispered.

He opened his eyes and uncurled his fingers. The three coins had been replaced by three small, deep blue pieces of azurite.

"Nice," Aysha complimented him.

"Yeah. *Morpho* solves the whole no-carrying-magical-items-around problem. Like, *why* didn't we think of that?" Mira said.

Even Div looked impressed. "Hmm, not bad. Okay, Torrence...so let's see you do *agnitionis* on Greta's scarf."

"Not me. *Us*," Torrence replied. He arranged the three azurite pieces on top of the scarf in a triangular pattern. "You all know that group spells are way more powerful than when it's just one witch doing the casting, right? We should group-*agnitionis* Greta's scarf and see what we can learn."

The other witches nodded in agreement. Everyone scooted in closer to form a smaller, more intimate circle.

"Join hands," Torrence instructed.

Greta held Iris's hand on her left and Torrence's on the right. Iris's hand was small, cool, and slightly sweaty; Torrence's was big, warm, and dry. Greta was picking up powerful emotions from both witches. But they were too ephemeral, too complex for her to decipher, and besides, she needed to concentrate fully on the task at hand. Magic was all about intention, and if the mind wandered, the spell could be compromised.

"*Agnitionis*," Torrence said, once again closing his eyes.

"*Agnitionis*," the other witches repeated after him.

The effect was almost immediate. Greta felt zaps of electricity course through her body, radiating from Iris's hand and from Torrence's hand, too. Images flooded her brain, blurry at first and then quickly sharpening into focus.

She, Greta, was in someone's living room. Dozens of candles flickered and glowed in silver candlesticks.

She was sitting in a red chair. Her wrists and ankles hurt...why?

Wait. She seemed to be tied to the chair with rope.

A woman hovered over her. Middle-aged, with grayish-blond hair... oh, right, she was the social worker from the high school. Mrs. Feathers.

Mrs. Feathers touched a cup of tea to Greta's lips. Greta took a small sip. The tea had a green, bitter taste, with a hint of sweetness.

Also poison.

"*NO!*" Greta shouted, spitting out the tea.

"I'm afraid you don't have a choice, Greta."

Mrs. Feathers poured more tea down Greta's throat. Greta tried to resist, and to keep spitting out the tea, but it was too hard. She could feel the poison seeping through her system. She could feel her brain shutting down.

As Greta's mind slowly, slowly faded to black, Mrs. Feathers told her a story. About a man named Maximus Hobbes, who was both a witch and a witch-hunter, from the nineteenth century. How he was still among them, magically staying alive on the heart-fire of the scions of Callixta Crowe. How Penelope had been a scion, which was why she'd had to die and sacrifice her heart-fire. And how Greta was a scion, which was why she had to die and sacrifice her heart-fire, too . . .

A cat—a gray cat?—rubbed up against her ankles. Another cat appeared . . . was that Gofflesby? He was quietly circling the room, batting at the candles with his paws and knocking them down.

Flames licked at the curtains and spread quickly. Soon the entire room was ablaze.

Now people were attempting to rescue Greta. Iris, Ridley, Binx, Mira, Aysha, and Div.

Suddenly, Mrs. Feathers raised her arms in the air and said something.

What was that word?

Oh, yes. It was *praetereo.*

Forget. She had erased all their memories. Wiped their memory banks clean of that horrible event—and what else?

"Greta! Greta, are you there? Are you okay?"

Greta's eyelids fluttered open. Torrence was sitting in front of her, his face lined with concern.

"I-I'm okay. Did you guys...did you see...?" Greta managed.

"Yes! The school social worker and the fire and your familiar," Diy said, rising to her feet. "She killed Penelope, and she was about to kill you, too. We need to find her immediately, before she hurts anyone else."

The eight witches stood in front of Mrs. Feathers's gray house at 158 Spring Street, debating what to do. The curtains were closed, and no sounds came from inside. A brown sedan was parked at the curb; it was half-covered with dead leaves, and one of its tires was flat.

Greta took a few deep, slow breaths and touched the place on her throat where her raw amethyst pendant usually hung. Her comfort stone, which was hidden away in her dresser at home. Now that she was here, she was remembering more and more about that awful day. The confusion. The terror. Saying goodbye to her family, her friends, her familiar. Mrs. Feathers, the bland, kind social worker from school, revealing herself to be a witch and a murderer.

It made no sense. Mrs. Feathers's house looked completely intact. No traces of fire damage. Had that fire been an illusion? The fire and what else?

Torrence put his hand on her arm. "Are you okay?" he whispered.

"Not really," Greta admitted. "I'm glad we're getting to the bottom of things, though."

"We all saw what you went through here. Are you sure you don't want the rest of us to just handle it?"

"I'll be okay. But thanks."

Binx was tapping furiously on her phone. "I'm trying to trace the license plate number to see if that's her car"—she nodded at the brown sedan—"but...*blurg*, the DMV site is offline, and I can't access anything. I'll keep trying, though."

"I think we should just ring the doorbell, and if she answers be like, 'Hey, remember us, lady?' and zap her with a group *obstupefacio*," Mira suggested. *Obstupefacio* was a petrifying spell.

"I say we should use an opening spell, like *obex*, to sneak in," Aysha said.

"Both of those could be dangerous. I've never met her, but she seems like she's a pretty powerful witch," Torrence pointed out.

Iris raised her hand. "Hello, people? Everyone? I'm trying to make another vision happen right now...you know, to figure out if she's in there cooking up more dastardly evil to spring on us. Except, the only vision that I'm getting is an image of cat food, which makes no sense... unless I forgot to feed Oliver P. and Maxina this morning? No, I definitely fed them."

Then Greta thought of something. "We could use *videre* to peek inside first?"

"Wait, I might be able to do that without using *videre*, like I did with that mansion yesterday." Ridley stepped up to one of the curtained windows and squinted. "Nope, I'm not getting anything. Sorry."

"What mansion?" Mira asked her.

"The mansion in the Kai forest. I—"

"The Kai forest where you and I were yesterday?" Aysha cut in, looking confused.

"Guys?" Div jiggled the doorknob. "It's unlocked. *Pleukiokus omnis*," she added quietly—a group protection spell. She pushed at the door lightly.

Greta heard the frantic meowing coming from inside.

Without thinking, she scooted past Div and rushed inside. Four cats ran up to her—three black kittens and a gray cat with—was she missing an eye? Yes, she was missing an eye. The cats stood up on their hind legs and batted their paws against Greta's legs. She felt the distress and hunger emanating from them.

Greta knelt down on the floor and petted them. "You haven't eaten in days, have you? Poor babies," she cooed.

The other witches had come inside and formed a tight semicircle behind Greta. Iris nodded at the gray cat. "I saw a picture of that cute little kitty in Mrs. Feathers's office. At school. I think her name is...I think it's Prozac?"

Mira screamed.

Div grabbed her arm. "What is it, Mira?"

"G-guys?" Mira pointed to the kitchen, which was just beyond the living room. "Is that...I mean, it looks like..."

Everyone turned in that direction.

Through the doorway, they could see a body lying on the floor. They all rushed to the kitchen.

It was Mrs. Feathers. Dead.

PART 2

FIFTY SHADES OF DEATH

What is death, anyway? Is it the end? Or the start of a different beginning? Or to paraphrase from my favorite movie: Am I asking the wrong questions?

(FROM THE GRIMOIRE OF RIDLEY M. STONE)

11

TAKE TWO

Relying on others can be occasionally
useful. Or deadly.

(FROM *THE GOOD BOOK OF MAGIC AND MENTALISM*
BY CALLIXTA CROWE)

R idley sat on the patio of the downtown Starbucks, warming her hands
over her pumpkin spice latte as she waited for Binx. The morning
air was brisk, and her fingertips were tender from her extra-long violin
practice sessions the past couple of days. She'd run through "Liebesfreud"
and also the first movement of the Tchaikovsky Violin Concerto multiple
times. She loved the Tchaikovsky, even though it was technically too hard
for her; in fact, her teacher, Mr. Jong, had suggested she wait a couple of
years before tackling it. But it was so lovely and bright and hopeful, and
trying to master its high-energy double-stops and triplets filled up the
sad, empty places in her mind.

The last time Ridley had seen Penelope alive was at this very spot.
One cool September afternoon, the day after they'd first met, Penelope

had invited Ridley for coffee. Pumpkin spice lattes, her favorite. She'd brought her familiar with her—a white standard poodle with big, doleful brown eyes named Socrates—and the two girls had talked, at first about light topics like the fall season and upcoming holidays and tennis, then about deeper, more personal things. Ridley had surprised herself by telling Penelope about Daniel's death, which she'd never shared with anyone, not even Binx, because the subject was just too raw and difficult. They'd confessed their witch identities to each other.

They were supposed to have lunch the next day, at school, but Penelope never showed.

That night, Ridley, Greta, Iris, and Binx had found her body at the construction site.

Ridley's hands shook, and she nearly knocked down her cup. She put them in her lap and drummed out a rhythm, the first line of the Tchaikovsky. *Better.* She'd read somewhere that he'd composed the concerto during a rare time of happiness in his life, and that he'd wanted to dedicate it to his violinist, a man with whom he'd likely had a romantic relationship. Being secretly gay in nineteenth-century Russia—what had that been like for him? How had he managed to create such beautiful music despite his oppression and hardship? Or did those things *inspire* him to create the beautiful music?

Ridley took a sip of her latte. The taste of it flooded her with sense-memories of that day—the end-of-summer chill in the air, Penelope's rose perfume, Socrates's soft fur as he leaned against the girls' legs under the table.

Poor Socrates. He must miss her so much.

And now Mrs. Feathers was dead, too, and the trail of secrets surrounding Penelope's death had ended with her. After finding Mrs.

Feathers's body, the girls and Torrence quickly placed an anonymous 911 call. Still, justice, closure, and healing seemed more elusive than ever.

They did have *some* answers, though. According to Greta's *agnitionis*-recovered memories, Mrs. Feathers had killed Penelope for her heart-fire—none of the girls knew what that consisted of, exactly...blood?...tissue?...magical energy?—in order to keep the long-ago witch and witch-hunter Maximus Hobbes alive.

But who, then, had killed Mrs. Feathers? Hobbes? One of the Antima? A member of the Jessup family?

Whatever the case, would Hobbes try to come after Greta again? Where *was* he, and what did he even look like these days? A zombie? A ghost? Or a regular old human? And how could he be both a witch *and* witch-hunter?

Greta had a small heart-shaped birthmark on her chest, which apparently was a sign that she was one of Callixta's descendants—*scions*, Mrs. Feathers had called them—and therefore a possessor of the special, life-extending heart-fire. Penelope had had one of those birthmarks, too. Ridley and the other witches had checked and double-checked and triple-checked, and none of them had the birthmark. Did that mean they were safe from Hobbes? Still, what about all the other descendants out there, including the mystery witch who'd posted the excerpts from Callixta's magic manual in March 2016?

I should talk to Aunt Viola about all this.

Ridley's aunt had arrived in Sorrow Point late last night after more travel mishaps, including her Los Angeles to Bellingham flight being rerouted to San Francisco because of a sick passenger, and then her rental car having engine trouble on the highway. But she was finally here and had settled into the guest bedroom and was sleeping in this morning.

Ridley was looking forward to spending some time with her for, well, however long she planned to stay in town—she hadn't said.

A dog barked, making Ridley glance up. It was Binx, finally. She was walking across the patio, her puppy tugging excitedly on his leash.

"Hey!" Ridley waved.

"Hey!" Binx set her drink down on Ridley's table, pulled out a chair, and sat down. The puppy jumped up on her lap, panting happily, as she glanced at her watch. "*Blurg*, it's after nine! Sorry I'm late. Hannah One called just as I was leaving the house."

"Hannah One?"

"There are two Hannahs on the Homecoming Committee."

"Yeah, I've been meaning to ask...why are you on that committee, exactly? It doesn't seem very you."

"It's not very me. It's the binary opposite of very me. It was Div's idea"—Binx peered around to confirm that they were alone on the patio—"you know, to fit in, adapt, camouflage ourselves."

"Got it."

"So how are you?"

"Not great."

"I hear you." Binx reached across the table and squeezed Ridley's hand. "Everything really, really sucks right now, doesn't it?"

"Yeah, it really, really does. It's nice to see you, though. It's been a while...I mean, since we've hung out alone without the...without everyone else."

"I know. Apologies. It's been pure chaos."

Ridley smiled grimly. "Understatement of the year."

"Yeah."

The puppy sniffed at the top of the table, in search of crumbs. He was cleaner and fluffier and bigger than the last time Ridley had seen him, nearly a month ago. A stray, he'd been hanging out in Binx's yard for a while. She'd tried to find his owner, but after having no success, she'd adopted him and made him her familiar.

"What did you end up naming him?"

"Lillipup," Binx replied.

Lillipup barked.

Ridley reached over to pet him. "That's a cute name. Is it a Pokémon character?"

"Yup. Gen Five, Normal Type. Its face fur has radar abilities."

"Nice."

"Yeah, well, *this* Lillipup isn't very good at the radar thing. If you throw a stick and tell him to fetch, he'll run in the opposite direction." Binx regarded her Starbucks cup, took off the lid, and inspected the contents carefully.

"What are you doing?" Ridley asked, confused.

"Just checking for mealworms. Long story. So, listen ... I stayed up late doing research on Maximus Hobbes and also Mrs. Feathers. Lots of records and documents seem to be missing, which is weird ... or maybe it's not weird, considering. *But.* I did manage to hack into the police file re: her death."

"And?"

"They're still investigating, but at the moment, their working theory is quote-unquote 'an accident.' Like, they think she fell and hit her head."

"Do *you* think it was an accident?"

"I don't know."

"Hmm. Maybe I'll ask my mom. She works at City Hall now, and she might be able to get some inside info from someone in the public-safety department."

Binx nodded. "Sounds good."

Ridley reached over to pet Lillipup. "So how's the new coven?"

"Um, you know. It's fine. Div's Div."

"Have you guys... I mean, have you made any progress on the Libertas front? And how's your friend ShadowKnight?"

Binx's eyes lit up. "Didn't I tell you? Ohmigosh, I didn't tell you! I'm finally going to meet him IRL later today... and some Libertas members, too."

"Wow! Where?"

"At the WitchWorldCon in Seattle."

"That's like a big annual convention for the *Witchworld* fandom, right?"

"Right. I've had a ticket to go since like forever, and it turns out he and some other Libertas people will be there, too, so...." Binx scrunched up her face. "Div is insisting on coming with me, though. I think she thinks I need babysitting or bodyguarding or hand-holding or whatever. I told her I'd be fine, but she never takes no for an answer, so..."

Ridley tried to picture Div at a video game convention. "Huh. Good luck with that."

"Yeah, I may need it," Binx said, chuckling.

Ridley had more she wanted to say. Like: *Can you please leave Div and Aysha and Mira and come back to us?* Also: *Be careful when you meet up with ShadowKnight in Seattle.* She'd never said as much to Binx, but she was kind of with Greta on this one. How could Binx trust someone that she'd met on the Internet? He knew she was a witch, and he knew about the existence of their two covens. Wasn't Binx putting them all at risk? What if he turned out to be an undercover cop or Antima or both?

But Ridley wasn't sure how to say these things without alienating or angering Binx. Things were fragile enough between them, now that they were in different covens. Besides, it sounded like Div was a little more skeptical about ShadowKnight than she'd originally let on? Ridley hoped she would keep Binx safe at WitchWorldCon.

Binx was saying something to her.

"How's the old crew? How's my replacement?"

"He's nice, and he seems to have some serious skills," Ridley replied. "He's not you, though. Plus, I might be imagining it, but there seems to be some sort of weird unspoken love-triangle vibe happening between him and Greta and Iris."

Binx's jaw dropped. "*What?* Spill the tea *immediately*! Who likes who?"

"I'm not sure. I think Iris likes Greta, and Greta likes Torrence? But I could be misinterpreting."

"*Verrrry* interesting. And who are *you* liking these days?"

Ridley stared at her.

Binx clapped a hand over her mouth. "Oh. Dumb. Sorry! That was the dumbest thing to say, ever. You like...*liked*...Penelope. Gah, sorry, I am an idiot!"

"It's okay."

"No, it's not. I *deserve* to drink mealworms with my mocha Frappuccino."

Ridley snort-laughed. "I still don't know what that means."

"One word: *Aysha*. Let's just leave it at that."

"Understood. Hey, speaking of Aysha...I need a favor."

"Sure, anything."

Ridley told her about the Kai Rain Forest field trip on Friday and the strange mansion she'd seen there.

"Aysha told us about that field trip," Binx said, nodding. "She said the history sub dude was wearing an Antima pin, which is, well, *disgusting*."

"Aysha didn't see the mansion. Only I saw it, I think. But I asked her to take pictures of that spot with her phone."

"I'm confused. Why didn't *you* just take the pictures?"

"Not important. The bottom line is, nothing showed up in the photos—nothing obvious, anyway—but I thought you might be able to do your cybermagic on them and look for clues? Also, Greta was thinking it would be great to research old historical deeds and find out if there ever was a real house there."

"Of course! Text me those photos and give me the GPS coordinates on the house. Or just tell me, like, where the house was—*is*—in the forest, like, ballpark."

"I will. Thanks. And this isn't a rush, since we have other priorities, obviously."

"No worries. I'm happy to help. Under one condition, though."

"What?"

"The Homecoming Dance. I know this is completely random, but... can you go with me? Unless you already have plans, that is."

"I don't...and sure!"

"Great! I have to be there for committee reasons, and I need someone not Div and not Mira and not Aysha to hang with. Although they're preferable to any of the other committee members...not to mention most of the Sorrow Point High population...." Binx sighed. "Honestly, I am so sick of humans."

Ridley frowned. Where had *that* come from? "Excuse me?"

"Don't get me wrong. I'm not planning on starting a hate group against humans. But that's just my point. *They're* the ones who don't want to coexist with *us*. They're bigoted and stupid and dangerous. Why should we waste our time and energy and powers hiding from them and defending ourselves against them, when we could be using said time and said energy and said powers doing useful stuff...cool stuff...*productive* stuff? Like reversing climate change? Or achieving world peace?"

"Umm..."

Ridley couldn't argue with any of that.

Still, she'd never heard Binx say these things before. Could this be Div's influence? Or ShadowKnight's? Or both?

As Ridley walked home, she thought over her conversation with Binx. She was glad they'd met up. Things were so off-kilter and broken in Sorrow Point, in the world, that rekindling her friendship with Binx was like a small flame of hope, even if she wasn't part of Greta's coven anymore. Maybe Ridley and Binx *could* maintain their best-friendship while being in rival camps. And then Ridley remembered Div's phone call on Friday. Maybe the two covens didn't have to be rivals. Maybe they could find a way to work together, not because they had to but because they wanted to? Because now more than ever, witches had to put their differences aside and stick together against their enemies.

Although, Binx's weird comment about humans troubled her. Witches and non-witches alike deserved equal rights under the law and in society's eyes. Neither group was better than the other.

Her phone buzzed with an incoming call as she neared her house. She checked the screen. Speak of the devil....

Ridley hit talk. "Hey, Binx!"

"Hey! This will be quick. Div's picking me up in like ten minutes to drive us to the con, and Her Highness does *not* like to be kept waiting. Anyway...I ran Aysha's pix through this special program I have on my phone. I enhanced them like a thousand times, and I found something interesting."

"*That* was fast. What did you find?"

"So I think it's a *lamassu*."

"A...what?"

"A magical sculpture from ancient Mesopotamia. This one had a bluish glow, like it was glazed, or like maybe it was made of molybdenum bronze, which is a bluish metal. Although did they *have* molybdenum bronze two, three thousand years ago? Hmm, I'll have to look into that."

"This thing is two or three thousand years old?"

"Maybe? Anyway, I literally didn't see anything else in the photo, which means that if there *was* a house there, some sort of superpowerful invisibility enchantment must have been in effect. I'm not sure why the *lamassu* itself was visible, though. Might be because it was activated when Aysha took that photo? Because that's what a *lamassu* does...protect someone's property, and maybe it perceived the photo taking as a threat."

"Who on earth would own a magical sculpture from ancient Mesopotamia?"

"A museum? Or a rich witch who collects stuff? Anyway, I'll do more research, plus I still have to hack into the county deeds office to find a deed for that property. I'll get back to you ASAP on that."

As she hung up, Ridley wondered how—and why—history seemed to be folding in on itself, conflating, creating a bizarre kaleidoscope of time periods. The 1870s...the Civil War...the Mesopotamian civilization... and the here and now in Washington.

She had a bad feeling about all of this.

History was catching up to them.

✳ 12 ✳

UNFAMILIARS

Trust is an asset, but only if one is committed to
the myth of honesty.

(FROM *THE GOOD BOOK OF MAGIC AND MENTALISM*
BY CALLIXTA CROWE)

"Lolli, no! *Bad* mouse! That is *not food*; that's for the magical talisman!"

Iris leaned over her desk, picked up her familiar, and tucked her into the pocket of her flannel shirt. Lolli McScuffle Pants had been nibbling on the pile of rosemary, clove, and other herbs that Iris had gathered for her special project: a kick-butt, turbocharged talisman of protection for Greta. The "recipe" was a combination of something from Callixta's manual and an item belonging to Jadora, one of Iris's favorite NPCs—nonplayer characters—in *Witchworld*. Or maybe even in all of gamedom. Jadora was Iris's role model—a smart, brave, powerful witch who said funny, clever things while dispensing with her enemies…things like: *Surrender now, or I shall turn you into cat litter!* and *Is that the best you can do? My wand is falling asleep from boredom!* Iris planned to combine the herbs and a few other ingredients, including obsidian chips—obsidian had strong protective properties, being an elemental combination of fire, earth, and water—and put them in a pretty little potpourri bag that Greta could keep under her pillow or wherever.

Because Greta had to stay safe from Maximus Hobbes. Just thinking about the group visions from last night's double coven meeting, followed by the discovery of Mrs. Feathers's very dead body, made Iris's skin crawl with cold, invisible spiders. Greta had been a target of Hobbes's sights before; he would no doubt try to come after her again. Iris had to do everything in her power to protect her friend. Her more-than-a-friend.

Although...Iris's more-than-a-friend seemed to be treating their new coven member as *her* more-than-a-friend. For a brief, dark moment, Iris wondered if she should cook up a potion to make Torrence turn ugly. Or mean. Or at least smelly.

Stop it, she told herself. The thought *was* intriguing, though.

Lolli poked her tiny pink nose out of Iris's shirt pocket and sniffed at the air. Iris stroked her delicate little whiskers. "I know, I know. As soon as I'm finished with the magical talisman, I'll go down and get you a banana for your breakfast, okay?"

Blueberries, Lolli seemed to answer.

"Okay, fine, blueberries. I'll have to see if we have enough, though, because they're Nyala's favorite, and if I don't leave her some, she might put shaving-cream slime in my backpack again and—"

"Who are you talking to?"

Iris spun around. *Argh*. It was Nyala, peering through the doorway.

"Hey! Hi! I was just talking to Lolli," Iris explained casually.

"Ms. Traitor Mouse, you mean."

Lolli used to be Nyala's pet. But she'd kept running away from Nyala's room to Iris's, and eventually, Iris had realized that Lolli was meant to be her familiar. To compensate Nyala, Iris had bought her a young Snakeskin Blue Moon crayfish along with a tank for him to live in. This meant their family had four pets now, including Lolli and the two cats, Oliver P. and Maxina. Nyala had named the crayfish Captain Notorious Blade Edge, or Blade for short.

"How's Blade?"

"He's good. I want to get him a friend, but I'm worried he'll eat it."

"Yeah, that might be a problem."

Nyala's gaze swiveled to the pile on Iris's desk. "Whatcha making?"

"What?" Iris shifted her body slightly to block the view. "Oh, it's just...it's just this homework thingama-whosit I have to do for biology," she improvised.

"I heard you call it a 'magical talisman.'"

Eavesdropping little sisters! Iris had to be more careful.

"No, what I said was, uh, *macro telomerase*. We're studying, uh, really, really big enzymes. Giganto ones."

"Whatever." Nyala walked into the room and perched on the edge of Iris's bed. "What do you think of Xandri?"

"What's Xandri?"

"It's a *who*, dummy. They're a Witchtuber."

"A...what?"

"They have a YouTube channel. They play that game you like—*Witchworld*—and do commentary and stuff. They have over a million subscribers. They're nonbinary; isn't that cool? Cameron at my school's nonbinary. So are Saffie and Tyler."

"Cool." Iris wondered why she'd never heard of this Xandri person. She reminded herself to look them up ASAP.

"Can you maybe teach me?" Nyala asked.

"Teach you what?"

"How to play *Witchworld*. I think magic's cool."

Iris blinked. Nyala never asked her for help or advice about anything, ever.

And she thought magic was cool? This made Iris really happy, and at the same time really worried.

"Sure, I can teach you."

"You're going to that convention today, right? WitchWorldCon?"

"Uh-huh. I thought about skipping it because there's a lot of other stuff going on. But then I changed my mind because, well, it's *Witchworld*."

"I asked Mom if I could go with you, but she said no because I have to babysit Ephrem while she finishes the yard work. Is that dumb or what? I mean, who cares about yard work?"

"Sorry. If you want, I could bring you back a souvenir?"

Nyala's face lit up. "*Yessss!* Xandri tweeted that they might be there. If they are, can you get me an autograph?"

"I can try."

"Noice!" Nyala glanced at her phone. "Oh, Reagan's texting me, so bye."

"Bye."

Nyala left, typing furiously. Iris spun around to face her desk again. She was puzzled—pleasantly puzzled—by her sister's behavior. Nyala's usual mode in Iris's presence was insults or indifference. Maybe she was coming out of her "terrible tweens" phase? Had *she* been like that when she was twelve?

The talisman. Iris needed to finish it up, and then she would morph herself into Jadora—nonmagically, of course—and head for downtown to catch the bus to Seattle. With a quick stop first to drop off her gift.

Blueberries. Lolli was staring pointedly at Iris.

"Right. I promised."

Iris remembered then that blueberries were good for protection, too. Maybe she should throw one or two into the mix along with the herbs and crystals?

An hour later, Iris stood in front of the Curious Cat, admiring the Halloween-themed window display. *Dracula* by Bram Stoker, *Frankenstein* by Mary Wollstonecraft Shelley, and other spooky novels were interspersed with jack-o'-lanterns, dried cornstalks, and skeleton candles. Wispy white-lace ghosts with black button eyes appeared to fly over the scene. Iris wondered if Greta had designed the display; in addition to being a skilled witch and gardener, she was incredibly artistic.

The sun emerged from behind the clouds, brightening the foggy morning. Iris caught her reflection in the windowpane. For a second, she didn't recognize herself in her Jadora outfit. With her high ponytail, black leotard and leggings, and silver quiver, arrows, and bow made of coat hangers and aluminum foil, she looked seriously B.A. Overpowered. Sexy, even. The effect was night-and-day different from Iris's usual flannel shirt, jeans, and glasses-falling-down-her-nose self. No wonder she preferred being Jadora the Justice Warrior Witch to Iris Evangeline Gooding.

She pushed back her shoulders, winked at her reflection, and pivoted toward the front door. She was ready to see Greta.

Opening the door, Iris was greeted by the wonderful smells of old books and freshly brewed coffee. Behind the counter, Mr. Navarro sat on a high stool, flipping through the *Sorrow Point Sentinel* while talking on the phone.

Iris waved to him.

"I'll see if I can order a copy of that for you...oh, hang on one sec," he said into the phone. "Hey there, Iris! Nice to see you. Great costume. Greta's in the back, I think, in poetry."

"Thanks, Mr. Navarro!"

Iris waved again and headed toward the poetry section. She flipped her ponytail over her shoulder and adjusted her glasses. "Hey, Greta! How are you?" she murmured under her breath. "Hey, Greta! I brought you a present! Nah, it's no big deal, it's just a little something I made myself...."

"The face of all the world is changed, I think, since first I heard the footsteps of thy soul...."

Iris froze. Someone was reciting a poem.

That someone was Torrence.

He and Greta were sitting cross-legged on the floor, close together, surrounded by boxes and crates. An old book was cradled on his lap. Greta was sipping from a blue ceramic mug.

"Move still, oh, still, beside me," Torrence continued.

Greta caught sight of Iris. She smiled in surprise. "Hello!"

Torrence glanced up from his book. "Hi!"

"Hey, Greta. And...hey, Torrence, I'm Iris!" Iris blurted out. "JK, we've already met lots of times, I'm a little out of it because...anyhoo, I didn't mean to interrupt you guys, I was just in the neighborhood...well, actually, I have a *reason* to be here, so it's not like I was randomly in the neighborhood...this was one of my stops...but at the same time it *was* kind of random because my main reason for being in the neighborhood was...is...oh, *argh*."

Greta gathered her green velvet skirt, rose to her feet, and put a gentle hand on Iris's arm. "Do you want to join us? We were just reading Elizabeth Barrett Browning, to cheer ourselves up. *Sonnets from the Portuguese.* Do you know them? They're really amazing. Also, we're drinking this special tea blend that Torrence made. Can I make you a cup, too?"

Torrence stood up, too. "Sorry, I don't think I brought enough. Next time, though."

"Well, we do have other kinds of tea up front, and coffee, too," Greta offered.

"It's okay. I can't stay, anyway, because"—Iris blinked, trying to remember where she had to be—*Greta is touching my arm*—"yeah, so I have to catch the Seattle bus. To get to WitchWorldCon. That's why I'm wearing this"—she waved at her outfit—"so, yeah."

Greta's smile morphed into an anxious frown. "WitchWorldCon? What is that? Is it some sort of public witch event? Will there be Antima there?"

Greta didn't play video games. How could Iris have forgotten that? She was old-fashioned, from another century. Like one of those beautiful sunlit girls in a Victorian painting.

"I don't think so. It's a convention for *Witchworld* fans, and *Witchworld* doesn't involve real witchcraft, it's just a video game, and it's super-popular with normal humans"—Iris face-palmed—"I didn't mean... it's not that witches aren't normal... we *are*... the point is, no one thinks *Witchworld* is a game for witches. It's like, you don't have to be a Pokémon character to play Pokémon video games, right? Sure, it's not possible to be a Pokémon IRL, but you know what I'm saying. Although I wish a person *could* be a Pokémon IRL, because if so, I would totally be Goodra because Goodra is cute plus O.P.... which means overpowered, which means superpowerful, not power*less*...." She stopped; she could feel heat in her cheeks and wondered if she was doing her ugly blushing again. "So, um... why do you needing cheering up? Did something bad happen? I mean, aside from all the bad stuff that's been happening, including finding *another* murder victim?"

"Yes, well... I talked to Ridley this morning. Binx told her that the police think Mrs. Feathers's death was an accident," Greta explained.

Iris digested this. "So the police don't think she was killed by the Antima or Maximus Hobbes or someone else who's connected to, you know, Penelope?"

"Exactly. And I don't think Maximus Hobbes is even on their radar, since..."

"...he's not even supposed to be alive," Torrence finished.

I'm talking to Greta, not you, thank you very much!

"How are Mrs. Feathers's kitties doing?" Iris asked Greta. Sweet, kind, protective Greta had taken the four orphaned pets home with her—the gray cat with the missing eye and the three black kittens.

"They're doing a lot better. I've been feeding them lots and giving them some healing herbs, too. Gofflesby"—Greta hesitated—"Gofflesby seems happy to see them. Which is weird, because he's always been kind of a loner. One time when my brother brought home his friend's cat for the weekend, to take care of her while their family was out of town, Gofflesby became really upset and aggressive."

"You saw—we all saw—Gofflesby at Mrs. Feathers's house in your vision," Torrence reminded her. "Is it possible he knows those cats?"

"I don't know. I can't imagine." Greta touched her throat—*she must be missing her raw amethyst pendant*—then let her hands fall to her sides. "I suppose I should do more scrying spells about that, though."

"I can help you. We can all help you," Torrence told her.

Greta smiled gratefully at him. "Thank you."

Iris started to make a gagging motion, then stopped herself. This wasn't a competition. Actually, it *was* a competition, and Torrence was winning. Still, she needed to be calm and mature about this. Maybe she should talk to her therapist, Deanna, about increasing her Zoloft. . . .

Zoloft.

A random memory flashed through Iris's brain.

"Loviatar!" she burst out.

Greta blinked. "Lo-vi-a-what?"

"The gray cat. I thought her name was Prozac, but actually, it's Loviatar. It just came to me. I was confused because Loviatar sounds like a medication, too. But Mrs. Feathers had that photo of the gray kitty in her office at school…and she told me she named her Loviatar after the… um, let's see…the Swedish goddess of desserts. No, not that…the Finnish goddess of death…no, not that, either…it was the *daughter* of the Finnish *god* of death."

"Oh!" Greta said.

Iris closed her eyes and tried to recreate the photo in her mind. The image was fuzzy at first, then sharper, more vivid. *Yes, that's it.*

"There's another cat in the picture, too. A little kitten. With long golden fur, kind of like"—Iris gasped and opened her eyes—"kind of like Mr. Gofflesby."

Greta turned ghostly pale.

"It must be a coincidence," Torrence reassured Greta.

"Haven't you had Mr. Gofflesby since forever? Since he was a baby?" Iris asked.

"N-no. I've only had him for a few months. Over summer vacation he kept coming to my garden, and he was obviously a stray…." Greta stopped and stared agitatedly past Iris and Torrence. "That day in Mrs. Feathers's house…I'm remembering now. She told me Gofflesby was *her* familiar, and that she'd sent him to spy on me. Which was a lie. He's *my* familiar. He would never do that to me!"

Greta's hands were shaking, and she looked as though she was about to burst into tears. Torrence put his arm around her shoulders and whispered something in her ear.

Time to make my exit. Iris didn't want to be there anymore.

"I have to go. I'm so, so sorry things are such a mess, Greta. Let me know what I can do to help. Oh, and I made you a present, 'k, bye!"

Iris had wrapped the magical talisman in pink tissue paper and tied it with a lavender ribbon from Grandma Roseline's sewing basket. She thrust the package at Greta and turned to go.

Greta said something to her, but Iris wasn't listening, because she was too busy trying to get away from the lovebirds and also recall the name of that app that that girl in the bathroom had told her about. *Oh, right. Krush.* She would search for a new true love during the bus ride to Seattle.

Iris rushed toward the doorway, but stopped abruptly when her foot made contact with something on the floor. Greta's tea had spilled.

"*Argh*, I'm sorry! I'm such a klutz!" Iris apologized.

"Honestly, it's fine," Greta assured her.

Iris bent down to pick up the mug at the same moment as Torrence. She got to it first and wiped up the spilled tea with the back of her sleeve.

The realization hit her like a wave.

The tea wasn't just tea. It was something else.

Could it be...a love potion?

"Here, let me get that!" Torrence said nervously.

As Iris handed him the mug, he wouldn't look her in the eye.

✳ 13 ✳

WITCHWORLDCON

Some humans think they have power, when
they do not. Some witches think they have
no power, when they could rule the universe
with what is inside them.

(FROM *THE GOOD BOOK OF MAGIC AND MENTALISM*
BY CALLIXTA CROWE)

"Over there! Quick, before someone else gets it!"

Binx sat up in the passenger seat and gestured wildly at an empty parking spot in the corner of level 5. She was as excited as if she'd tracked down a super-rare Lunicorn in the Dominion of Subcrystals, which she—or rather, Ms. Magius, her *Witchworld* avatar, whom she'd named after a Pokémon ghost-type character—had yet to do in the game. She and Div had been circling the convention center's underground garage for nearly half an hour.

Obviously, everyone in the entire country had decided to show up for WitchWorldCon this year.

"Finally! Good work, Binx," Div said. She drove her white Audi to the spot, parked, and cut the engine.

"We should have used a parking-spot-finding sp—I mean, *enhancement*. Is there such a thing? If not, there should be."

"Perhaps. It's good for us to hone our real-life skills without resorting to the enhancements, though, don't you think?"

"I guess?"

"So what's first on our agenda?"

"We need to pick up our passes and go through security and stuff."

Binx consulted the WitchWorldCon schedule on her phone. *Good*... they were still well within the check-in and registration window. She opened the car door and stepped out, slowly, because it wasn't easy to maneuver in her thick, padded ski pants with the gazillion tiny rainbow-colored pom-poms stapled precariously onto them. Not to mention that the ski pants used to be her father's, so she kept having to pull them up and recinch the belt. Also, her plastic headband with the papier-mâché demon horns pinched, and her black sequined spandex top scratched and itched. And her plastic ax, which she'd found in the basement along with a box of other childhood toys, was just sad. *Why* had she agreed to this nonsense? Not only was she incredibly uncomfortable, but honestly, she looked more like a failed clown than a fearsome Hodge-demon from the Brandlewycke Dimension.

If only she'd been allowed to just buy a costume from Target or such. Cosplaying apparently involved making everything from scratch. What was she, a pioneer girl? On top of which, she'd had like twenty minutes to pull all this together.

"Please explain again why you're wearing that outfit. Is it a disguise?" Div asked her as they headed for the elevators.

Binx glanced around to make sure they were alone. They were.

"I told you before. I arranged to meet ShadowKnight at the cosplaying competition, although I won't be competing because, well, I'd rather eat one of those orange parking cones than get up on a stage in *this* and be judged by a panel of nerd fashionistas," she said in a low voice. "He'll be in costume, too, and so will the other Libertas members. It's to blend in with the crowd better. Sort of like the Homecoming Committee thing. Although he and the other people in his group may be competing... I don't know."

"Cosplaying," Div repeated. "I think Caitlin and Cassie were talking about that the other day."

"Oh, do they do cosplaying?"

"No, but they seem to want to get into it. Maybe you can teach me about it so I can help them make costumes, and whatever else this activity entails?"

"Sure. I'm hardly an expert, but I can share what I know. Websites, et cetera."

"That would be useful."

They got into the elevator and Binx pressed L. It was weird, hearing Div talk about the Jessup twins in a big-sisterly way... not that Binx knew what it was like to be a big sister, despite technically being one to her super-annoying half-brother, Lucas. Before switching covens, Binx had thought of Div as the ice-cold, ruthless, and extremely powerful leader of the enemy camp. Someone to be avoided at all costs, especially when she was accompanied by Prada, her terrifying boa constrictor familiar. Did she actually have a beating heart under that frosty exterior? Of course, maybe the big-sister vibe was part of *her* disguise, her fake persona as Hunter's girlfriend, a way to ingratiate herself with the family. Binx shuddered to think about what Div *really* thought about the Jessups and what she was planning to do to them. For being Antima. For being the force behind the New Order. And for maybe having a connection to Penelope's murder, too?

The elevator stopped at parking level 2, but no one got in. Div sighed impatiently, jabbed at the L button, and glanced at her watch. "What time did you arrange for us to meet up with ShadowKnight, exactly?"

Us?

"Umm...so...he's expecting to see me, not you. I thought I could talk to him alone first, and then you can join us later?" Binx said vaguely.

"Binx."

"Hmm?"

"Did you tell him I was coming to this convention with you?"

"Umm..."

Div sighed. "Fine. I understand you're trying to protect his privacy. But as coven leader, I need to protect you, protect our coven. Besides, Libertas and we—and by *we* I mean our coven and Greta's coven—have a common goal. Working together will provide a considerable mutual benefit."

"Got it."

"I certainly hope so."

Binx fiddled with a loose sequin and said nothing. At least Div wasn't insisting on accompanying Binx to the initial meetup. Still, Binx hoped ShadowKnight would be okay about Div being here. She hadn't given him the heads-up that Div would be accompanying her to WitchWorldCon, in part because she hadn't wanted to scare him away. The most important thing was that she, Binx, would get to see him face-to-face...*finally*. She didn't want anything to jeopardize that moment.

When they reached L, the elevator doors whooshed open, and the two girls stepped out into a three-story glass-and-steel lobby. The air smelled like hot dogs and fruit punch and hand sanitizer. The lobby was jam-packed with people—kids, tweens, teens, adults...even parents with strollers. The *Witchworld* theme blasted over the loudspeakers, interrupted by occasional announcements: *"Cosplaying weapons must be cleared by our security staff."*... *"Those with VIP passes can go straight to Table A."*... *"There are a few spaces left in this afternoon's* Witchworld *voice-over stars' meet and greet, so sign up now!"*... *"Make sure you stop by and check out the hundred and fifty vendors we have in our Artists' Alley."*...

Binx felt a frisson of excitement; she hadn't been to a con in over a year. Staring out at the crowd, she noted that more than half had dressed as a witch, elf, troll, goblin, demon, vampire, ghost, zombie, halfling, or other character type from *Witchworld*. Even the babies were wearing *Witchworld*-themed clothing, like tiny knit caps with dominion affiliations or onesies with images of Draska, Ilyara, or one of the other High Council witches.

Despite her anti-human feelings of late, she had to admit that this seemed pretty fun. Of course, she didn't know what percentage of the attendees were actually humans. Maybe she and Div were in the majority here, not the minority? *That* would be cool.

"I appear to be underdressed," Div remarked, peering around. "Perhaps I, too, should have cosplayed."

"I don't think that's how the word is used, but okay. Maybe we can buy you a *Witchworld*-themed hat or cape at one of the booths?"

"Perhaps. Or perhaps not."

"Binx!"

A man in a purple polo shirt and khakis, no costume, was making his way toward her and Div. The shirt bore the distinctive *Witchworld* logo—a big *W* and a small *w* strung together to look like a jagged line.

An unwelcome human. *Her father.* Binx groaned. Even though this was his con, she hadn't expected to run into him; she'd figured he would be overseeing the operations from somewhere far away and letting his many minions deal with the on-the-ground details. She hadn't seen him since July, when he'd insisted on flying her to his fancy vacation house in Aspen to spend a week with him, Sloane, and Lucas. She'd holed up in her room the entire time, gaming nonstop and trying to tune out the baby's incessant crying...and also avoid having to conversate with Sloane while pretending she hadn't had an affair with Binx's dad and broken up the Kato-Yamada family.

"Is that ShadowKnight?" Div asked, confused.

"Ew! *No!*"

Her father dodged a small band of Enochian Elves, walked up to Binx, and hugged her. She patted his back and carefully extricated herself.

"Binxy, you should have told me you were coming!"

"It was super last-minute," Binx fibbed. "How did you recognize me in this, um, outfit?"

"Don't be a goose. I'd recognize you anywhere." He turned to Div and thrust out his hand. "Hi there, I'm Stephen."

"Div, this is my dad. Dad, this is my friend Div," Binx mumbled.

Div shook his hand. "So I guess you're a *Witchworld* fan as well?"

Stephen laughed. "Yes, you could say that. Do you live in Sorrow Point, too?"

"Yes."

"That's terrific. Hey, let me set you guys up with VIP passes...unless you bought them online already?"

"We bought regular passes because the VIP ones cost, like, a fortune," Binx replied.

"Come with me, then. I'll grab you some VIP *Premium* passes; they're for industry only."

"I'm confused. Does your dad work here?" Div whispered to Binx as they trailed behind him through the lobby.

"Um . . . yeah. Kind of," Binx whispered back.

"What does that mean, 'kind of'?"

"Yeah, so he kind of owns Skyy Media, the company that created *Witchworld*."

Div raised one eyebrow. "Really?"

"Yes, but that's not why I'm a fan. We're not exactly close. He and my mom split up a long time ago, and he lives in Palo Alto now. I hardly ever see him."

"I understand. I have a father like that, too."

"You do?"

"Yes. I'll tell you about him sometime."

Binx nodded. Div was full of surprises today.

On the far side of the lobby, Stephen spoke to one of the minions, who left and returned a moment later with a pair of platinum-and-purple passes. Binx and Div slipped the lanyards around their necks.

"Are you two free for dinner? I'd love to take you out," Stephen offered. "Sloane and Lucas are visiting her parents in Portland, so I'm on my own. There's a terrific ramen place down the street, and it has a live DJ."

"Maybe. I don't know. Why don't I text you? We kind of have to rush off now because we need to get to the"—Binx glanced at a nearby poster and picked a random event—"Beeble's Bazaar minitournament in room two forty-three."

"Sure, of course. Have fun. And no need to go through security; I've cleared you." Stephen's gaze dropped to Binx's plastic ax. "Say, didn't I buy that for you in kindergarten?"

Binx felt herself blushing. "I don't know, maybe?"

"You were cute as a button then. Still are. I'm so glad you're here, Binxy."

"Yup."

"Text me, okay?"

"Yup."

"Nice to meet you, Div!"

Div smiled and waved.

Binx grabbed Div's arm and pulled her toward the main floor. "Whew, that was close."

"What was close?"

"Having to deal with parental social interaction when we need to focus on...you know, super-important, life-or-death, world-on-the-brink-of-disaster stuff." Binx didn't add that seeing her father had made her feel awkward and weird and also a little sad.

"Yes, I agree with your priorities. Now, are we really going to room two forty-three for this bizarre minitournament, whatever that is, or are you going to go find ShadowKnight?"

"The latter, and it's *BA-zaar*, not *BI-zarre*. The cosplaying competition starts soon. Why don't you stay close, and I'll text you when the, um, coast is clear?"

"I won't be far. And...Binx?"

"Yes?"

"Be on your guard."

"I'm always on my guard."

"I *mean* it."

As Binx made her way to the auditorium where the cosplaying competition was happening, she passed a police officer talking to two twentysomething guys who were holding hands.

She almost dropped her plastic ax. The two guys weren't in *Witchworld* costumes. They were wearing matching jean jackets. With Antima patches.

Binx stifled a swear. She'd known there might be police and Antima presence at the convention, but still. The police officer and the Antima couple were busy talking. Binx thought she heard the words *arrest warrant*. What the hex? She kept her head down as she passed them. *Keep walking. Act natural. Blend in.*

Then one of the Antima guys called out to her, "Excuse me, miss?"

Crap. Crap. Crap.

Binx stopped in her tracks. All three of them were looking at her. She fake-smiled, trying to hide her terror. Was she about to be arrested? "Yes. Hi?"

The Antima guy pointed to the floor. "One of your pom-poms fell off."

Binx followed his gaze and exhaled. *Just a pom-pom.* She scooped it up and stuffed it quickly into her pocket.

"Thanks. I suck at sewing."

"Hey, I think I know you," the other Antima guy piped up. "Is your name...you're Astrid Wong, right? You work at Abercrombie?"

Astrid Wong? Binx stifled her annoyance. He was apparently one of those people who thought all Asians were basically indistinguishable from one another, that Japanese and Chinese were basically the same thing.

Also, *Abercrombie*?

"Nah. But I think I know who you mean. Okay, it's nice to meet you all, bye! And thanks for keeping things safe, Officer!"

The police officer replied, but Binx didn't stick around to hear what she'd said. *Blurg.* The little encounter with the threesome—the *witch-hating* threesome, assuming the police officer leaned that way, which she no doubt did—had rattled Binx to the core. Her hands shook, and sweat beaded her brow.

Stop it. Get a grip. Everything's fine.

Still, she wondered how many other police officers and Antima were on-site here at the convention. Maybe Div was right. Maybe she *did* need to be on her guard, more than she'd realized. As it turned out, she passed four more police officers and a dozen Antima-patch wearers before reaching the auditorium. *Not. Good.* She wondered if she should text Shadow-Knight and reschedule, or meet off-site, or at least warn him.

Once at the auditorium, she stood in one of the doorways, debating what to do. Inside, witches, elves, goblins, and other *Witchworld* characters in their elaborate homemade costumes were bustling around and getting ready.

And then she saw him standing a little ways away from everyone else. ShadowKnight.

She recognized him in part because he'd told her that he would be dressing up as Dargon, a half-human, half-witch assassin. ShadowKnight was wearing Dargon's signature baggy olive shirt, riding pants, and scuffed leather boots. His brown cape bore the partly ripped-away scarlet insignia of the kingdom of Vandervallis, from which Dargon had been exiled for his various crimes.

But more than the Dargon attire, she recognized ShadowKnight because he'd clearly been watching for her, and he looked as nervous and excited as she felt inside. He raised his hand slightly in an almost inconspicuous wave. She did the same. They smiled at each other.

The police and the Antima, though. She pulled out her phone and saw to her annoyance that it was almost dead. She didn't dare use a spell to remedy the situation; she'd have to do so the old-fashioned way, at a charging station. *Ugh.*

She composed a quick message to ShadowKnight via their secret server:

LOTS OF TEAM ROCKET COSTUMES HERE. ALSO TEAM GALACTIC.

Team Rocket and Team Galactic were two of the villainous teams in Pokémon. Team Rocket was her and ShadowKnight's code name for the Antima, and Team Galactic was their code name for the police.

ShadowKnight replied:

I'M AWARE. NO WORRIES MY POKÉMON'S EVASION STATS ARE PRETTY HIGH.

Okay. So ShadowKnight was telling her that that it was safe—or safe-ish, anyway—for them to meet. She looked up from her phone and saw him chin-nod at the rear left corner of the auditorium. It was pretty much empty; all the action seemed to be up front. Binx gave ShadowKnight a thumbs-up and began walking in that direction. When they were a few feet from each other, she sized him up. He wasn't just cute, which had always been her impression of him during their videochats. He was down-right...well, *hot*, which was a word she rarely used, because hotness was not something she really cared about. He was also much taller than she'd expected.

It occurred to her just then that he was one of only two male witches that she knew of IRL, the other being her replacement-slash-Greta's-maybe-crush, Torrence.

Oh, and that homicidal freak Maximus Hobbes. Binx had spent hours digging for info on him last night. One new tidbit she'd gleaned was that he'd gone missing in 1878 and never been found. He'd gained a sort of legendary status among witch haters, especially in the past few years with the rise of the Antima.

But Binx didn't want to think about Hobbes right now. This was a happy moment, and she wanted to keep it that way.

"Hey, ShadowKnight4811!"

"Hey, Pokedragon2946!"

They stood grinning at each other for what seemed like forever.

"So this is okay?" she asked him.

"This is definitely okay."

"Where's the rest of your crew?"

"Around. I'll introduce you soon."

"Are you actually competing in this?" Binx gestured at the stage.

"Yeah, but later. They had too many contestants for the one-thirty round, so I got bumped to three thirty. Which is fine. When are *you* competing?"

"I'm not."

"Got it. Your costume's cool, though. You're a Hodge-demon, right? From the Brandlewycke Dimension?"

Binx touched her papier-mâché horns. They felt crooked, so she adjusted them slightly. "How can you tell? My crafting skills—my costume-crafting skills, anyway—aren't exactly, well, *skills*."

ShadowKnight laughed. Binx noticed that his eyes lit up when he laughed. It was a surprising sight...and it was nice, really, given how he was usually sad or mad or subdued whenever they spoke.

"I think you look awesome. So, listen...I scouted things out, and there's a conference room one floor below that's not being used at the moment. We should go down there so we can have more privacy."

He thinks I look awesome. "Yup, good idea," Binx said out loud.

"Great. Let's go."

They left the auditorium, and Binx followed ShadowKnight to a nearby stairwell. As they headed down, several more pom-poms fell off her ski pants—she really *did* suck at sewing. She thought about not picking them up, then changed her mind; she didn't want to leave a trail of bread crumbs for anyone to find her.

Once in basement level 1, ShadowKnight led her down a long hall-way to the last door on the right. A handwritten sign had been taped to it: DRASKA'S DUNGEON #1, WITCHWORLD PLAYING CARD TOURNAMENT ROUND 1 @ 2 P.M. NO PRE-REGISTRATION NECESSARY. *Hmm, sounds fun.* Binx wondered if she might have time to participate. But, *nah*...she'd probably be too busy engaged in a *real* battle against evil.

Inside the conference room, she and ShadowKnight closed the door and sat down at a folding table.

"*Calumnia*," he said quickly. "Just in case."

Binx held up her phone. "So from your message, it sounds like you're not worried about the police and the Antima?"

"I'm *always* worried about the police and the Antima. My people have taken measures to stay safe, though. And you and I should be fine. If we run into any authorities, I have a plan A and a plan B."

"What are they?"

"Not important. Hopefully we won't have to deploy them. Let's get down to business since our time is limited. Tell me what's been going on in Sorrow Point."

"Sure."

Binx took a deep breath, then launched into a long, detailed update about everything. The escalating Antima presence at the high school, including many more students plus Mr. Terada, the history sub. The arrest of the English teacher Mr. Dalrymple. The New Order, and Dr. Jessup being their leader. The discovery of Mrs. Feathers's body last night and their belief that she'd killed Penelope for her heart-fire, which would prolong the life of Maximus Hobbes, who happened to be a witch *and* witch-hunter.

She was about to tell him about the witch database that the New Order was compiling when something niggled at her brain. Something about ShadowKnight. Something off.

"ShadowKnight?"

"Yes?"

She studied his very cute face, trying to decode his expression. Decode *him*.

"How did you know I'm from Sorrow Point?"

14

THE STING THAT BINDS

Truth and fiction are often the same thing.
So are life and death.

(FROM *THE GOOD BOOK OF MAGIC AND MENTALISM*
BY CALLIXTA CROWE)

"And see these leafy green things growing under the deck? You'd think they were just plain old nuisance weeds that need pulling," Aunt Viola said to Ridley. "They're called stinging nettle, and if you touch them without gloves, they can give you a mean rash. But they're actually very good for you, when used properly. Witches like myself love to make tinctures and teas out of them for medicinal purposes. You can also make a tasty soup out of them. Cream of nettle. I'll teach you the recipe while I'm here."

"Sure!"

Ridley knelt down on the grass next to Aunt Viola and studied the nettle plants up close. Aunt Viola was right; they *did* look like weeds. In fact, she had a vague memory of accidentally touching one of them over the summer and getting super-itchy.

She opened her grimoire—a plain old black-and-white composition notebook that she'd labeled CREATIVE WRITING JOURNAL for deception purposes—and found a blank page. There, she sketched a quick picture of the nettle plants in pencil—she didn't have Greta's drawing skills, but she was improving—and added some notes underneath:

Stinging nettle

Use gloves to pick (otherwise rash!)

Medicinal tinctures and teas (get recipes from Aunt V)

Cream of nettle soup (ditto)

Ridley closed her grimoire, stood up, and brushed the dirt and grass off her jeans. Her not-Ridley jeans, which were slim-hipped and a darker, stiffer denim than she preferred. She'd almost forgotten that she was in her untrue form. She'd done *muto* on herself on her way home from meeting Binx at Starbucks. Even though Ridley was in these ugly jeans plus had the ugly stubble on her face, Aunt Viola was aware of who she really was. She'd known for years, just as she'd known about Ridley being a witch.

Everyone should have an aunt Viola in their lives, especially queer kids. And especially queer Black kids.

Aunt Viola picked a few pieces of the stinging nettle, put them in her basket, and rose to her feet. Ridley noticed then she wasn't wearing gloves.

"Wait! Aren't your hands—"

"I'm fine, darling girl."

Probably a protection spell.

"Thank you for teaching me about stinging nettle," Ridley said. "I don't remember Callixta Crowe writing anything about them." She felt comfortable speaking openly without *calumnia* since Daddy, Momma, and Harmony were at the grocery store, and none of the neighbors were in their yards at the moment.

"Ah, yes, *The Good Book of Magic and Mentalism*. Callixta actually does have a section on stinging nettle—quite a long one, in fact—but that part hasn't been uploaded for public eyes."

That part hasn't been . . .

"I don't understand. If it wasn't uploaded by that one descendant of Callixta's, how do *you* know about it?"

"I never mentioned this to you. But last spring, my ladies' group back in Cleveland"—Ridley assumed that "my ladies' group" meant her coven—"well, we discovered a few lost pages that were not part of Callixta's descendant's original upload in 2016."

"Seriously? Where?"

"At a flea market of all places. We were shopping for old bottles and jars—you know, for storing potions—when we stumbled upon a box of vintage gardening books. Well, we bought the whole lot, and when we were going through the books back at my store, we found Callixta's pages all folded up and wedged inside *Formal Gardens for the Informal Gardener* by Neville Austin-Biss." Aunt Viola sniffed. "Not a very good book, by the way."

"Wait . . . so . . . you have actual pieces of paper with Callixta Crowe's *handwriting* on them?"

"That's right."

"That is . . . *amazing*! Can I see them?"

"I don't have them with me. They're in an interdimensional vault, and the only access is through a portal behind my store. But maybe you can come visit sometime soon, and I can share them with you?"

An interdimensional vault. A portal. On the rare occasions when Aunt Viola brought up these things, doubt seeped into Ridley's mind. Having powers was one thing, but this stuff sounded like science fiction, like something wacky and made-up from Binx's favorite video game.

"Ever the skeptic, aren't you?" Aunt Viola said with a knowing smile.

"Maybe a little? I mean, you didn't have a portal back when we lived in Cleveland. Or an interdimensional vault, either."

"They're new since you all moved out here. Remember, darling girl... everything is possible. Magic is only limited by your imagination."

"I guess I have a lot to learn, then."

"Yes, you do. We all do. After all, the craft is infinite."

Everything is possible.

Magic is only limited by your imagination.

The craft is infinite.

Ridley wished she could reflect on these intriguing concepts, follow their trajectories in her head, maybe even write about them in her grimoire. This was the part of being a witch that she missed. The luxurious swaths of time and space to study, to discuss, to grow. These days, with the New Order people bulldozing full-speed ahead with their magic-hating agenda, Penelope's death, a new death—Mrs. Feathers's—and the prospect of Maximus Hobbes being alive, Ridley felt like she was in triage mode. She was just trying to get through the day without being discovered or losing herself in the despair of what was happening and what was yet to come. Lately, even the coven meetings at Greta's house had become all about strategizing and putting out fires and forestalling disasters.

Aunt Viola's voice interrupted Ridley's thoughts.

"You haven't asked me why I'm here."

Ridley blinked. Her aunt's unscheduled appearance in Sorrow Point *had* caught her by surprise, especially since this was her first and only visit in over a year. Her father, on the other hand, was just glad to see his sister, and likewise with her mother.

"Okay. Why are you here?"

"I had a vision last week. In my scrying mirror."

"What about?"

"About your parents. They know about you."

What is she saying?

"They . . . know that I'm a witch?"

"No. They know that you're trans."

"What?"

Ridley rocked back on her heels, dizzy with shock. She felt as though she might pass out. This was the absolute last thing she'd expected to hear from Aunt Viola . . . from anyone. Momma and Daddy *knew*? How could they, when she'd been so, so careful around them?

Aunt Viola reached over and gave Ridley a long, fierce hug. "Darling girl. It's okay. Breathe."

Ridley took a deep breath. Then another. The dizziness subsided a little.

"They know, but they don't know how to talk to you about it. They both love you so much, and they don't want to mess it up," Aunt Viola explained.

"But . . . Daddy and Daniel . . ."

"Your dad isn't exactly Mr. Woke, that's for sure. When we were in high school and college . . . well, let's just say we had our share of arguments about the meaning of 'equal rights.' But there's not a day that goes by when he doesn't beat himself up about his last conversation with your brother. I truly believe he wants to be more open-minded, be a better man . . . be a better father. Just give him a chance."

Ridley nodded into Aunt Viola's shoulder. She didn't know what to say.

Aunt Viola leaned back and ran a loving hand across Ridley's hair.

"That's why I'm here. Not to push you into coming out to them—that's entirely your choice, and you should do it on your own timetable, whether it's tomorrow or next year or ten years from now or never. But I wanted to let you know in person that they love you, that we all love you. And I wanted to be here to support you guys if you want my support. And if you don't, well, we can still have a nice visit, can't we? I can help out with the cooking and other household chores, too. I'll make a big pot of my nettle soup!" She winked.

Ridley clutched her grimoire to her chest. There was so much to process. "I've been trying to learn *vertero* and *dissimulatio* because I didn't think I would ever be able to come out to them," she confessed.

"Well, now you have some options."

"Yeah. I do."

A shadow seemed to pass across Aunt Viola's face. "There's another reason I'm here."

"What?"

"My ladies' group has been keeping tabs on all the negative activity in this area. The hate groups, the death of that girl…"

Ridley winced.

"…and your teacher who's missing. The substitute history teacher."

"You mean Ms. O'Shea?"

"Yes, that one. My group thought I might look into all that, and help if needed."

"We've been investigating all this stuff," Ridley told her. "My coven, that is, and another coven at our school. In fact, I really wanted to talk to you about what we've learned, get your advice."

"Well, fire away. But first, you should call your friend. Bicks?"

"You mean Binx? Why?"

Aunt Viola closed her eyes and fluttered them open again. "I'm not sure. But something tells me that she might be in trouble. I call it my seventh sense. I know most people call it their sixth sense, but in my case it's different because—"

But Ridley wasn't listening anymore. She pulled her phone out of her pocket and composed a text to her best friend, in all caps:

IS EVERYTHING OKAY?

No answer.

Ridley hit call. It went straight to Binx's voice mail.

"*Profundus,*" Aunt Viola said.

"What?"

"It's a powerful new spell of protection that my ladies and I created. I can teach it to you now, and we can cast it together for your friend. My seventh sense is telling me that she may need it."

15

DUNGEONS AND DISGUISES

Be wary of shadows, especially the ones
you have conjured.

(FROM *THE GOOD BOOK OF MAGIC AND MENTALISM*
BY CALLIXTA CROWE)

Div stood in front of a booth in the so-called Artists' Alley and checked her phone. Aside from a reminder from Hunter about the next New Order meeting, there were no messages. Out of curiosity, she picked up one of the small paintings on the display table. The subject was an odd-looking purple creature—half-human, half-cat?—posing against a yellow sky splattered with raindrop-shaped runes. *How peculiar.*

A young woman sat behind the table, dressed in a hooded green satin cape. She leaned forward and smiled at Div. "*Krimlock!* I'm Elysia. If you're interested in that series, I can give you a deal. Buy two, get the third painting free. That way, you could own all three of the Mid-Council Magical Scribes."

Div cocked her head. "I'm sorry, you must be mistaking me for someone else. My name isn't Krimlock."

Elysia laughed merrily. "No, I didn't mean...*krimlock* is Ongolean for 'hello.' You were probably confused because the Ongolean language didn't used to have vowels. But the Ork queen changed that after the second Ragamong Revolution."

"What is a...and what does a revolution have to do with...never mind. In any case, I'm not interested in these paintings."

Elysia's face fell. "Oh."

Div noticed then that all the artwork had been signed with a dramatically curlicued *E*.

How annoying. This Elysia person must be the artist.

Sighing, Div scanned the other items on display, feigning interest. Buttons, stickers, postcards, posters, handmade soaps...

Her gaze landed on a beanie cap. It was black and crocheted and had one star-shaped blue rhinestone for an ornament. It didn't seem too dreadful. And besides, it might help her to better fit in with the convention masses.

"How much is that?"

Elysia's face lit up. "Oh, that's an excellent choice! It's twenty dollars. I'm sure you recognize the symbol of the Symsarian witch army?"

The what?

"I have another version of that hat from when the Symsarians were more of a motley rebel squad...remember? And their star symbol was green, not blue? That was before Aksandria the Space Witch decided to organize an uprising against—"

"Yes, very interesting, here you go," Div said, pulling a twenty-dollar bill out of her white designer backpack. "There's no need for a bag. I plan to wear it."

"Lovely! And here's a complimentary Ilyara sticker and a sample-sized bar of Feykarn soap. The recipe is an almost exact copy of the Feykarn tribe's recipe, except that I had to substitute lemon balm leaves and sea salt for tallen beetle wings because—"

"Fascinating. Must run now, goodbye."

Grabbing her purchases, Div continued down the jam-packed row of artist booths and headed toward the concession stands and restrooms. *Good…* that area seemed relatively artist-free. *These* Witchworld *fans are odd people. Perfectly harmless, but odd.*

After a few minutes, Div found a secluded corner. She leaned against an ATM, pulled on her new hat, and checked her phone again. Still no messages.

Her brow furrowed. Binx should have texted by now. According to the time frame she'd given Div, the cosplaying competition should be underway. Surely she'd made contact with ShadowKnight?

Div typed:

Need to talk where are you?

No response.

Are you okay?

Still no response.

Div frowned. She didn't like being put in this position—waiting and in the dark—and she didn't entirely trust this ShadowKnight character. Hopefully she was just being paranoid. As coven leader, she always had to err on the side of caution. And of course, if ShadowKnight turned out to be who he said he was, he *would* be an excellent ally in the war against the Antima.

Things would be much easier if Binx was more…compliant. Obedient. Respectful. Granted, she'd been with Div for less than a month, so she was still finding her place in the coven and getting a sense of the hierarchy—not the obvious hierarchy, with Div as leader, but the subtle infrastructure of the roles the witches played. Mira was the social one who was good at interacting with the outside world, like the Jessups and the Homecoming Committee. She was also good at following the rules when it came to coven business. Aysha was more of a loner, preferring her Alaskan noble companion dog familiar, Nicodemus, to humans or even witches, but she possessed impressive telekinetic powers and other skills, too. And although she might lack Mira's obsequiousness, she knew at the very least not to defy or question Div's authority.

Ever since meeting and recruiting the two girls over a year ago—Div smiled slyly at the memory of when she'd overheard their plans to magically alter their report cards and pretended she would turn them in to the authorities—she'd developed their coven into a formidable group, focusing on dark sorcery, which in her opinion was far superior to the "love and light" nonsense in Crowe's manual. Of course, Div had used some of the knowledge in those pages; they weren't entirely frivolous. But she'd tweaked most of those spells and potions to give them an…*edge*. Magic wasn't for the timid or the faint of heart. That's why she and Greta had ended their intimate little coven of two in junior high; that girl had no guts.

Div waited one minute, then five minutes, then ten. Still no response from Binx.

Then a text popped up—finally! Except it was from Ridley. Div would have to deal with her later; she had to concentrate on finding Binx.

Time to be more proactive. Glancing around to make sure no one was looking—she'd noticed police and Antima members wandering through the crowd, which was highly disturbing—she held her phone to her ear and pretended to be having a conversation.

"*Locus*," she whispered, picturing Binx in her mind.

The location spell worked almost immediately, although the results were somewhat vague. Downstairs—maybe one level?—but nothing more specific than that.

"*Locus*," Div repeated. The enchantment revealed no new information. Impatient, she pocketed her phone and started toward the elevators.

"Div! Krimlock, greetings, hello!"

Now what? Div spun around.

A familiar figure stood behind her, waving awkwardly. Ponytail, glasses, black leotard, black leggings, a lot of aluminum-foil accessories . . .

"*Iris?*"

"Affirmative! Wow, I didn't know you were a *Witchworld*er. I just made up that word; do you like it? *Witchworld*er?"

"I am not a . . . never mind, have you seen Binx?"

"Binx is here, too? How cool is that?" Iris exclaimed.

"Yes. But I need to—"

"Do you guys want to hang out? I took the bus; did you guys take the bus? Except, you must have been on a *different* bus, because I didn't see you on the ten-forty express, which by the way smelled funny. Like bleach and sunscreen and scrambled eggs. Speaking of . . . have you tried the big concession stand way over at the end? They have Haruyn doughnuts just like the ones from that tavern in Valkyrie Valley; can you believe it? And they're pretty yummy, which is saying a lot because they had that mashed sweet potato filling, and my mouth usually can't stand mashed foods. It's the SPD, I'm super-sensitive to textures *and* tastes *and* smells. . . ."

Div groaned. Was she *destined* today to be socially entrapped by people who never stopped talking?

"Thanks for the culinary recommendation. So I gather you haven't seen Binx?"

"No. But, full disclosure, I spent the last half hour trying to track down Xandri—do you know Xandri?—so I could get their autograph for my little sister. Well, I finally found them, and I bought an autographed headshot. It cost a fortune, but I guess it's worth it because it'll make Nyala happy. She's a *humongous* Xandri fan."

Xandri. Cassie and Caitlin's obsession. Div made a mental note to purchase some autographed headshots for them, too. "That's very nice. Come with me, please. I really do need to find Binx."

"Sure! By the way, that's a supercool hat! You're a member of the Symsarian witch army, amiright? Did you know that the leader of the Symsarian army was actually a set of identical twins? During the Battle of Carthagria, she—I mean, they—fooled the enemy because one of them would be, like, at the eastern citadel, and the other one would be all the way across the kingdom at the western citadel, and..."

Div wondered if she should break her no-magic-in-public rule yet again and deploy *silencio*.

When the elevator reached basement level 1, Div and Iris started to exit. At the same time, a young guy in a purple polo and khakis—the same outfit Binx's father had been wearing, perhaps a corporate uniform?—got on.

"Need any help?" he asked Div and Iris in a friendly voice.

Iris raised one of her aluminum-foil contraptions in the air. "Krimlock! Yes! We're looking for—"

"No, we're fine, thank you," Div cut in. She didn't want to draw any extra attention to themselves or to Binx.

"Okay. Welcome to WitchWorldCon; enjoy yourselves!"

"Thank you! They're so friendly here. Aren't they friendly here?" Iris gushed to Div.

Div didn't reply but instead started down a long hallway. Binx had to be here *somewhere*. Some instinct made her look behind her, though. Turning, Div saw that the elevator doors were still open, and that the WitchWorldCon employee was speaking quietly into his headset. And watching Div and Iris with a not-so-friendly expression. *What the hex?* He wasn't reporting them to someone, was he?

"What are we looking for, boss?" Iris asked Div.

"Please don't call me that. *Calumnia*," Div added under her breath; the spell was unavoidable, given the circumstances. "I believe Binx is around here, possibly with ShadowKnight."

Iris's eyes grew enormous. "*The* ShadowKnight? The one Greta yelled at Binx about, and then Binx broke up with our group to go to your group, and the whole thing caused a big, huge, messy drama?"

"Yes, that ShadowKnight."

"What's he doing here?"

"At the moment, hopefully discussing strategy with Binx. But I'm not entirely certain. That's why we need to find her. She hasn't been returning my texts. And I'm concerned she's not entirely objective about him. For all I know, she has personal feelings for him."

"Oh!" Iris plucked at her sleeve. "Speaking of personal feelings... what's your opinion on love potions?" she whispered.

"Love potions?"

"I mean, if a person uses one to make someone like them, that person must be pretty desperate, right? Not to mention deceptive? And on a related note...if you knew your friend was being fed love-potion tea without her knowledge, wouldn't it be your duty to tell her?"

Div sighed. "Can we discuss this matter later? We need to focus on our task at hand."

"Sure, boss. I mean, *not*-boss."

They continued walking down the hallway, passing a dozen doors with cutaway windows. Div paused and peered inside each. Some of the rooms seemed to be hosting *Witchworld*-themed tournaments or workshops. Others were empty. She looked back to see if the employee guy was still lurking at the elevator; he wasn't.

At the end of the hallway was a red door with a handwritten sign that said: DRASKA'S DUNGEON #1. Div peeked in.

Inside the room, Binx was talking to someone with his back to the door. Longish brown hair, brown cape, boots. ShadowKnight, no doubt.

Div squinted, trying to better assess the situation. Binx looked angry. Or scared. Or both.

"Come on, Iris!" Div pushed open the door and ran inside.

Binx turned toward them and gasped in surprise. "What are you... how did you know I was here?"

ShadowKnight whirled around. He was reaching for something under his cloak—for a wand? For a weapon?

"What's going on?" Div demanded. She reached into her pocket for *her* wand, which she'd disguised as a tube of lipstick via *morpho*.

ShadowKnight closed his eyes briefly, then opened them. "Oh. You're Div"—he glanced at Div, then pivoted to Iris—"and you're Iris." His hand fell to his side.

"Guys, I'm okay. ShadowKnight and I were in the middle of an interesting conversation." Binx crossed her arms over her chest and narrowed her eyes at him. "He was just about to explain how he knew I lived in Sorrow Point."

Iris raised her hand. "Um, question? How is that interesting? Because, no offense, but people's home addresses aren't exactly...well, *riveting*. Also, I like your Dargon costume," she said to ShadowKnight.

"Because he and I only know each other from online. I never told him where I live," Binx explained.

Div took a step forward, keeping a grip on her lipstick-wand. Her paranoia had been spot-on; ShadowKnight *was* trouble. "Oh. That *is* interesting. Please continue."

ShadowKnight regarded Binx. "It's not what you think. One of Libertas's most important tasks is to keep track of anti-witch crimes. After you told me about the murder of your witch friend Penelope, I mentioned it to the group, and a member found Penelope's obituary online. He noted that Penelope lived in Sorrow Point, Washington, that she went to Sorrow Point High, and that she was buried in the Sorrow Point Cemetery. I'm sorry; I didn't mean to freak you out or make you feel like I was spying on you or whatever."

"Oh." Binx's face relaxed. "Sorry. I guess I'm kind of on edge. Before I met up with you upstairs, this Antima dude stopped me, and I thought I was toast."

"So I take it that you've told Div and Iris and your other coven-mates about me? About the group?" ShadowKnight said, frowning.

"Kind of. I had to. Now it's *my* turn to apologize. I know I promised to keep your identity and the group totally confidential." Binx turned to Iris and waved. "Hi! I didn't know you were coming to this thing, although I should have figured. Are Greta and Ridley and my replacement here with you?"

"No. I saw Greta and Torrence this morning, though." Iris's cheeks flushed a deep red; Div wondered what *that* was about. "At the Curious Cat. That's her dad's bookstore, but you probably already knew that. Sorry, redundant. I had to drop off a, well, anyhoo, there was a tea situation. We mostly talked about her cats."

"You mean *cat*, singular, right? Gofflesby?" Div said, confused.

"No, cats, *plural*, not cat, *singular*. Five of them, total. Mr. Gofflesby and the scary social worker lady's four cats. Greta's taking care of them while we figure out who killed her and why." Iris clapped a hand to her mouth. "And am I supposed to be saying all this in front of him?" she mumbled, glancing nervously at ShadowKnight.

"It's fine, Iris. I already told him about Mrs. Feathers, and he knows about Penelope, obviously," Binx reassured her.

"Oh. Whew."

Div regarded ShadowKnight, or whatever his real name was. Binx's friend, if he *was* that, was tall and slender, with a thin, handsome face. He looked to be about their age, perhaps a couple of years older. Binx wasn't aware, but Div had spent considerable time trying to find his real name online and via scrying spells, with no success, and also any information regarding Libertas—again, no success. For a brief moment, Div contemplated deploying a mind-reading spell—*psychicona* or perhaps *lectio mentis*—to suss him out more thoroughly, now that he was physically present; proximity was always an advantage with this category of magic. Maybe later. Right now, her instincts told her that she needed to proceed with caution. He *seemed* to be on the up-and-up, but appearances were always deceiving. She didn't want to take any chances and escalate the situation unnecessarily.

And then she realized that he was scrutinizing her, too. It was unsettling. Was he trying to use *psychicona* or *lectio mentis* on *her*? In any case, she sensed that he was unusually powerful. He exuded the same intense, dark energy that Div's mother used to give off, and Daniela was a formidable witch—even more formidable than Div herself.

Iris was still babbling about Mrs. Feathers and her cats.

"...and Greta and I were talking about the photo the scary social worker lady had in her office at school...or used to have, I don't know. I mentioned it to you guys, remember? The photo had her gray kitty in it. I told you then that her name was Prozac, but it came to me just this morning that her name was actually Loviatar. There was another kitty in the photo, too...a kitten...not one of the three little black ones Greta rescued, but a floofy golden-orange one that looked kind of like—"

"Loviatar?"

Binx had practically shouted the name. Her expression exuded shock and outrage, and she began backing away from ShadowKnight. "When we were videochatting last month, you had a cat with you—a *gray* cat—and you said it was your friend's and that its name was Loviatar."

Div felt the blood draining from her face. ShadowKnight had known Mrs. Feathers?

He also began backing away. His expression had changed, too; he looked afraid.

"Pokedragon...*Binx*...I can explain...," he began.

He stood just a few feet from Iris. Before Div could stop her, Iris jumped forward and touched ShadowKnight's arm...

...and jumped away just as quickly.

"*Guys!* He's...I mean, I don't know how...but he's *two* people. He's ShadowKnight *and* he's Maximus Hobbes!"

"*You're Hobbes?*" Binx burst out.

Div's eyes widened. *Oh god, we walked into a trap.*

She pointed her lipstick-wand at ShadowKnight, Hobbes, whoever he was. But she was momentarily distracted by something in the doorway. A small, shiny object in the cutaway window. Was that a cell phone? Or just the light playing tricks on her eyes?

Also, Binx had beaten her to the punch. She had retrieved her gaming console–wand and was waving it in ShadowKnight/Hobbes's direction. Apparently she, like Div, had ignored the no-magic-items-in-public rule for the day.

"You are *so dead*," Binx hissed at him.

"You don't understand; I'm on your side!" ShadowKnight/Hobbes insisted. "Callixta Crowe sent me here to try to save you all!"

"Nice try, jerk. *Focus Energy! Frozen!*" Binx chanted.

With Binx's spells—Div didn't recognize them—ShadowKnight/ Hobbes cried out, and his body jerked unnaturally. A silvery-white film of ice spread swiftly across his skin. Seconds later, he toppled to the ground, unconscious.

Binx turned to Div, breathing heavily. "Do you want to finish him off, or shall I?"

16

TOIL AND TROUBLE

The revelation of a true name can yield
tremendous power.

(FROM *THE GOOD BOOK OF MAGIC AND MENTALISM*
BY CALLIXTA CROWE)

Greta tried to get up from her living room couch, but the three black kittens wouldn't let her.

"You guys are very silly," she said, laughing as they somersaulted and tumbled over her lap. "Hey, that tickles!"

Torrence smiled at her. He was sitting on the rug with a deck of tarot cards and drinking a cup of herbal tea. This time, it was Greta's special blend, made of dried rose petals, blackberries, ginger root, star anise, and cinnamon. Each ingredient had multiple magical properties, but she'd selected them for specific effects—the rose petals for good luck, the blackberries for healing, the ginger root for prosperity, and the combination of star anise and cinnamon for enhancing dreams and divination.

She'd sweetened the tea with a little sorghum syrup rather than honey, since honey wasn't vegan.

After Iris's departure from the bookstore, Greta had been eager to come home to check on her cats, and Torrence had offered to accompany her. She was glad he was there; she didn't want to be alone right now. Or rather, she didn't want to be without Torrence right now. He made her feel safe…and something else, too. Warm. Nervous. Excited. Had she developed a crush on him? The evolution from platonic to not platonic had happened seemingly overnight and caught her unawares.

It had been a long time since she'd liked anyone that way. Freshman year, she'd dated here and there—Malik Nasser from her English class and Eliza Weissmueller from choir—but neither had become her boyfriend or girlfriend. Actually, she'd never really *had* a boyfriend or girlfriend, and getting "married" to Taylor Chao in kindergarten didn't count.

And, speaking of her short, short list of romantic experiences…there was Div. Back in junior high school, they'd formed a coven with just the two of them, making elaborate potions out of the herbs in Greta's garden, creating a private language of spells and incantations that were a combination of English; Latin phrases they found online; Romanian, which was Div's family's native language; French because they were studying that at school; and threads of random poetry. Also ideas from different mythologies. Callixta's magic manual hadn't appeared in the world yet, but they'd managed nevertheless, fueled by the energy of their own growing powers and their delight in having found each other in what seemed to be a witchless world.

But then their paths had diverged. Div had become interested in using her abilities for dark purposes, like communicating with the dead and manipulation of others…also revenge, like the Furies from Greek mythology. Greta had preferred—and continued to prefer—using her skills for healing and nurturing, love and light, which was Callixta's way.

When Div had made Greta participate in a necromancy ritual to bring a dead gerbil back to life, only to feed the newly reborn creature to her boa constrictor familiar immediately after, Greta had quit their coven and their friendship without a second thought. And likewise, Greta's romantic feelings for Div had died in that instant, when she'd been forced to watch Prada devour the poor, innocent creature. By then, Greta had been crushing on Div for ages. They'd even kissed once, while watching a movie together right here in this very living room. On the very spot where Greta now sat. She still remembered cuddling under the afghan, the taste of Div's strawberry lip gloss on her own lips, the breathless excitement and thrill and wonder of it all.

But no more. Those feelings were gone—well, 99 percent gone, anyway—as was any semblance of collegiality between them. Div was her rival, and she absolutely couldn't be trusted. Greta could barely stand having their two covens working together, even for crucially important reasons like solving Penelope's murder and protecting themselves against the Antima…and now, also, solving Mrs. Feathers's death and protecting themselves against the mysterious Maximus Hobbes.

Hobbes. Greta shivered at the thought of him. Was he still alive? Was he still after her and other Callixta descendants in order to harvest their heart-fire?

Greta reached into the pocket of her skirt and extracted the protective talisman Iris had made for her. What a sweet gesture. As with Torrence, she was glad for Iris's presence in their coven. A month ago, the coven had been just herself, Binx, and Ridley. Now Binx was gone, having defected to the other side, but Iris and Torrence had filled the void. It was a powerful group. They would do a lot of good in the world... assuming they survived Maximus Hobbes, the Antima, and the rest of it.

Torrence was petting one of the kittens. "So what are you going to name the little furballs?"

"Well, I'm not sure. I've been doing some scrying spells to figure out what their real names are, but I haven't had any luck." Greta turned to the one-eyed gray cat, who was asleep in front of the fireplace. "Iris said her name is Loviatar. I'm not sure if I should honor that or if I should rename her."

At the sound of her name, Loviatar stirred in her sleep.

"Hmm, that's a tough one. Maybe you could make up a new nickname?" Torrence suggested.

"Maybe."

"Let's see. You could do Lovebug, Atar, or Atari."

"Isn't Atari a kind of computer?"

"Sort of? It's a company that makes video games and stuff."

"Oh!"

Greta picked up one of the kittens and kissed her on the nose; she wriggled happily and began purring like a motor. The three kittens, all girls, all black, had a few distinguishing features. One had a white blaze on her chest and also extra toes; another had white paws as though they'd been dipped in white paint; and the third had heterochromia, which meant two different colored eyes—in her case, one light blue and one sea green.

Loviatar had kept her distance from Greta since coming to live in this house. She ate, drank water, and used the litter box, but that was it. She ignored the kittens unless they jumped on top of her, whereupon she'd bat them away gently with her paws.

The gray cat's demeanor around Gofflesby was interesting, though, and vice versa. Sometimes, they sat in meatloaf positions just a few feet apart, facing each other, and seemed to conduct a silent conversation with their eyes and their whisker twitches. Gofflesby didn't act in a territorial or defensive way. Loviatar likewise displayed no aggression. They had a quiet, mysterious connection that Greta couldn't quite decipher.

Because of what Mrs. Feathers said. Because Gofflesby used to live with her . . . used to be her familiar.

No. Gofflesby was *her* familiar. They were bonded . . . had been ever since she'd found him in her garden, Bloomsbury, nibbling on the silver vine and valerian. She'd prayed he was a stray so she could keep him, and she'd done her due diligence, posting flyers in the neighborhood and checking at the SPCA daily to see if his owner was looking for him. After two weeks, when no one had claimed him, she'd bought him a cozy little cat bed as a present and christened it with catmint. She'd also made him a celebratory collar out of marigolds and Johnny-jump-ups; he'd tolerated it for about twenty minutes, then wriggled out of it, torn up the blossoms, and eaten half of them.

Greta knew his soul. Or maybe not? Had she been deluded by her love for him? Worse, had Mrs. Feathers been telling the truth about how he'd come to Bloomsbury? Had she sent him to Greta to spy on her and confirm that she was, indeed, a descendant of Callixta? Tears filled Greta's eyes as she regarded Gofflesby, Loviatar, and the kittens. Were they *all* spies? Were they still tied to Mrs. Feathers somehow, even in her death? If so, were they a danger to Greta? Should she give them up for adoption, even Gofflesby?

She shook her head back and forth, back and forth. Gofflesby was *her* cat, *her* familiar . . . and for now, Loviatar and the kittens were her charges, her responsibility. She would find a magical way to discern if Mrs. Feathers still had influence over them from the otherworld, and use spells and potions to separate her from them if necessary.

"The Furies," she said out loud.

"What?" Torrence looked up from his tarot card spread. Greta saw that the card in the center was called the Lovers, which made her blush.

"Greta?" he prompted her.

"What? Oh, yes. The Furies. Do you know them?"

"Yes. Aren't they evil?"

"It depends on the interpretation. They were dark forces, for sure. They were vengeance spirits. At one time, they were believed to be ghosts of humans who'd been murdered."

"Sounds delightful," Torrence said, making a face.

"There were three of them. Allecto, which means 'anger'; Megaera, which means 'jealousy'; and Tisiphone, which means 'avenger.' Together, they were the Erinyes, aka the Furies…except some people were too scared to call them that, so they gave them nice names, positive names, to make them seem less terrible."

"Clever."

"Well, maybe I'll do that with these little Furies." Greta scooped up the three kittens in her arms. "Alex instead of Alecto"—she kissed the one with the white blaze—"Meg instead of Megaera"—she kissed the one with the white paws—"and Tessie instead of Tisiphone"—she kissed the one with the two different-colored eyes. "And I shall call Loviatar Love-bug, like you suggested. There, done!"

Torrence grinned. "You're brilliant!"

Greta blushed again. "Why, thank you."

Her phone trilled with a text. Perhaps it was Iris, reporting in about her witch video game event in Seattle.

But it wasn't Iris…it was Mira. *Mira?* Why would she be contacting Greta?

Oh, Goddess…what if something happened to Div?

Greta quickly opened the text. Mira had written:

Is it okay for me to call you?

Greta typed:

Yes of course.

The phone rang a second later. Greta hit talk.

"Hi, is Div okay?" she asked, jumping to her feet and scattering kittens everywhere. Torrence stood up, too, his brow furrowed in concern.

"Div? She's at WitchWorldCon with Binx. This is something else," Mira replied in a high, nervous voice. "I can't talk very long. Aysha and I are at my dad's campaign headquarters. Div wanted us to spend some time here quote-unquote 'volunteering' so we could suss out any Antima activity. We're outside on a break."

"Are you and Aysha okay?"

"Yes? No? I don't know... not really. This isn't exactly a happy place for us. And I'm beyond furious at my dad for... but that's not the reason I'm calling. So Aysha found a piece of paper in the printer tray. It looks like someone was trying to print it, but then the printer jammed up. A lot of the words are too smeary and faint to read, but some of them are legible."

"And?"

"We think it's a list of names and addresses."

"Like a list of volunteers or donors or whatever?"

"No. Like..." Mira hesitated. "Greta, your name was on it. Your address, too. Aysha and I think it's that list Div heard those New Order people talking about... you know, the database of suspected witches in Sorrow Point."

"What?"

"Greta, what's wrong?" Torrence whispered. He put his hand on her shoulder.

"You should...you should do whatever you need to stay safe. Like, hide your, um, items..." Mira was saying.

Greta's heart was hammering frantically in her chest. She pictured her room—had she put away the potion bottles she'd been filling with her latest brews? Was her grimoire in its usual spot? What about her scrying bowl and her herbs? Was her wand, Flora, still magically disguised as an antique fountain pen?

"I'd better go. Let me know if you find out anything else. Thank you for the heads-up, and please stay safe...both of you," she told Mira.

"We will. You too."

Greta hung up and tried to calm herself. Her thoughts were racing and pinging and crashing into one another. Would the police come to question her? Arrest her, even? Or had the list not made its way past the printing queue of the "Neal Jahani for Mayor" campaign headquarters? Also, what was the list even *doing* there? Was Mira's dad in that deep with the Antima, with the New Order? If so, what did that mean for Mira, not to mention the rest of them?

It occurred to Greta, too, that they needed to warn whoever else was on that list. She started to text Mira about it, then stopped. She had no idea if Mira still had privacy—what if she was back inside the building with her phone in plain sight of the others? And besides, she needed to focus on getting her room in order and locking up her magical belongings.

She realized that Torrence was asking her a question.

"What did you say?"

"What did Mira want?"

"Oh! She had bad news. Really bad."

Greta bent down and scooped Gofflesby in her arms as she explained the situation to Torrence. Gofflesby nestled against her, purring, and she once again fought off the impulse to cry. Nothing could happen to her or her familiar. Or her witches and *their* familiars. Or *any* witches and their familiars, either.

"Let me help you," Torrence said when Greta had finished, at the same time kicking his tarot card spread under the couch. Greta noticed that one card remained visible—the Wheel of Fortune, upside down. Didn't that configuration mean bad luck?

"Thank you. At the moment, I need to go upstairs and—"

Greta was interrupted by fists banging on the front door. It was a malevolent presence. Greta sensed it immediately. She could feel the waves of dark energy, the cruel intent. She froze, terrified.

No. I have to act, now.

"Can you grab Lovebug and the babies? We need to hide," she told Torrence.

Then, voices. Greta heard her mother's among them.

Mama. She thrust Gofflesby at Torrence, wriggling and meowing and complaining, and rushed to the front door. When she opened it, she found two police officer with Ysabel, who was balancing bags of groceries in her arms. Ysabel and the officers—their badges said Correa and Babel—all turned toward Greta at the same time.

"Are you Greta Navarro?" Officer Correa asked brusquely.

Fear coursed through Greta's veins, and she was unable to speak. *It's happening. Mira's warning came too late. They have the list.*

"We need to bring you in for questioning, Greta. You've been accused of violating Title 6 of the US Comprehensive Code, Section 129," Officer Babel added.

"No!" Ysabel set her groceries down on the porch and stepped between

Greta and the officers; she was short, so the two men towered over her. "There's been a big mistake. *I'm* the one you're looking for, not my daughter."

"Mama!"

"Hush, now. I'll go with these officers. Teo is doing family swim at the Y with Papa; just take care of them until I return."

"But—"

Ysabel gave her a warning look. "I'll be fine, mijita. Officers, let's go."

Greta watched as the officers led Ysabel to their car, which was parked across the street. Now the tears were flowing down her cheeks. Was this the beginning of the end?

It couldn't be.

She glanced over her shoulder; she was alone. Torrence had obeyed her instructions and was hiding somewhere with Gofflesby and the other cats. *Good.*

Mama had lied to save her. And now, she had to save Mama. She pulled out her phone and texted the only witch who had the skills to deal with a crisis as dire as this.

Div.

17

PRISONER'S DILEMMA

Even one's enemies have souls, or
they at least pretend to.

(FROM *THE GOOD BOOK OF MAGIC AND MENTALISM*
BY CALLIXTA CROWE)

nside the Kato family's beach shack, Iris leaned against a tower of oars and crates. She tried a few therapy breaths, although without breathing *too* much, because the place smelled like dead fish and moldy things. Also salt and rotting wood. Plus there were lots of spiders and other creepy-crawly critters, too, like silverfish, which weren't fish at all, so why were they called that, and centipedes...needless to say, animals with a hundred of *any* appendage were, by definition, super-scary and not welcome.

The whole situation was less than ideal for Iris's SPD and anxiety and other issues. Maybe if she held her nose and therapy-breathed through her mouth, for starters.

She tried this now. *Nope, negatory, doesn't work.*

Her SPD and anxiety were also not helped by the sight of

ShadowKnight's very unconscious, very tied-up body on the damp plank floor. Earlier at WitchWorldCon, Div had made the decision to smuggle their prisoner into the trunk of her fancy white car, using a series of concealment and invisibility spells, and drive back to Sorrow Point to interrogate him. Binx had suggested that they take him straight to her family's beach shack, which was apparently never used and located in an out-of-the-way spot.

Too out-of-the-way, in Iris's humble opinion. If they screamed, would anyone hear them?

Although, Iris wasn't sure which worried her more—the possibility that he might wake up any minute and zap them all with his Maximus Hobbes magical murder powers, or that Binx and maybe Div might do the same to him. Kill or be killed.

"C-can we go soon? I don't like it here," Iris blurted out.

Binx shot her a *just deal with it* look. Div ignored Iris entirely; she was frowning at her phone and tapping at the screen.

"Besides, how are we going to interrogate him when he's, you know, not conscious?" Iris went on. "Also, not to be a buzzkill, and maybe this is just a minor side issue... but aren't we committing a crime by bringing him here? Like kidnapping? Are we criminals now? Of course, we were *already* criminals according to 6-129, except as we all know, we—"

"Is there no signal out here?" Div interrupted.

"Nah. I've been trying to create a magical app for that, but it's still in the beta stage," Binx replied.

Iris raised her hand. "I'm having phone issues, too. I texted Greta before, to tell her where we were, but I didn't hear back."

She's probably having a make-out sesh with that love-potion-wielding loser.

"I also need to get hold of Mira and Aysha and tell them what's happening here," Div murmured. "And they were supposed to report to me about what's going on at Mira's father's campaign headquarters. Perhaps I should run up to your house quickly. You did reach Ridley, right, Binx?"

"Yup. While we were driving. She was *super*-relieved to hear we were all safe. She should be on her way here."

On the floor, ShadowKnight stirred and moaned. His eyelids fluttered.

"He's waking up!" Iris whispered frantically.

Div put her phone away. "Wands ready, both of you!"

Iris and Binx obeyed. The three witches proceeded to form a circle around their prisoner and pointed their wands at him.

He opened his eyes and blinked at the girls' defensive stances. "Th-that's not necessary," he said in a weak, croaky voice.

"I would say it's *very* necessary, given that you had Penelope killed... and you tried to have Greta killed, too. Not to mention all the witches you murdered during your witch-hunting days," Div countered.

"What *are* you? A shapeshifter?" Binx demanded.

ShadowKnight didn't answer.

Maybe I can summon a vision and figure it out? Iris squeezed her eyes shut and therapy-breathed. Unfortunately, it was hard to achieve clarity when the dead-fish smells and the noiseless skittering of spiders and silverfish swirled and collided with each other in her brain. She wished she had an off switch so she could filter out the sensory static.

No vision came to her, but she *did* manage to conjure up some ideas.

"Yeah, so...it makes sense that he's Maximus Hobbes, given what we know. But it also *doesn't* make sense, because how can a guy from the nineteenth century be a teenager now? And which version of him needed Penelope's heart-fire? ShadowKnight or Mr. Hobbes? What even *is* heart-fire, anyway? Hmm." Iris tapped her chin with her index finger, hoping it would make her look wise and detective-ish.

"Good questions, and I have more questions of my own." Div turned back to their prisoner and aimed her wand right between his eyes. "You'll answer them all, Hobbes, ShadowKnight, whatever your name is. But if you make the slightest move, magical or nonmagical, I'm prepared to use *cruentus caecus* against you. As you may know, there is no counterspell or cure for *cruentus caecus*."

ShadowKnight paled. "*Cruentus caecus?* Where on earth did you learn that?"

Iris tried to remember what *cruentus caecus* was. Something having to do with eye gouging and lots of blood and maybe permanent blindness, too. *Ouch.*

"Explain to us, please. How do you happen to be both a witch and a witch-hunter? That's illogical," Div went on, her wand still laser-focused on its target. "Also, are you in league with the Antima? With the New Order? With the Jessup family? Did *they* help you and Mrs. Feathers kill Penelope? Who was Mrs. Feathers, and did you kill her after you were done with her? How exactly does heart-fire work to prolong life?"

"I have zero, *nothing*, to do with the Antima or New Order or this Jessup family. To answer your other questions, though, I need to go back to the beginning."

"Fine. Begin."

"Can you untie me? I promise I won't—"

"*No.* Your promises are garbage!" Binx cried out, waving her wand in his face.

Iris was worried about her friend, who looked like Draska before she sliced the fake prince Lagorian in half with her magically charged Draggidian steel ax for betraying the Wildcat Folk. If things didn't turn around fast, Binx really *would* murder ShadowKnight for betraying her, and for everything else, too. And as far as Iris knew, there was no spell to *un*murder someone.

"Pokedragon, I'm sorry." ShadowKnight hoisted himself up on his elbows, leaned against a broken kayak, and cleared his throat. "I'll explain everything."

"Fine. Talk," Binx snapped.

"When I was a teenager—a human, or so I thought—I saw my parents killed by witches. From then on, I dedicated my life to avenging their deaths. When the government initiated the Great Witch Purge of 1877, I volunteered to help round up witches."

"I've read that the government did this because they blamed—actually, *scapegoated*—witches for a terrible virus. A plague," Div remarked.

ShadowKnight nodded. "It's true. I…" His voice broke. "I lost loved ones in the Gray Plague. So did many others. I knew there was an actual virus at work, and that witches had nothing to do with it. I was a medical student back then, specializing in sepsis and surgery. Still, I was more than happy to join the government's cause and make witches suffer for what they'd done to my parents. I became a witch-hunter, one of the best."

"And you were having so much fun that you decided to keep yourself alive and continue with your evil witch-hunting into the twentieth and twenty-first centuries?" Binx spat out.

"No, not at all!" ShadowKnight insisted. "You see, during the Purge, I encountered Callixta Crowe. I knew who she was, and that there was a tremendous bounty on her head. I was about to capture her and turn her in to the authorities when she told me an astonishing story. She said…" He paused and shook his head. "She said *I* was a witch, and that both my parents had been witches, too. And that it was humans, not witches, who'd murdered them."

Iris, Binx, and Div exchanged shocked glances.

"She explained that I was part of an ancient prophecy that had been memorialized in a magical scroll. According to the prophecy, I, Maximus

Hobbes, was destined to stop the extinction of all witches in the year 2017."

"2017, as in now?" Iris asked, confused.

"Yes. She showed me the scroll, and when I touched it, I knew she was telling the truth."

"Soooo…you time-traveled to the present to save all our butts or whatever?" Binx asked skeptically.

"Yes and no. Callixta sent me through a magical portal to fulfill the prophecy, but it glitched. Like, seriously glitched. I went back and forth through time—I became a baby, and then an old man, and then a baby again, and then an old man again…before the portal finally spit me into the present as my eighteen-year-old self. By then, I was practically dead from the space-time dis-continuum and disruption. My internal organs had begun to disintegrate and atrophy."

Binx swiveled to Div. "I think he's lying. I think we should just throw him into the ocean and be done with him."

"Yeah, I deserved that," ShadowKnight acknowledged.

"*Deserve*, present tense. I'm not joking, you jerk," Binx told him coldly.

ShadowKnight stared at her.

"Perhaps Binx has a point. Can you back up your account? Do you have proof?" Div asked ShadowKnight.

"Not exactly. But I'm happy to subject myself to whatever scrying rituals you want to put me through."

"What about the heart-fire thing?" Iris spoke up. "Also, why does my stomach hurt suddenly? Is it the doomsday vibe in this room? Or is it the Rage-Mage Nachos with a side of Goblin Guac I ate back at WitchWorld-Con?" She clutched her sides. "Sorry. TMI, right?"

"Let me explain about heart-fire," ShadowKnight went on. "When I landed in the present, Mrs. Feathers was already here, waiting for me.

Callixta had sent her through the portal, too, from 1877, to help me with my mission and to fast-track my magical training. But as I mentioned before, I was very sick. In fact, as a person with medical training, I could tell that I would likely be dead within the year. Months, maybe. Callixta had foreseen this and warned me that the only possible cure would be to harvest the heart-fire of her descendants. Scions, she called them. Heart-fire is…well, to obtain it, you have to cut out a scion's heart, perform a spell to extract its essential energies, and make a potion out of those energies and other ingredients."

"Now I *really* have a stomachache. Correction, I want to throw up," Iris moaned.

"*That's* your excuse for having Penelope killed? A so-called prophecy?" Div snapped at ShadowKnight. "Was Mrs. Feathers a scion, too? Is that why you killed her?"

"I didn't kill Mrs. Feathers! And as for Penelope…I…" Shadow-Knight hesitated. "So she's not dead. Not exactly."

"*What?*"

Everyone turned. Ridley stood in the doorway.

"Hey!" Binx rushed up to her best friend and hugged her.

Ridley was visibly shaking. "Binx, what does he mean Penelope's not…is he saying she's still alive?"

"He's been telling us quite the tale, Ridley. We still need to sort out what's true and what's not," Div spoke up.

Iris was about to jump into the discussion when her overly sensitive ears picked up a barely audible sound. A word. *Evanescetio.*

She turned back around to face ShadowKnight.

A heap of loose ropes lay next to the broken kayak where he used to be.

"Guys? He's gone!" Iris cried out.

PART 3

IDENTITY THEFT

Transformation can be achieved using
muto, but that spell has limits. *Vertero*
is the more advanced form and difficult
to achieve. Also, there are side effects. I
should know, right?

(FROM THE GRIMOIRE OF PENELOPE RUE HART)

18

THE GAMING ROOM

Science and magic often collaborate
in interesting ways.

(FROM *THE GOOD BOOK OF MAGIC AND MENTALISM*
BY CALLIXTA CROWE)

"Die!" ShadowKnight yelled as he tapped repeatedly on his computer mouse, directing his Staff of Eternal Night at a roving band of Ongolean Orks. "Die, die, *die!*"

The staff glowed blue and then red as a bolt of lightning shot out of it, zapping the head Ork. "*Fzdtp!*" it screamed before falling to the ground with a great thud. No vowels, which told ShadowKnight that these were outlaws from the pre–Ragamong Revolution days.

"Yeah, *fzdtp* to you, too, you parasitic slimeball! That'll teach you to steal my Golden Rocks of Retrograde Teleportation!"

ShadowKnight finished off the rest of the rogue Orks, this time switching to the more efficient method of casting Poison Splash at the lot of them. He watched as the creatures dissolved into a collective pool of oozing purple liquid, shouting various vowel-less Ongolean obscenities as they perished.

"Ugh. Finally!"

He slumped back in his chair, took a long sip of Mountain Dew, and debated what his next move should be. Shop for new magical weapons at Beeble's Bazaar? Chase down the rumor about buried treasure in the Skirnysh Zone? Pay his former-enemy-turned-mentor Arestipolla of Yorn a visit? He wondered if Binx's avatar, Ms. Magius, was online. He hadn't been able to locate her so far, but it was possible to hide one's presence in the game with a simple hack. He wondered, too, where Binx herself was IRL, and what she was thinking about—or rather, what she was thinking about *him* after today's events.

Their WitchWorldCon meetup had not gone as planned. Not even close. It was supposed to have been his great, grand opportunity to tell her the whole truth—well, *most* of it, anyway—and win her over to his side forever. He hadn't expected Div to show up; Binx had assured him she'd be at the con alone, and he'd believed her.

He was lucky he'd managed to get away from Binx and the others at the beach . . . *really* lucky. He'd used the temporary distraction of Ridley's sudden appearance and the big reveal about Penelope to cast an advanced form of *evadere*, and fortunately for him, it had taken effect before the four witches could perform a counterspell. If he hadn't escaped, who knows what they would have done to him? Binx had threatened to kill him—throw him into the ocean—and she may have gone through with it, too. He recalled the look of shock and horror in her eyes at Witch-WorldCon when she realized he wasn't the person he'd claimed to be.

I'm sorry, Pokedragon. I really am.

He truly liked her. She reminded him so much of his beloved Beatrice. Smart, spunky, a wicked sense of humor, and beautiful in her own defiant way. The coincidence of the names—Beatrice and Beatrix—hadn't been lost on him, either. Of course, Binx had no idea that he'd been aware of her full name—Beatrix Akari Kato—since the beginning, even when he'd supposedly known her only as Pokedragon2946.

Beatrice had perished during the Gray Plague. So had many others close to him. Over that horrific winter, a hundred thousand American souls had been lost to the mysterious disease, and the government, looking to cover up their own incompetence in handling the crisis, had falsely blamed witches and called for their immediate capture, arrest, and executions.

As a witch-hunter, his name and reputation became legend across the nation. Especially when he came up with the idea of burning witches in giant birdcages over a bonfire. The symbolism had taken hold along with the methodology; Crowe's familiar was a black crow, so the image of witches in birdcages had possessed an elegant sort of logic. Vengeance artistry.

And then he'd met Crowe face-to-face.

When he finally managed to track down her hiding place—a stone cottage deep in the forest, a silly fairy-tale cliché, really—he'd been enormously pleased with himself and grimly eager to present her to the authorities in chains before performing her execution himself. Crowe was picking flowers in her garden when he arrived...another fairy-tale cliché. Roses and lilies and anemones, he recalled. She hadn't even flinched when she saw him standing at her gate, his rifle slung across his shoulders and murderous intent written across his face. What followed had shattered his entire world.

His whole life had been a lie.

A noise startled ShadowKnight from his reverie. He jumped up from his chair, knocking down his bottle of Mountain Dew as he did so, and did a quick sweep of the gaming room. Everything was in its usual place…the multiple high-def TVs…the Xbox, PlayStation, Wii, and Switch equipment…the elaborate routers…the boxy old PCs running Pac-Man and other vintage arcade games…the pinball machines…the VR corner with the Oculus and HTC headsets.

And just past the gaming room, on the other side of the Chinese screen, thirteen candles flickered on the round mahogany table. Next to it, Penelope Hart lay unconscious on the velvet settee. The other body—Mrs. Feathers's, which was not quite as far along—was still stored in the greenhouse among the jasmine and black nightshade that he grew for his lunar sorcery; he was still contemplating what to do with her. Near Penelope, two large vials of reddish liquid bubbled on Bunsen burners. The *lamassu*, too, was in its usual place on the bookshelf next to the latest editions of *Vigilante Bots* and *Princess Tokyo*, two of his favorite manga series.

Where had the noise come from? ShadowKnight did another sweep, inspecting everything carefully. Nothing was awry. It must have been one of the gaming machines, then. Sometimes, he felt as though they were autonomous and sentient, that they had lives of their own. Which they did in a way, which was why gaming was everything. He only wished they'd had video games back in his century; perhaps he would have been a happier person.

On his way back to his main desktop, where he'd paused his *Witch-world* game, he passed his favorite scrying mirror hanging on the wall; it was one of a dozen in the house. He peered at his reflection and smiled, then unsmiled, then smiled again. He was glad to be here in the twenty-first century, alive and intact. Although he wished he hadn't had to dabble in this heart-fire business. Why would Crowe concoct such a perverse "cure" in the first place? Or had that little detail been out of her control, and she'd simply been following a predestined path—for herself, for him—which involved sacrificing several witches to save *all* witches? What had Spock said in one of the *Star Trek* movies? *The needs of the many outweigh the needs of the few.* What was the loss of a few lives compared with the salvation of many, many more?

Whatever the case, he'd killed witches before, and he'd do it again, albeit much less enthusiastically. He already believed in the truth of the prophecy. Its veracity, its universe-shattering importance, had burned bright inside him when he touched the scroll. And so, with Mrs. Feathers's help, he'd built his magical mansion in the forest—not like Crowe's silly cliché fairy-tale cottage, but a 2.0—then set about to locate the scions. He'd taught himself about computers and hacking to try to unearth this information. And along the way, he'd developed a passion for video games. And for *Witchworld.* And for his favorite *Witchworld* friend, Pokedragon2946.

Like him, Binx was devoted to witches' rights and had a deep hatred of the Antima movement, and so he tried to gain her trust by telling her about Libertas. Not the real Libertas, which she wasn't ready to hear about yet, but a made-up version that would make her like and trust him, and that would have achieved a similar goal, had it really existed. And, underhanded as it was, he solicited her assistance to find Callixta's scions so that he and Mrs. Feathers could harvest their heart-fire ASAP and restore his ailing health. Little did he know that the first two scion victims would turn out to be Binx's friends Penelope and Greta.

And little did he know that Mrs. Feathers would give him trouble, too. ShadowKnight hadn't realized how her trip to 2017 affected her cerebral cortex, slowly changing her. But he knew things were over once she'd started hearing "voices" telling her that the two of them had to confess their "sins" and turn themselves in to the police. He hadn't wanted to kill her, but he'd had to. And he'd had to make it look like an accident.

But now that he'd harvested Penelope's heart-fire, ShadowKnight was certain he could fix the harm he'd done to her, and simultaneously fulfill the prophecy. In the short time they'd spent together back in 1877, Crowe had convinced him unequivocally that witches were not the enemy. Humans were. *They* were the petty, power-hungry, violent race... not witches.

"Now, where did I leave my laptop?" he muttered out loud.

Ah, yes... somewhere near the Bunsen burners. He'd been keeping most of his scientific notes on the laptop, and ditto his notes on the true Libertas project. That, too, had a scientific component as well as a magical one. If Libertas was successful, he and Binx and their kind would all become free. No more 6-129, the old edition, or President Ingraham's proposed "upgrade" known as 6-129A. No more Antima or New Order.

And not only would witches become free—they would rule, forever. Just as the prophecy stated. Just as Crowe had intended.

He picked up the laptop and pressed the power button. As he waited for it to boot up, he glanced down at Penelope's still body, which he'd managed to move from her grave via *lacus*. A magically induced illusion of her corpse was still in her grave, in case anyone checked.

The necromancy spells had not worked perfectly. Her heart—her *new* heart—beat only intermittently. And some of her cells seemed to have an aversion to oxygen, which might be a side effect of the *vertero* he'd used to help with her transformation. Perhaps he needed to experiment with different herbs—maybe the ones from the Himalayas he'd read about that germinated only once in a decade, or the so-called cyber-botanicals Binx had told him about?—and also rewrite some of the incantations.

It might help, too, to have other witches join in the necromancy effort. Group spells tended to be more powerful than solo ones. He would have to keep trying to win back Binx. And Ridley, her best friend, seemed to have feelings for Penelope, which would be an advantage. Div should be a natural because he sensed she'd already dabbled in necromancy and other dark arts. And if Div could be convinced, then the other witches in her coven—Mira and Aysha—would surely follow? He wasn't sure about Greta, though, or Iris. Or the new one, Torrence.

He sat down at the edge of the velvet settee and touched Penelope's cheek. It was ice-cold. He then touched the tiny heart-shaped mole on her sternum, the mark that had identified her definitively as a scion. It seemed to have changed color from yesterday, from blue to lavender. It was also warm.

Hmm. This was new. And perhaps scientifically relevant.

He opened the corresponding document on his laptop and began to type.

✳ 19 ✳

TRUTHFUL LIES

Enemies can sometimes turn into friends.

(FROM *THE GOOD BOOK OF MAGIC AND MENTALISM*
BY CALLIXTA CROWE)

"Hey there, Mira, the councilman is on a call, so he'll just be another min. How's school going?"

"Fine, thanks, Ms. Ortega. How is your family?" Mira asked politely.

"Can't complain. Why don't you girls have a seat?"

Mr. Jahani's assistant waved to a row of red vinyl chairs, across from a closed door with a plaque that said COUNCILMAN NEAL JAHANI. As Mira and Div checked their phones, Greta glanced around the room. This was her first time in a councilperson's office; actually, it was her first time in the Sorrow Point City Hall building, period. Framed certificates covered the wood-paneled walls—awards and accolades from the Downtown Business Association and the Chamber of Commerce and the League of Women Voters—and a lone plant dangled from a macramé hanger. Devil's ivy, *Epipremnum aureum*. Next to Ms. Ortega's desk, the October page of a calendar sported a menacing-looking jack-o'-lantern with the word *Boo!* inside a dialogue bubble. Greta touched her throat. Her amethyst pendant wasn't there, so she pretended to rub the back of her neck.

It's okay. Everything's going to be okay.

She crossed and uncrossed her legs, then plucked a loose thread from her sweater, which was a happy, messy jumble of colors: lavender, pale pink, moss green, cornflower blue. Mama had knitted it for her last winter out of half skeins of yarn left over from various projects. She'd added a heart design on the pocket because that's what she used to do when making clothes for Greta and Teo when they were little. She'd made this particular heart very small, so no one but Greta would see it.

"Please let me do most of the talking," Div whispered without looking up from her phone. "Both of you."

"But he's *my* dad," Mira whispered back.

"I'm aware of that. If you must speak to him, please keep it very brief. We can't afford to get emotional and have the conversation degrade into an argument."

"O-kay." Mira shrugged and returned to her texting.

Greta started to protest, too—*we're here because of* my *mom*—then changed her mind. She'd asked Div to help with the daunting task of getting her mother out of jail for a reason. Div excelled in impossible situations. Nothing seemed to scare her. She could charm a deadly snake or outmaneuver a hungry panther without breaking a sweat. Greta and Mira really did need to follow her lead and obey orders, stay in the background.

Greta closed her eyes briefly and tried to feel her mother's presence. *Nothing.* Ysabel had to be in this building, too, perhaps deep in the basement or subbasement. Papa had explained that when a person was arrested, they were typically kept in a cell until a judge could decide whether or not to release them on bail.

The police officers had taken Ysabel away on Sunday at approximately five p.m. It was now four p.m. on Monday, which meant she'd spent almost twenty-four hours in jail. Papa's lawyer friend Lionel was trying to help, but so far, he hadn't made any progress on speeding up the arraignment or getting the charges dropped. In the meantime, Div had suggested that they appeal to Mira's father to intervene; as a councilman and possibly the next mayor of Sorrow Point, he could surely pull some strings? At first Mira had objected to the plan, saying that he was a stickler for rules and never granted special favors, even when it came to friends and family. But Div had insisted and Mira had relented, and had asked her father to meet with the three of them. For once, Greta was grateful for Div's alpha personality and general bossiness.

The door with the name plaque swung open, and Mr. Jahani poked his head out. "Hi, Mira, honey. Hey, girls. Come on in!"

Mira stood up, smiled tensely at her father, and headed into his office. As she passed him, he gave her a quick kiss on the cheek, which she accepted wordlessly. Div and Greta followed. Greta didn't know Mira that well, but whenever she saw her at school or a joint coven meeting or the like, she was usually charming and talkative. The discovery that her dad was so anti-witch must have devastated her...

...not to mention the news about ShadowKnight/Maximus Hobbes, which had devastated *all* of them. Right now, the other witches—Iris, Ridley, Binx, Torrence, and Aysha—were at Binx's house strategizing about how to find him ASAP and make sure he was no longer a threat to Callixta's descendants. He'd apparently claimed that Penelope was still alive, too, although surely that was just a ruse, a red herring, to confuse them?

I tried to warn you about him, Binx. And you didn't listen.

Inside the inner office, Greta, Mira, and Div sat down on a couch.

Across from them, Mr. Jahani perched on the edge of his very large, very cluttered desk. Greta had never seen him in person before, although she'd glimpsed his face on political posters and on TV a couple of times. He was tall and slender and bore a strong resemblance to Mira. His eyes were sharp and bright, although his face seemed strained by worry...or overwork...or both.

She tried to sense his emotions, his inner state. He *was* worried and overworked. But there was something else inside him.

Fear.

What was he afraid of?

"How's school going? You two are sophomores like my Mira, right? What kind of sports and clubs and other extracurriculars are you involved in?" he asked Greta and Div.

"Well, I'm in choir," Greta replied.

"I'm on the Homecoming Committee, like Mira. And after that wraps up, I hope to run for student government," Div said with a hair flip.

Greta stared at her, as did Mira. *Student government?* That didn't seem like Div at all. Neither did the hair flip. Or perhaps this was all an act for Mr. Jahani?

"Wonderful! I was president of student government when I was a senior. Very fulfilling work." Mr. Jahani crossed his arms over his chest. "So what can I do for you girls today?"

"Well, Daddy—" Mira began.

"We're here on behalf of Ysabel Navarro," Div cut in. "Greta's mom. She's been arrested for supposedly violating 6-129. But there's been a terrible mix-up."

Mr. Jahani raised an eyebrow. "Oh?"

"The police came to the Navarros' home last night because Greta's name was on a list of suspected witches. Mrs. Navarro let herself be arrested to protect Greta because, well, that's what any parent would do, right? Protect their children?" Div paused and leaned forward. "Mrs. Navarro isn't a witch. Neither is Greta. She and I have been best friends since junior high school, so I should know."

Div turned to Greta and squeezed her hand. Surprised, Greta squeezed back. Was this more acting, or...

"Councilman Jahani, we believe Greta's name ended up on that list because one of the Antima activists at our school asked her out and she turned him down, and he got mad and decided to lie and accuse her of witchcraft," Div went on.

Greta blinked. That was *definitely* not true.

"That's not good. Not good at all. Who was it?" Mr. Jahani asked.

"Honestly, I don't feel right naming names," Div said apologetically. "I have no interest in getting him into trouble. I understand how important the cause is and that sometimes people can get carried away. In fact, my boyfriend, Hunter, was telling me just the other day that—"

"Hunter Jessup?"

Div beamed and hair flipped some more. "Yes! Hunter was telling me just the other day that when it comes to witches, it's best to cast a wide net. Some innocent victims, like Greta and her mom, are bound to get caught up in it, but they'll eventually be freed when the facts get sorted out. Don't you agree, Councilman Jahani?"

"Yes, yes, of course...."

Greta glanced over at Mira, who was biting her lip and scrolling absentmindedly through her phone. The poor girl, having to watch her friend and coven leader pose as Antima to deceive her father, who actually *was* Antima...or pro-Antima, anyway. If there was a difference.

Mr. Jahani reached behind him, picked up his phone, and pushed a button. "Cindy? Yup, I'm aware...but first, can you find out for me if

Chief Myrick has contacted the US Attorney's office yet about the case of Ysabel—" He paused and peered at Greta.

"Navarro," Greta said quickly.

"Ysabel Navarro. If yes, get me Keisha Anderson. No, I don't want to speak to one of the AUSAs. I need to speak to Keisha herself."

He put his hand over the mouthpiece and winked at Greta. "Don't you worry, we'll take care of this. If all goes well, your mom should be home by dinnertime."

Greta exhaled. *Oh, thank Goddess.*

"And that's how it's done," Div whispered in her ear.

"Thank you," Greta whispered back.

"You owe me, Gretabelle."

"Gretabelle" was Div's old nickname for her, from back in their junior high school days. Div used it only occasionally now, mostly to disarm or distract Greta. At the moment, though, Greta was neither disarmed nor distracted. Just grateful to her former BFF.

She reached over and squeezed Div's hand. This time, it was Div's turn to be surprised.

20

NECESSARY DANGER

Never stop seeking the new or revisiting the old.
The craft is infinite.

(FROM *THE GOOD BOOK OF MAGIC AND MENTALISM*
BY CALLIXTA CROWE)

inx leaned back against her Princess Zelda throw pillow—the B.A. *Breath of the Wild* Princess Zelda, not one of the other, wimpier incarnations—and fanned her Pokémon deck in her hand. Around the circle, the other witches—Aysha, Ridley, Iris, and Torrence—were gathering their own materials for the calling of the quarters ritual. Nearby, Lillipup was napping in his little dog bed next to Binx's desk and making adorable snuffling noises in his sleep.

She picked a random card. Slugma, the fire-based lava slug. *Figures...* Slugma's stats were super-weak across the board, everything from HP to Attack to Defense to Speed. Plus, if it ever became exposed to the cold, the magma inside its body would harden and slow it down. Normally, Binx would be willing to work with a less-than-stellar card; she enjoyed having to be resourceful and creative that way. But this was a serious coven meeting with serious stakes—they needed to locate ShadowKnight ASAP so that she could cast a double, triple, quadruple *aegresco* on him, for starters—which meant that she needed to line up an all-star Pokémon roster if possible.

"Sorry, buddy," she told the Slugma card, and picked again. Charizard, the final form of Charmander. *Much better.* She set it down on the rug next to a flickering candle. Charizard would represent the fire element, corresponding with the South.

"Let's begin," she said once the others had arranged their magical items, too.

"Wait…why are *you* the coven leader today?" Aysha asked, sounding vaguely annoyed.

"*Because-Mom-likes-me-better,*" Binx singsonged. "JK! Div asked me to fill in while she and Mira and Greta deal with the City Hall sitch."

Aysha rolled her eyes. "Whatevs."

"I hope Greta's mom is okay." Iris picked up a piece of rose quartz, moved it to the right, then moved it back again. "I hope they were able to free her. If not, well…maybe we could cast a big ol' group spell to make it happen. Like maybe *liberum*?"

"Or maybe *liberandum*? It's more advanced," Torrence suggested.

"*Liberum* is better," Iris sniped back.

Binx glanced at the pair. *Hmm, Ridley was right. There's definitely a love-triangle vibe happening.*

"Guys, can we…can we please start the meeting? We really, really need to find ShadowKnight and"—Ridley looked down and twisted her hands in her lap—"and Penelope, too."

"Of course," Binx said gently. Her best friend had been a mess since ShadowKnight had revealed this little nugget to them, if it was even true. Which Binx seriously doubted, since ShadowKnight was an evil, lying liar. Besides, how in the hex could Penelope possibly be alive? They—Binx, Ridley, Iris, and Greta—had found her very dead body at that construction site in the Seabreeze development. Days later, they'd attended her funeral and paid their respects as she lay in an open casket covered with pink roses...and Iris had accidentally touched her and been blasted with an unwelcome vision that the girl's heart was gone. *Gone.*

Time to find that self-important jerk and blast him back into the past for good. Because what's going to happen if and when he needs more heart-fire? Also, I need a revenge fix.

Binx initiated the calling of the quarters ritual, which they often used to begin a meeting. Charizard was definitely the right card for today; she sensed the magical energy in the room spark and buzz and elevate. Ever since her discovery moment at age nine, when she'd wished that her favorite Charmander stuffy would talk to her and it had, she'd made up her own style of craft that combined her considerable computer skills with her love of Pokémon. These days, post the 2016 upload by the anonymous descendant, Binx's system had grown into a complex hybrid of cyber, Pokémon, and C-Squared's spells and potion recipes. Which worked for her. And these days, she could feel her skills, her powers, growing at hyperspeed.

Maybe she could even be a *real* coven leader someday? For now, though, she was cool with being just a sub. For now.

After the calling of the quarters, she launched into the urgent matter at hand—finding ShadowKnight.

"So in the last twenty-four hours, since our 'beach party'"—Binx made big, extra-sarcastic air quotes—"I've been trying to develop a new geolocating spell that combines GPS technology, a *Witchworld* username search function, and one of C-Squared's classic location spells, *inveniet.*"

"Any luck?" Aysha asked.

"It's buggy, but I'm hoping to have it operational ASAP."

Iris raised her hand. "Excuse me, fellow witches? I've been trying to make myself have a magical vision about where ShadowKnight might be hiding or not hiding or whatever. Nothing was happening—no vision, nix, nada—but then when I got home from school today, I came across *this*." She uncurled her palm, displaying a small, crumpled scrap of brown cloth.

"What is it?" Ridley asked her curiously.

"It's a piece of fabric. My little sister found it in my silver Jadora quiver that I made for WitchWorldCon because she was going through my stuff like she's not supposed to but she always does, anyway. And *I* originally found it on the floor of Binx's family's beach shack when we were there yesterday. I must have tossed it into the quiver and forgot."

"Uh-huh, but *what* is it?" Aysha prompted her.

"My guess is...was...still is...that it must have ripped from Shadow-Knight's Dargon costume. It's the exact same color. Plus, it was at the spot by the kayak where he was our prisoner and then not our prisoner. Near an old life preserver that smelled like an expired tuna-salad sandwich. Dargon, for those of you who don't know, is a half-human, half-witch character from *Witchworld*. He was exiled by the High Council for try-ing to K-I-L-L all the members of the Low Council with a deadly potion made from the breath of an ice dragon. And his *mom* was one of the Low Council members, can you believe it?" Iris snort-laughed. "Anyhoo...I was going to mention it at the time, but he'd *poof!* vanished into thin air and all heck was breaking loose, so I threw the thing into my quiver and totally forgot about it. Until an hour ago, because of Nyala."

"Did the cloth inspire any visions, then?" Binx asked.

"Yes. A mini-vision, more like a micro-vision actually, because I had to stop with the visioning to help Ephrem—he's my little brother—and then I had to leave for this meeting, and I wasn't sure I could get a ride with...well, anyhoo, I saw some shiny gems in my micro-vision. Something black and also bloodstone...I *think*. Wait...bloodstone isn't made from blood, is it? Because that would be gross. Oh, and I saw a pinball machine—you know, like one of the ones in the arcade at the mall—except this one was antique-y or vintage or whatever. The theme was bride of Frankenstein or bride of something, or someone, else. But then Lolli tried to eat the cloth—she's my familiar, for those of you who aren't familiar with her—get it, familiar with my familiar?—sorry, old joke, right?—so I had to, um..."

"Did you say 'bloodstone'?" Ridley spoke up.

"Affirmative. Well, affirmative-*ish*. Why?"

"When you said that, it reminded me of...I don't know, I'll try to remember."

Iris sat up. "Yes, that's it! Weren't you and I and Greta talking about bloodstone at our last coven meeting?"

"Right! Sorry, my brain's kind of shot right now."

"Can I see that?" Torrence asked Iris.

"Ummm...I guess?" Iris reluctantly passed the cloth to him.

As Torrence studied the cloth, Binx wondered if he would have preferred being part of the Greta's-mom-rescue-squad at City Hall versus hanging out with the B-listers here. Probably, right? Especially since Iris was throwing so much hostility and shade his way? Whatever the case, Div had texted her earlier with a progress report, saying that Mr. Jahani was making some VIP phone calls to try to fix the situation, adding that if for any reason that should fall through, she planned to enlist Hunter's help when she saw him at a New Order meeting later tonight.

We should be focusing on destroying the New Order, and all the rest of the Antima scum, too. But instead, we have to spend our valuable time chasing down that vile super-villain man-boy to make sure he doesn't kill more scions or whatever. This is all on me, since I totally fell for his lies.

"Would there be a benefit to repeating the group *agnitionis*, like we did the other day? With Greta's scarf?" Torrence offered. "I could conjure up three pieces of azurite again."

Iris side-eyed him.

"Yeah, that might be worth a try. Although there's no need to conjure the azurite, Torrence. I have some here." Binx leaned over and retrieved the stones from a shelf. "Done! Now let's set the Dargon cloth down in the middle of the circle."

"I'll do it!" Iris reached over to grab the cloth from Torrence.

Honestly. These two.

Binx arranged her azurite pieces on top of the cloth in a triangular pattern. Then the five witches joined hands and closed their eyes.

"*Agnitionis*," Binx said quietly.

"*Agnitionis*," the others repeated.

Silence. Binx's mind was blank; she wondered if anyone else was having a vision.

"I'm not getting anything," Aysha announced after a moment.

"Me neither," Ridley added.

"Me neither, three," Iris piped up. "Maybe we should start over?"

"*Wait!*"

Binx's mind was no longer blank. A strange plan of action was fomenting, seemingly of its own accord. She let go of Ridley's hand to her right and Iris's to her left, then laid her Charizard card on top of the cloth and azurite. She added her phone/grimoire, first making sure that her beta-stage ShadowKnight-locating app was open.

She closed her eyes and concentrated. *Come on, come on, come on.* She felt in her bones that she was onto something.

Seconds later, a frigid wind rushed through her. Cold...she was so cold. Her body was freezing, turning into stone. But then a flame erupted out of nowhere, and her body became pure heat. What was happening to her? She was liquid magma...no, liquid molybdenum....

There he is. ShadowKnight. He was sitting at a table and lighting candles...thirteen of them...and also arranging gems in a circle. At the sight of him, fury and sadness and regret coursed through her, mingling with the river of molten fire. She'd liked him. As in, *liked* him. And she'd invested in him all her hopes and dreams of destroying the Antima and the New Order and liberating witches forever.

Maybe he still wants to destroy the Antima and the New Order and liberate witches forever. But the heart-fire stuff is definitely a deal breaker.

Suddenly, energy zapped her fingers where they hovered over the cloth and other items. She yelped and opened her eyes. A bizarre blue light was sparking and crackling from her phone screen like some sort of reverse lightning.

Lillipup woke up from his nap, spun around and around, and began barking like mad.

Binx grabbed for her phone and then dropped it; it was burning hot.

"*Frigidum!*" she shouted. *Cool down.*

The phone morphed to icy white. Binx picked it up again—the cold was bearable—and stared at the screen.

47.8 something, something, something and 123.9 something, something, something

Below them was the image of a small bluish sculpture.

She recognized the numbers as partial GPS coordinates and matched them quickly against a map.

Yessss! Gotcha, you conniving catfisher!

"Ridley!" she said suddenly.

"What's happening? Are you okay?" Ridley demanded.

"Those photos you showed me. The ones Aysha took. From your field trip."

"You mean the Kai Rain Forest trip?" Iris asked.

"Yes. I think he's there. At that invisible mansion!" Binx told Ridley.

Torrence's gaze bounced between them. "Invisible mansion?"

Ridley held up a hand. "I'll explain in a sec, Torrence.... Binx, how do you know ShadowKnight is there?"

"I saw the *lamassu*. The magical sculpture from ancient Mesopotamia, remember? And I have partial GPS coordinates, too. I looked them up just now; they correspond with the northwestern part of the state, where the rain forest is located. That way." Binx pointed, and at the same moment realized that Lillipup was facing in that direction, too. *Good dog!*

Ridley's eyes widened. "Oh! Of course! That explains the bloodstone and the black gems . . . they were black onyx. I'm remembering now; I saw them at the mansion, too, along with some herbs."

"Excellent." Binx picked up her phone—it felt normal again, *whew*—and fired off a text to Div explaining the situation. A moment later, Div wrote back:

Can you all head over to that location immediately? All is well here but I must head over to the Jessups' house for a meeting within the hour.

Binx typed:

Sure, no problem. I can drive us. Is Greta's mom free?

Div replied:

> She should be shortly. Re SK, please use care to assess the
> situation. Don't put yourselves in unnecessary danger.

Binx wrote:

> We won't.

"Guys? Road trip," Binx announced as she pocketed her phone.
Already, she was formulating a possible strategy to inflict maximum damage points on ShadowKnight and defeat his sorry butt. Which should be
within Div's parameters... after all, she hadn't said anything about *neces-*
sary danger.

* 21 *

THE DESCENDANT

The work of healing is often misunderstood.

(FROM *THE GOOD BOOK OF MAGIC AND MENTALISM*
BY CALLIXTA CROWE)

"You're on the list, Ms. Florescu. Please go on through."

"Thank you, Douglas."

The Jessups' security guard opened the electronic gates, and Div proceeded down the long gravel driveway. Even though it was a moonless night, there were many stars in the sky. Div thought she recognized several constellations, including Cassiopeia, the beautiful Greek queen, and Scorpius the scorpion...she wondered, briefly, if any witches in history had ever had a scorpion for a familiar. *Could be interesting.*

The long, majestic pine trees that flanked the driveway began thinning out as Div's Audi approached the vast, pristine front lawn. The house—or more accurately, estate—was just beyond the marble fountain and the semicircular driveway, which was lined with cars. *The New Order members must have started arriving for the meeting already.*

Div parked in her usual spot near the family's eight-car garage, pocketed her smart key, and headed briskly for the front door. As she walked, she checked her phone. No further messages from any of her witches. Hopefully, no news was good news, or at least not *bad* news.

Out of the corner of her eye, she saw two officers standing on either side of the Jessups' front door.

She bit back her alarm as she slowed her steps and continued scrolling busily through her phone. What in the hex were they doing here? And then she remembered there were police at Saturday's New Order meeting, too. *This group is really serious about security.*

"Good evening, miss," one of the police officers—a woman—called out.

Div smiled and waved. "Good evening, Officers."

"Your name?" the woman asked her.

"Divinity Florescu. I'm here for the meeting."

"Right. Douglas has already cleared you. Please go on in."

"Thank you."

The second officer, a man, had been silent during the entire exchange. Now he stared at Div with a curious expression and rested his hand casually on his gun holster. *What the hex?* Just to be safe, she mentally cast *animo legere* in her head, to glean his thoughts and make sure he didn't know about her witch identity. *No, he doesn't seem to.* Then she switched to *transpicere* and quickly scanned him from head to toe. *Aha.* He was wearing a T-shirt under several layers of uniform, and on the sleeve of the shirt was a patch. An Antima patch.

Actually, not the usual Antima patch. This one had the image of the birdcage burning over a fire, except that the fire part consisted of the letters *N* and *O* in the shape of flames.

The New Order.

Both officers stepped aside as Div rang the bell, still pretending to check her phone, all the while furiously assessing and analyzing. The New Order rebranding of the Antima had obviously begun. And the *police* were part of the effort now? The entire situation was spiraling out of control. Not to mention the fact that any day now, the US president planned to sign an even more draconian version of 6-129, called 6-129A, into law. On top of which, Div and her coven, and Greta and her coven, too, had to deal with Maximus Hobbes aka ShadowKnight and this heart-fire business. He seemed unhinged, dangerous. And what did he want beyond just staying alive? Power? Wealth? World domination? All of the above? Something else entirely?

At least Div finally knew the true leader of the New Order. She'd tasked Binx with researching Dr. Jessup's background and trying to hack into her private emails and such. So far, Binx had turned up little beyond available public information. Jane L. Meritt, born in Sorrow Point . . . top of her class at the medical school at the University of Pennsylvania . . . head of pediatrics at Sorrow Point Hospital . . . married to real estate mogul Jared Jessup since 1981 . . . mother of Hunter, age seventeen; Colter, age sixteen; and the twins, Cassandra and Caitlin, age ten. And now, she was the head of the most powerful anti-witch organization in the country.

The door opened. Hunter stood there. Grinning, he pulled Div inside and swept her into his arms.

"I am so glad to see you!" he murmured, hugging her tightly. "I had two midterms today, so I'm ready to chill. Well, the meeting first, *then* we can chill."

"How did you do on your midterms?" Div asked, hugging him back.

"I won't know until Professor Brody and Professor Sayed do their grading. But if I had to guess, probably A's?"

"So you're basically a genius."

Hunter laughed. "Yeah, but we already knew that. Come on in."

As soon as he'd closed the door behind them, he pulled her in closer and kissed her. Div allowed herself to enjoy the physical sensation for a brief moment. It really was too bad that he was the enemy. Otherwise, he would be the perfect boyfriend—not the falling-in-love-with kind of boyfriend, or the "I-can't-wait-to-marry-him-someday" kind of boyfriend, either, but a hot guy to go on dates with and make out with whenever the urge might strike. All fun and pleasure and entirely dispensable.

As it was, she was just relieved he had bought into her ruse so completely. He truly believed she was sympathetic to the cause. As for Mira... she was still fake-dating Colter. Although, Div could tell that a part of her was having a hard time accepting that her faux boyfriend and his family, or at least the family minus Cassie and Caitlin, were card-carrying Antima-now-New-Order members who believed in 6-129 and that humans were superior to witches. That witches shouldn't exist.

I need to have another conversation with her...ASAP.

Hunter took her by the hand and led her through the entryway, which was thick with the scent of gardenias, hyacinths, and other flowers from an elaborate bouquet on the antique half-round table. Voices drifted from the living room...not conversations, though, but what sounded like yelling and shouting.

"Has the meeting already started? Is everything okay in there?" Div asked Hunter nervously.

"What? Oh, that's from the TV. The meeting hasn't started yet, but some people got here early, and they're watching the news because of the rallies that kicked off today."

"*What* rallies?"

"You don't know? Sorry, I must have forgotten to mention it; it came together pretty much overnight. The New Order leadership has organized a series of rallies across the country to roll out the new name and to support the passage of 6-129A. In fact, there's going to be one in Sorrow Point on Wednesday. Orion Kong from your school is helping to organize it. Why don't we go together?"

"Oh! Sure."

Div peered through the living room doorway. Mr. Jessup and a dozen or so other New Order members—she remembered most of them from the last meeting—were milling in front of the eighty-five-inch wall-mounted TV. The screen was split between half a dozen cities—Los Angeles; New York City; Chicago; Washington, DC; Boston; and Miami—then it shifted to six different cities, including some small ones in the Midwest and South. Each shot showed protesters wearing shirts with the new symbol, marching down Main Streets and in front of state capitols and city halls. They carried signs that said THE NEW ORDER IS HERE TO STAY! and 6-129A NOW! and HUMANS FIRST! while chanting "Witches don't belong here!" through bullhorns.

"Isn't it great?" Hunter murmured. "The rallies are totally nonviolent, too. That's *true* activism. Democracy in action."

"Absolutely."

Div felt sick to her stomach. She had to get away. "Can you excuse me a sec? I want to say a quick hello to your sisters. I still have a few minutes, right?"

"Sure, of course. That's sweet of you. They've been super-grumpy lately...maybe you can cheer them up."

"Are they okay?"

"Yeah, well...ten-year-old girls, right? They think they know everything."

That's kind of sexist, Div wanted to say. *Are only boys allowed to be opinionated and sure of themselves?* Instead, she squeezed his arm and headed upstairs, running a hand across her hair to smooth it even though it didn't need smoothing. She was usually the epitome of calm, cool, and collected—she didn't believe in wasting time and energy on emotions—but right now, she was fighting to keep her feelings in check. True activism? Democracy in action? These rallies were nothing but hatred and prejudice, pure and simple. Hatred and prejudice against *her kind*.

And was she really going to march in one on Wednesday with her pretend boyfriend? Did she have any other choice?

Upstairs, Div found the twins in Cassie's bedroom, sitting on the floor with their tablets. She took a deep breath to center herself before poking her head through the door.

"Knock, knock."

"Hi, Divvy," Cassie called out. Caitlin waved without looking up from the screen. Hunter was right; they were definitely not their usual cheerful, chatty selves.

"Hey, you two. What's up?"

"Well, I'm playing the *Untitled Duck Game* and Caitlin's playing *Animal Land*," Cassie replied.

"We're not allowed to play *Witchworld* anymore," Caitlin added. "Dad says."

"Oh! I'm sorry." Div sat down cross-legged on the floor next to them. "Why won't he let you play?"

Caitlin shrugged. "Dunno. Hunt is on his side, too. He told Dad *Witchworld* was a 'correcting influence.' Or 'corrupting.' Whatever. Anyway, it's *so dumb*."

"I'm sorry. Hey, tell me about these new games of yours. I've missed you guys! I haven't been here in a couple of days because Hunter was busy studying for his midterms."

"I hope Hunter *flunks*," Cassie snapped.

"Yeah. I hope they throw him out of college for being a total *jerk*," Caitlin added. "Oops. Hey, Hunter. Actually, *not* oops. I hope you heard *everything*."

Startled, Div glanced over her shoulder. Hunter stood in the doorway, scowling at his phone.

"Div, I need to speak to you. Now, please."

His demeanor had completely changed from five minutes ago. He seemed angry—*really* angry. Puzzled, Div rose to her feet. "Of course. We'll continue this conversation later, girls."

Hunter put his hand on Div's back and nudged her into the hallway, not gently. What was *wrong* with him? She had to resist the impulse to say a few choice words and storm off. Perhaps instead, she should cast a quick *cessabit*, to calm him down?

"What's up, Hunter?"

He held up his phone. "Would you like to explain this to me?"

Div leaned closer to take a look.

She almost stopped breathing.

It was a video. Of her and ShadowKnight in that conference room at WitchWorldCon. The quality was fuzzy, and the sound was barely audible, but it was clear she was pointing her lipstick-tube-wand at him. Binx and Iris were out of the frame.

Worst of all, Binx was yelling incantations at ShadowKnight, but because she wasn't visible, it sounded as though the magical words could be coming from Div.

"Huh. Weird. Where'd you get this?" she said innocently.

"It's all over social media. Colt saw it just now and sent it to me."

"What is this place? And who are these people?"

"What do you mean? That's you, isn't it?"

Div pretended to squint at the screen. *Quick, think of something.* "I guess that could be me? Hmm, maybe. You know, I didn't mention it to you before, because I respect how you feel about *Witchworld*. But I went to this gaming convention yesterday, in Seattle—my friend Binx practically begged me because her other friend who was supposed to drive her bailed at the last minute—and it turned out to be a *Witchworld* convention."

"*Witchworld*? You mean that pro-magic propaganda I told my sisters to stay away from?"

"It's not propaganda. It's just a silly game, like your mom said. And the convention was silly, too... just a bunch of gaming nerds spending a lot of money on autographs and posters and stuff. Anyway, there was this... I don't know, they call it a 'cosplaying competition'... cosplaying, as in costumes... happening, and Binx convinced me to dress up and participate. And this is probably me with some random cosplayer, although it's hard to tell for sure from the terrible video quality. In any case, it was all just pretend and playacting."

"Div." Hunter touched her chin and tipped her face up to meet his gaze. "Tell me the truth. Are you a witch?"

"Honestly, this is all just a—"

"Answer me!"

Panicked, Div took a step back from him; should she do a memory-erase or a time-reverse? But before she could decide, she saw over Hunter's shoulder that someone was coming toward them, shrouded in shadow.

"*Praetereo,*" the person called out softly. *"Rado."*

Div tried to hide her surprise. Who *was* that?

A second later, Hunter blinked and cleared his throat. He gazed down at Div with a confused expression. "Oh. Hey! I came up here to... I totally forgot. Sorry, too many all-nighters lately, studying for... anyway, I think I need to help put out extra chairs for the meeting. I'll see you down there in a few?"

Div forced a smile. "Yes, perfect."

Hunter kissed her quickly on the lips and then hurried past her toward the stairs. But Div was no longer interested in his movements. She craned her neck and peered down the hallway, wondering who had rescued her. Who in this house full of New Order members could possibly be casting spells?

The person stepped out of the shadows, wielding a wand.

"Hello, Div," Dr. Jessup said quietly.

Div gasped. Hunter's mom was a witch?

Not possible.

Maybe it was a trick? A trap to make Div confess to being a witch herself? Maybe Dr. Jessup had pretended to cast *praetereo* and *rado*, and maybe Hunter had pretended to lose his memory. The whole thing could be a setup.

Dr. Jessup motioned for Div to follow her into a nearby bedroom. Div had no choice but to obey and play along. Once inside, Dr. Jessup made sure they were alone, then closed the door. Her face was lined with tension. "*Calumnia.* And I expunged that video off the Internet just now, with *deleanta.* Div, I only have a minute, so I'll make this quick. The New Order meeting is about to begin downstairs, and as you know, I'm in charge of it."

Div nodded slowly.

"I know you saw Penelope's name in my journal. On Saturday, in my study. And incidentally, the letters O-N-E-G stand for her blood type. O-negative."

What. The. Hex.

"Are you aware of Callixta's descendant who posted that letter and the excerpts from her magic manual? You must be," Dr. Jessup went on.

Div crossed her arms over her chest and didn't answer.

"Well, I'm her. I'm Callixta's great-great-great-granddaughter."

This is insane. "You're lying."

"It's true. I can offer you proof."

"You're telling me that you're a witch *and* Crowe's great-great-great-granddaughter *and* the leader of the New Order," Div said incredulously.

"I had to do that in order to"—Dr. Jessup lowered her voice to a whisper—"in order to protect my daughters from my husband...and from my sons, too, now. You see, Cassie and Caitlin don't know it yet, but they both possess the power."

So I was right about the girls.

"I wasn't lucky like you and your friends. I didn't know about my true identity until I was a wife and a mom. By then, it was too late. I was worried that if I told Jared that I was a witch, he'd try to take the children away from me." Dr. Jessup smiled sadly. "You may find this hard to believe, but my husband wasn't always against witches. That happened over time. He made a lot of money at his business and fell in with a different crowd...a very rich crowd that was mainly interested in protecting their wealth and their power. They saw, and continue to see, witches as a threat to that."

"Why are you telling me all this?"

Dr. Jessup stood up a little straighter. "Because time is running out. I will explain more later, but...suffice it to say that things are about to get very, very bad. We witches need to organize and help each other starting immediately. Or it will be too late for all of us."

22

THE GIRL WITH THE ROSE PERFUME

Even the illusion of love can seem
better than no love at all.

(FROM *THE GOOD BOOK OF MAGIC AND MENTALISM*
BY CALLIXTA CROWE)

The Kai Rain Forest was a very different place at night. During the
school field trip, they'd had the benefit of daylight. Now, as they
drove past the sign that said CLOSED FROM DUSK TO DAWN, Ridley peered
out the passenger-side window and saw only darkness, punctuated by
occasional flashes of headlights winking ghostlike across the blur of trees
and dirt road.

And somewhere in the middle of all this was a witch-hunter from
another century.

"Yeah, so, does anyone else feel we should have waited until tomorrow because of the dark-and-scary factor?" Iris said nervously. She was in the back seat of Binx's Prius, sandwiched unhappily between Aysha and Torrence.

"Div's orders. Besides, we can't give him time to escape *again*." Binx white-knuckled the steering wheel and accelerated slightly.

"He might already be gone," Aysha pointed out.

"Nah," Binx replied. "I put a magical tracer on his IP location so I can keep tabs on the exact geographical coordinates of his sign-ins. Last I checked, he was here playing *Witchworld*. Because that's what psycho-gamer-rats like him do, right? Get in a few rounds of plunder and carnage in the kingdom of Vandervallis while plotting his next IRL witch murder? He hasn't done a counterspell on my tracer yet, which tells me that he's too busy stealing treasure from helpless goblin orphans to know that we're closing in on him."

"Fantastic," Torrence spoke up. "The tracer part, I mean...not the plunder and carnage and orphans part. What's our plan when we get there?"

"Maybe we should cast a *love* spell on him," Iris said sarcastically.

Over her shoulder, Ridley saw Torrence blush and turn away. *Love spell?*

"I'm assuming that's a joke. So what's our *real* plan?" Aysha prompted Binx.

"Well, as soon as we get to ShadowKnight's invisible fun house, which will hopefully be visible or semivisible to at least one of us, we're going to blast it and him with a group *claudo* spell, like, immediately. Does everyone know *claudo*? Imprisonment?"

There was a chorus of yeses.

"Good. With all of us on the spell, it'll be super-O.P."

Hmm. Ridley considered this. Binx's strategy *might* work since it would be five witches to one. On the other hand, perhaps he was monitoring them right now via a scrying bowl and lying in wait with an arsenal of deadly magical weapons. And what about his claim that Penelope was alive or almost alive, whatever that meant? That must have been a lie to throw them off... *right?* Honestly, this whole situation was beyond confusing and overwhelming. They had so much to tackle right now—ShadowKnight, the Antima and New Order, Greta's mom being in jail, and the mystery of Mrs. Feathers's death.

And Penelope. Always Penelope.

This is crazy. I have feelings for a dead girl.

Ridley began tapping out a melody on her leg, to distract herself. What was it, though? It wasn't the Kreisler or the Tchaikovsky or any of her other violin pieces; in fact, it sounded chaotic and random and almost arrhythmic. A tune out of nowhere. It reminded her of music from a pinball machine or a video game. Was it ShadowKnight–related?

Last night, she and Aunt Viola had taken a walk around the neighborhood, and Ridley had caught her up on the events at the Kato family's beach shack. In response, Aunt Viola had promised to communicate with her coven back in Cleveland so she could offer Ridley advice on how to proceed—which would be helpful on many fronts, including the fact that Aunt Viola and her friends were experts on interdimensional portals and time travel and such.

Ridley was so glad her aunt was here. And not just for her magical wisdom and mentorship, either. She made Ridley feel safe, accepted, and loved. Ridley wasn't sure yet if she would come out to her parents while her aunt was in town, or if she would wait a while. It was a *huge* decision, and she didn't want to rush things. In the meantime, though, she knew Aunt Viola would have her back, no matter what.

She brought her musical leg tapping to a close as Binx parked her Prius in the empty lot at the end of the dirt road. " 'K, I have ShadowKnight's IP location on my phone, so we can follow that," Binx announced as everyone got out. "And Ridley and Aysha...you can confirm my data with whatever you can remember about where that house was and/or where the photos were taken." She added, "I already cast a mega-protection spell on each of you—'cuz that's what coven leaders do, right?—so we're all set with that."

"Don't we need flashlights?" Torrence pointed out.

"We can do *malorna* with our wands and turn them into flashlights. We do this all the time—it's kind of an insider coven thing. I guess you had to be there, Torrence," Iris said, shrugging.

"Cool. I know *malorna*, so I'm all set."

"Oh. Okay, whatever."

Binx caught Ridley's eye and mouthed, *Love triangle.* Ridley nodded and attempted to smile, but she wasn't in the mood to dwell on love triangles at the moment, or anything having to do with love, for that matter.

After casting *malorna*, the five witches proceeded into the woods. Binx was at the front of the line, checking and tweaking her geolocating app every few seconds. As they walked, invisible creatures chirped and croaked and whirred in the darkness, becoming suddenly silent whenever the group passed by and then starting up again in their wake. The air smelled damp and loamy the smell of growth but also the smell of decay. Living things and dead things coexisting. Ridley found the juxtaposition at once unsettling and strangely comforting.

At one point, something far away uttered a shrill scream, and everyone jumped.

"B-bobcat?" Torrence guessed, looking this way and that.

"Or, could have been a red fox. Or a barn owl. Or a bunch of other wild animals, too," Aysha said.

After a few minutes, Binx stopped in her tracks and squinted at her screen, then pointed her phone toward a faint light through the trees. "*There.* I think? Ridley and Aysha, does this seem familiar?"

Aysha peered in that direction. "I'm not the one who had the magical mansion sighting, although this *does* look like the area where I took those pictures. Ridley?"

"Agreed."

"Okay, then. Everyone, have your wands ready. *Claudo*, on my mark," Binx instructed.

They continued down the path. The faint light grew brighter and brighter as they approached it.

They came to a halt when they were about thirty feet from the light. Ridley could just make out the shimmering suggestion of walls and windows and doors, like before...although *unlike* before, she couldn't see the interior at all.

"That's it," she whispered to the others.

"What's it? Because I don't see anything except for that light," Aysha said, craning her neck forward.

"Me neither," Torrence added.

"Ditto," Iris spoke up.

Binx frowned. "Same. That location's an exact match on my app, though. And he's still signed on to his *Witchworld* game."

Ridley was about to reply when the faint outlines of the house brightened and became sharper, more defined. Gradually, it morphed into an actual building.

"I can see it now!" Aysha exclaimed, and the others nodded.

Just then, the front door opened, and a figure stepped out.

ShadowKnight.

"Wands!" Binx hissed. "*Claudo* on three. One, two—"

"Don't!"

ShadowKnight raised his hands in a gesture of surrender. "Please, I just want to talk. Will you come inside? I'll stand down, I promise."

Inside the house, the five witches tied up ShadowKnight in a rocking chair via *ligibus*, not just with ropes but also with chains and steel cuffs around his wrists and ankles; Binx had insisted. The interior of his house was bizarre...a vast array of computer monitors, screens, gaming devices, pinball machines, and fantasy and anime collectibles combined with antique furniture, gas lamps, silver candelabras, and old-fashioned wallpaper with tiny birds and roses on it. Also, a painted Chinese screen sat to one side of the room. The place looked like a mash-up of a Victorian museum and a twenty-first-century gamer's paradise, which, granted, made a surreal kind of sense since ShadowKnight himself was from both eras. Ridley wondered about the velvet settee, the fireplace, and the mahogany table with the candles and herbs and gems that she'd seen on the field trip; perhaps they were in another part of the house?

Now Binx was pacing, touching an Xbox here and a VR headset there, picking up Pokémon figurines, checking out the *Witchworld* maps on the walls. The others perched on the edge of a couch, waiting on her orders, unsure of what to do next. Next to Ridley, Iris was gnawing on her thumbnail and humming quietly.

Binx eventually stopped and turned to ShadowKnight. Her face was hard with anger, but her eyes revealed something else, at least to Ridley, who knew her best friend well. Disappointment. Hurt. Vulnerability.

Her crush turned out to be a disaster, too.

"Tell me the truth. Did you use me to try to locate C-Squared's descendants? Is that how you found Penelope? Greta, too? Who *else* have you harvested for heart-fire so that you can keep your sorry self alive? And who's next on your hit list?"

"Mrs. Feathers and I found Penelope on our own, and Greta, too," ShadowKnight explained. "But I swear to you, Pokedragon...*Binx*... Penelope is the only one who I"—his voice caught in his throat—"and since then, I've been working hard to create synthetic heart-fire in my laboratory. In fact, I think I'm almost there."

"So you're a witch-hunter *and* a witch *and* a gamer *and* a mad scientist," Binx said sarcastically.

"I'm not a...I told you, I went to medical school."

"Oh, yeah, that's right. You're also a doctor. Plus, now you can add 'fraud' and 'murderer' to your résumé." Binx sighed in disgust and shook her head. "What about Libertas? Was that another lie, too?"

"No. I mean, yes, in a way. I don't have a group of witches' rights activists who are ready to march on Washington, DC. I wish I did, and maybe someday I will...." ShadowKnight hesitated. "Libertas does exist, though. It's the name of a super-spell I've been developing to defeat our enemies once and for all."

"'Our enemies'...you mean the Antima or New Order or whoever?" Aysha spoke up.

"Yes."

"How would this spell...this *super*-spell...work?" Torrence asked.

"It's complicated, and it's still in beta. I'm hoping to have it ready before President Ingraham signs 6-129A in a few weeks. In any case, I'm convinced this is what Callixta had in mind when she directed me to fulfill my prophecy. Witches—*we*—are under threat of extinction due to all the hatred and prejudice that's sweeping across our country right now. Like the Great Witch Purge, but much worse. I have a chance to stop it with Libertas and attain the freedom and respect that we all deserve. Which would lead to a—"

"What did you mean when you said that Penelope might still be alive?" Ridley blurted out before she could stop herself.

ShadowKnight stared at her. Ridley squeezed her fists. *Oh, hex... WHY did I ask him that? I'm not sure I want to know the answer.*

"I can show you, if you'll untie me from this chair. You can keep these things on my wrists." He indicated the steel cuffs.

Okay, so maybe I do *want to know the answer.*

Ridley glanced uncertainly at Binx. Binx nodded.

"Fine, but the five of us will have our wands trained on you at all times," Binx informed ShadowKnight coldly. "If you make the slightest wrong move, you are going to know a world of pain."

"Understood."

Binx twirled her wand at his restraints...all except for the ones on his wrists. *"Solvo!"*

The ropes and chains and cuffs disappeared. ShadowKnight stood up slowly and rolled his neck. "This way," he said, starting across the room. The others followed, wands out pointing at his back.

Binx fell into step beside Ridley and hooked arms. "Are you sure you're okay to see this? Whatever *this* is?" she whispered. "For all we know, he built a Penelope bot out of spare computer parts. Or designed a video game with her as the main character. I wasn't joking when I called him a mad scientist."

"It's okay. I'm just...I'm curious. Well, maybe 'curious' isn't the right word."

"No worries. I understand."

At the painted Chinese screen, ShadowKnight turned sideways and squeezed past it, then indicated for the others to do the same. The screen seemed to serve as a divider between two rooms that had no separating wall.

The area on the other side was dimly lit—just a few candles—and the air smelled faintly of roses. Blinking, Ridley could make out a settee in the middle of the room. The mahogany table and fireplace. *Everything from the field trip.*

She moved closer to the settee and peered tentatively over the back of it.

A girl was sleeping.

Penelope.

Ridley clapped her hand over her mouth and silent-screamed.

The others came up behind her. There was a collective gasp.

Binx marched up to ShadowKnight and touched her wand to his head. "Explain. *Now.* Is this some sort of illusion spell?"

"N-no. It's necromancy. I've been trying to bring her back."

Necromancy?

Ridley circled the settee, her steps faltering, and gaped at the still form of her friend. Her sister witch. Her crush. The rose scent was her perfume, and she wore the same pink dress with gold buttons that she'd been buried in. A strand of her honey-blond hair had fallen across her pale, pale face; Ridley had to resist the urge to reach over and push it back. She saw that Penelope's chest was rising up and down slowly. *Too* slowly...and unevenly, too. She was clearly breathing, though.

"Div's used necromancy spells to bring back insects, mice, small birds, stuff like that...but never a human," Aysha said, gazing in wonder at Penelope.

"Well, I still have a way to go with her," ShadowKnight explained. "This is my first time, so it's been a lot of trial and error. Anyway, I want to gather some different ingredients and write some new incantations, too. I also want to try this as a group spell. Maybe your two covens could join me? That would make, what? Nine of us, total?"

"Aren't there repercussions with necromancy spells? Like karmic side effects?" Torrence asked.

"I'm looking into that, too. I was hoping to use a spell to prevent or neutralize those," ShadowKnight replied.

Ridley twisted her hands. She tried to look away from Penelope, but she couldn't.

They're talking about her like she's a lab experiment.

But bringing her back might be a mad-scientist move worth trying.

"A group necromancy spell. We'll definitely need to run that by Div," Binx said.

"And Greta, too," Iris added. "She is *not* going to like this. I mean, she'll be glad that Penelope is alive or semi-alive or quasi-alive or whatever. Is there a difference between 'quasi' and 'semi'? Anyhoo, she doesn't like necromancy spells. She told me. She says they're against the natural order of things."

ShadowKnight shrugged. "Who's to say it's against the natural order of things, though? I mean, if you really believe that, then *all* magical intervention could be interpreted as being against nature, or at least against 'nature' as perceived and defined by humans."

"But we're talking about life and death here," Torrence said, frowning.

"Life and death are not simple, finite concepts. They're fluid."

ShadowKnight paused and glanced down at his cuffed wrists. "Listen. I know you guys don't trust me, and I don't blame you," he went on. "But believe me when I say that I want to right all wrongs, here and now. I want to fulfill my promise to Callixta and save our kind from extinction. I'm *this close* to doing that. And I want to undo the harm I did to your friend and bring her back. Will you let me do these things? And will you join me?"

Ridley gazed down at Penelope's sweet, beautiful face and breathed in her rose perfume.

Yes.

At that moment, she was willing to do just about anything to help ShadowKnight.

23

SLEEPLESS IN SORROW POINT

The work of magic must involve both careful
planning and carefree improvisation.

(FROM *THE GOOD BOOK OF MAGIC AND MENTALISM*
BY CALLIXTA CROWE)

On Tuesday after school, Greta hurried across the large courtyard in the middle of the Sorrow Point Hospital complex. She hadn't been to the hospital in years, not since Teo broke his arm falling from the maple tree in their backyard—he was a fan of high, forbidden branches—and she, Mama, and Papa had to drive him to the ER during a freak snowstorm. That night at home, he'd cried and cried, unable to fall sleep because of the pain, and neither Mama's guided breathing exercises nor Papa's rendition of "*sana, sana, colita de rana*" had helped...so Greta had made him a tea out of lavender, chamomile, lemon balm, and skullcap, and he'd finally drifted off, cocooned in the soft glow of his *T. Rex* nightlight.

Greta had made herself the same tea last night because she'd been too restless and agitated to sleep, even though her mother was back home safe and sound, thanks to Div and Mira. The tea hadn't worked, though, and neither had the spells she'd tried after that, *cessabit* and *somnia*. And so she'd stayed up, watching the minutes and hours tick by on her alarm clock, envying Gofflesby and Lovebug and the three kittens, Tessie and Meg and Alex, who were zonked out together in a furry puddle at the foot of the bed. At around four a.m., she'd poked them with her toes—her brain was no longer working properly at that point, and she was feeling exhausted and peevish—and they'd woken for only a few seconds before rearranging themselves into a new pile and falling right back to sleep.

Lovebug and the babies. Since bringing them home, she'd been trying to figure out if they were still linked to Mrs. Feathers somehow—maybe via a mystical pipeline from the dead to the living?—but so far, she'd found no evidence to support that. They seemed to be sweet, silly cats, grateful to have a home and food and one another, and also to be reunited with their old buddy Gofflesby. Who was *her* familiar and no one else's. Greta had considered gently probing Gofflesby's memories—via *conimentium*, a special mind-melding spell she'd been teaching herself—to find out what really happened to Mrs. Feathers. Maximus Hobbes aka ShadowKnight had apparently denied having anything to do with Mrs. Feathers's death, but there was a good chance he'd been lying. *He's Maximus Hobbes, for Goddess's sake.*

Although he *hadn't* been lying about Penelope. Iris, Ridley, Torrence, Binx, and Aysha had seen Penelope's undead body at Hobbes's mystery mansion in the forest. It—*she*—was breathing. The five witches had performed a series of scrying spells to verify that it wasn't an illusion.

It wasn't.

All of which explained Greta's never-ending insomnia.

Seriously, I may never sleep again.

A text popped up on her phone. It was Div, checking on her status:

Where are you?

Greta stopped and peered around the courtyard. She could just make out two people sitting together at a secluded picnic table, their heads bent close in conversation. Div and an older woman dressed in white hospital scrubs, her blond hair swept back in a neat ponytail.

Dr. Jessup. Callixta's descendant. *The* Descendant.

At least we have a super-witch on our side now.

Greta rushed over to join them. "Hi! Hello!"

Div and Dr. Jessup glanced up. Greta couldn't help but stare at the doctor. This was Callixta's descendant...her great-great-great-granddaughter. Of course, Greta was a descendant, too, which was why Hobbes had targeted her. But Greta was probably just one of many random descendants, whereas Dr. Jessup was a legend—albeit an unidentified one—in the witch community. She'd risked everything to try to bring witches together, to make them realize that they weren't alone.

"Greta, this is Dr. Jessup. Dr. Jessup, Greta," Div said.

Dr. Jessup smiled tersely and nodded. "Hello."

"Hello! It's an honor to...wow, I never expected to see—"

"Can we fan-girl some other time? We have a lot to discuss," Div cut in.

Blushing, Greta sat down on the bench. "I'm sorry."

"It's fine. We can get to know each other properly and have a more leisurely conversation later. And Greta, it's wonderful to meet another descendant," Dr. Jessup said. "But I have a few urgent matters that I need to discuss with the two of you, as the leaders of your respective covens."

Greta peered around. A few other hospital workers were hanging out on the other side of the courtyard; other than them, there was no one else around.

"It's fine. I've already cast *calumnia*. Also, I often take my breaks out here, so no one will be suspicious. If any of my colleagues asks me later about the two of you, which they won't, I'll explain that I happened to run into my son's girlfriend and her friend. That's another reason I wanted to keep this meeting small, so we don't call any unnecessary attention to ourselves." Dr. Jessup clasped her hands and leaned forward. "Several things. Needless to say, I happen to have all the inside knowledge about the workings of the Antima, now called the New Order, because of my position in the organization. *So.* As you know, there's going to be a New Order rally downtown tomorrow, at four o'clock. What you *don't* know, and what I just learned, is that some anti-witch agitators from out of town will be crashing the rally and making trouble—like harassing anyone who looks 'suspicious'—and that our local police intend to look the other way."

"What?" Greta cried out.

Div scowled but said nothing.

"They will certainly be targeting anyone whom they suspect to be witches or witch-sympathizers. But I'm wondering if they might also target other marginalized people, like BIPOC and queer people," Dr. Jessup went on. "In any case, they apparently plan to start on Main Street and spread outward to the side streets—Pleasant, Church, and so forth."

The Curious Cat is on Pleasant Street. Greta had to make sure that her father stayed safe. And of course, her witches. And everyone else.

"There's more, and it has to do with Maximus Hobbes," Dr. Jessup continued. "I've been searching for him ever since I learned that he was still alive. In fact, I owe you a big apology, Div, about the fundraiser for Neal Jahani at our house last month. I saw you in my study looking at my board of information about Hobbes—I had it under a *corium* spell, but obviously, you managed to see it nevertheless—and I was forced to cast *nescium* on you, to render you temporarily unconscious, and also *praetereo*. I'm very, very sorry."

"*Nescium*," Div repeated. "Hmmm. I'll have to learn that one for future use."

"Again, my apologies. Anyway, I got wind about Hobbes-slash-ShadowKnight's time-travel journey to the twenty-first century a few days ago, through my own channels"—Dr. Jessup turned to Greta—"and Div just told me that some of your coven members tracked down his physical location, his residence, just last night. And that he has Penelope with him and is attempting to bring her back to life."

"Greta isn't a big fan of necromancy," Div told Dr. Jessup.

"Neither was Callixta!" Greta said defensively.

"Actually, it turns out that my great-great-great-grandmother was more"—Dr. Jessup hesitated—"*complicated* than we'd all thought. That's a whole other conversation. What's important is that we know Shadow-Knight believes he's been tasked by Callixta to stop our extinction, which was prophesied to happen this year. It's not hard to imagine that prophecy coming to pass, with our current president and the new anti-witchcraft law he's working on, and of course the rise of the anti-magic movement."

"How does ShadowKnight intend to fix all this? What's his grand plan? One of my girls—Binx—said he's developing a 'super-spell' called Libertas," Div said.

"Yes. I've heard rumors of a super-spell, too. Do you and your witches have any information or even theories about what it will do?" Dr. Jessup asked.

"No. But Binx said that back when she thought he was just Shadow-Knight, and they were good friends, he used to talk about how witches should rule over humans rather than the other way around," Greta offered.

"Well, he does have a point," Div murmured under her breath.

Dr. Jessup gave Div a sharp look. "Do you really believe that?"

Div met Dr. Jessup's look. "You must admit, witches are much smarter and more powerful than humans. Also, humans don't care about anyone or anything but themselves. Look at all the damage they've done to the planet, to each other, and to us. If witches were in charge, we could fix all those wrongs."

Greta blinked. She absolutely didn't agree with Div on this. Witches should strive for equality, not world domination. Sometimes, though, Div made it very hard to argue with her. Like now. She was right that witches had superior intelligence and powers. She was also right that humans had inflicted a lot of harm throughout history, and were continuing to do so now. But still...

"The rally is a priority. Keeping everyone safe," Dr. Jessup went on. "As soon as we've dealt with that, we'll need to go to ShadowKnight's mansion and take care of things there, including Penelope and—" She stopped abruptly and glanced at a new message on her phone. Her expression fell. "Oh, *no!*"

"What is it?" Div asked, concerned.

"I just got a text from Jared. This is bad... *very* bad."

Greta could feel a bright red wave of panic emanating from Callixta's descendant. "What's wrong?"

"Jared says here that President Ingraham is in Seattle for an international trade conference. Apparently, he's decided to make a surprise appearance at our New Order rally tomorrow. This will surely rile up the anti-magic crowd and attract even *more* haters to the rally." Dr. Jessup took a deep breath. "And it looks as though the president has decided to move up the signing of 6-129A. It was supposed to take place at the end of the month, on the anniversary of Callixta's death, so I thought we had a few more weeks to strategize and defeat the bill. However, he's announced it will be happening in exactly twenty-four hours. In Sorrow Point. At the rally."

Greta and Div stared at each other in horror.

"That means—" Greta began.

"—that means that starting tomorrow, we will be in more danger than ever before. If the language in the new law is as severe as it's rumored to be, we may be talking about the Great Witch Purge of the twenty-first century," Dr. Jessup declared.

"I'm calling this emergency meeting to order," Div announced, lighting the last of the candles in the middle of the circle. "Thank you all for being here on such short notice."

Greta and the other witches—Iris, Ridley, Torrence, Binx, Mira, and Aysha—swiveled around to face Div. Greta hadn't been to Div's house in ages...not since eighth grade. Div's bedroom was different—it used to be all pink, but now it was all white, including the plush rug on which they sat and the sheer, gauzy canopy that cascaded over the queen-size bed. Greta wondered if Prada was around; Div usually liked to keep her familiar close.

"I still can't believe Colt's mom is *the* Descendant," Mira murmured, turning a piece of smoky quartz over in her palm. "I mean, who could have guessed *that*?"

Torrence nodded. "Right? I was just saying in my podcast that I thought it might be the president's daughter, Karine."

Everyone stared at him.

"Excuse me? You have a *podcast*?" Div demanded.

"Isn't that kind of, um, dangerous? Actually, a *lot* dangerous? I vote we kick him out of our coven immediately!" Iris said, raising her hand.

"No, no...it's not like that!" Torrence said hastily. "It's a brand-new project. I've written and recorded the first episode, but literally the *only* one who's heard it is my best friend back in Ocala Heights. His name is Mad Dog, and he's a witch, too." He added, "Someday when all this is over and witchcraft is legal again, I'll launch it. But for now, absolutely not."

"You will need to clear it with your coven leader before you launch. Is that understood? Now let's get back to business," Div snapped. "As you're all aware, there's going to be a massive Antima–New Order rally tomorrow in our town, and it turns out that the president of the United States is making a last-minute guest appearance. We need a plan. *Several* plans. First, we need a plan to prevent violence. Second, we need a plan to stop the president from signing that law. Likely we'll have to use magic to accomplish these things, which means that we also need a plan to evade the police and other authorities." She turned to Binx. "Will Shadow-Knight be attending the rally?"

"And on a related note, why did you guys just leave him at his house last night?" Greta asked worriedly. "Won't he try to escape again? What if he goes after other descendants, too?"

"He claimed the only reason he used *evanescetio* at the beach was because he thought we were going to kill him. Which, to be fair, was pretty spot-on," Binx replied, her eyes flashing. "He also claimed he's been working on a synthetic form of heart-fire. If that's true—and that's a *big* if—he won't need to target descendants anymore."

"About the rally...he said he needed to finish up his Libertas spell before the president signed that law," Aysha added. "Not sure if he knew about the rally then...I mean, *we* didn't even know about it until later, when you told us, Div...but I bet he knows now, and about the president, too."

Div considered this. "Did he describe what the Libertas spell does, will do, exactly?"

Iris raised her hand again. "He said it's a *good* spell and not one of his evil, apocalyptic spells. That it will help to quote-unquote 'liberate our kind.' He also said it's a solo spell and not a group spell. Was he telling us the whole truth and nothing but the truth, though? Maybe we should go back to his scary Scooby mystery mansion and *ligibus* him and interrogate him some more."

"No! We can't! He promised us he'd bring back Penelope, and I don't want anything to jeopardize that," Ridley spoke up.

"He wants us *all* to bring back Penelope, remember?" Aysha reminded her. "He specifically said that we should attempt a big group necromancy spell tomorrow at midnight. Because there's gonna be a dark moon."

Mira frowned. "You mean a *new* moon, right, Aysh?"

"Yeah, no, he specifically said 'dark.'"

"So, some witches believe the dark moon and the new moon to be one and the same, but others believe they're different, and that the dark moon directly precedes the new moon," Torrence explained. "A dark moon is completely invisible. A new moon can often show the faintest hint of a crescent. The dark moon is supposed to be a time of great power."

"Wow. I'd never heard that," Greta murmured. Torrence was full of surprises. In the very short time she'd known him, he'd revealed himself to be quite smart about interesting and sometimes obscure corners of the magic world.

It was strange, though. Over the weekend—at her father's bookstore, specifically—she'd been fairly certain she was developing a crush on him.

But today, those feelings were gone. Just...*gone*. Was she *that* fickle and mercurial with her affections? It was as though she'd had a love spell cast on her, then uncast. Which sounded crazy.

But now was not the time to be thinking about her love life, such as it was.

"Listen up. Here's what we should do regarding the rally," Div was saying to the circle. "Mira, you and I will stick with the Jessups, especially Dr. Jessup, so we can get as close to the main stage as possible. That's where the president will be, and there'll be a ton of security, obviously. Binx, can you get us a copy of the proposed new law? Dr. Jessup hasn't seen it, but she's heard it's *not* good."

"On it." Binx pulled out her phone and began pushing buttons. "Just a heads-up, anything president-related will have a bazillion fire walls, so it may take time."

"Understood. And let's all brainstorm about ways we might keep him from signing it," Div said. "Greta, Iris, Torrence, and Aysha—I need the four of you to work together to stop any harassment or violence against bystanders. Split up as necessary. Dr. Jessup will be working on that, too. And...Binx, can you contact ShadowKnight and ask him to meet you and Ridley at the rally? It would be good for the two of you to keep an eye on him."

Binx made a face. "Ugh, okay. I'm not sure if I can pull this off, though. He thinks I hate his guts."

"Pretend that you've forgiven him. Put on the charm," Div suggested. "Moving on. I'm almost done developing a new and improved version of *calumnia* that will hopefully shield our magical activities from the crowd, including and especially the authorities. It should be ready to deploy by the time the rally starts. It, too, will be in beta mode. But we'll have to roll with it because we'll require every ounce of protection, every advantage, that we can garner for ourselves. We can't take the enemy for granted. Dr. Jessup described this time as potentially being the Great Witch Purge of the twenty-first century, and I believe it. We *all* need to believe it."

Greta hugged her knees to her chest and tried to deep-breathe through the sense of dread that Div's words had inflicted on her. Inflicted on them all.

Tonight was going to be another sleepless night.

24

LIFE, LIBERTAS, AND THE PURSUIT OF HAPPINESS

The taking of a life is only justified
if the Goddess wills it.

(FROM *THE GOOD BOOK OF MAGIC AND MENTALISM*
BY CALLIXTA CROWE)

By three thirty on Wednesday, hundreds of New Order, Antima, or whatever they were calling themselves now, members had gathered at the park in downtown Sorrow Point, along with plenty of randoms. Adjusting his EarPods and nodding to the beat of a nonexistent song, ShadowKnight reached into his hoodie pocket—*good, still there*—and wondered if he should grab a quick slice before initiating the end of civilization. Ned's had decent pizza, and so did D'Angelo's around the corner.

Although "end of civilization" wasn't accurate. It was more like the end of *un*civilization, the start of a *real* new order.

Really, it was a major, major stroke of luck that President Ingraham had decided to make a surprise last-minute visit to the rally. Sure, it meant that downtown was now crawling with even more police officers and other security, and that it would be tricky getting anywhere near the main stage. It also meant that ShadowKnight would have to deploy Libertas before it was totally ready. The original plan had been to travel to Washington, DC, for the bill-signing ceremony on the 140th anniversary of Crowe's death. That would have given him enough time to perfect his super-spell.

It's ready enough, though. It has to be.

He glanced around, wondering if Binx or any of her witch friends were here yet. No sign of them. Last night, Binx had messaged him on their secure server, saying she wanted to meet up at the rally and talk. Unexpectedly, she had added an Excadrill icon. Was that a signal? Excadrill, a Gen 5 ground-and-steel-type Pokémon, had famously forgiven its former trainer after a major fallout. Maybe it was just wishful thinking on his part. Or maybe...

Later. They would talk later. Right now, he needed to concentrate on his very important task at hand, and he couldn't risk Binx and her covenmates stopping him.

"Excuse me."

A young woman was trying to maneuver around him on the narrow path that bisected the park, carrying a sign that said: HUMANS FIRST! As he stepped back to let her pass, she gave him an odd look—unfriendly, suspicious even. *I need to do more to blend in.* After she was gone, he slipped behind a nearby gazebo and whispered, "*Persequor.*" When he emerged again, he was holding the exact same sign.

Now the New Order members and other anti-witch protesters were starting to funnel onto Main Street and march toward City Hall, where the official rally kickoff was scheduled for four o'clock. The protesters chanted and moved forward as one with their obnoxious shoulder patches and signs. Some even carried pitchforks—was that a new prop? If so, what did it symbolize? And on the subject of symbols, the birdcage over the bonfire had been subtly tweaked to incorporate the letters *N* and *O* into the flames. *Yeah, we get it, people.* You're *in charge of burning the witches now.*

No matter. The New Order, and the persecution of his kind, would end today.

It was a *Witchworld* mod that had given him the idea for the super-spell. In the "WWW," aka "WitchWorldWar" variation, the rebel witches from Kasorkya were engaged in an epic battle against their mortal enemies, the elf clans of Dirrogh. To defeat the elves, the leader of the rebel witches came up with something called a W-move, which involved attaining an extra-rare W-stone from the undercaves of Glinore. The W-stone was used to megacharge a spell that specifically targeted the elves through the unique coat of arms design on their clothing, first sickening and then eventually killing them.

ShadowKnight had decided to create Libertas, his own version of a W-stone, out of hematite, angelite, and nanites. He planned to use his stone to strategically deliver a virus that he'd developed in his lab. The virus, which was highly lethal, would wipe out the worst of the witch haters within a hundred-mile radius…maybe even farther. He'd wired the W-stone with nanotechnology to seek out the image of the birdcage burning over the fire. Anyone wearing the arm patch, carrying the sign, or otherwise bearing the symbol, with or without the letters *N* and *O*, would be hit with the virus, fall sick, and die.

Including President Ingraham, who, according to the press, had recently begun sporting a black-and-gold lapel pin with the symbol.

That little fashion choice is going to cost you, dude.

ShadowKnight hoisted his sign high in the air and followed the masses down Main Street, moving his lips as though chanting with them. As he marched, he kept an eye out for Binx and her friends. Among the crowd, he noticed TV cameras and microphone booms. The media presence was going to be through the roof, which was perfect.

A scream. ShadowKnight did a 360, trying to locate the source. *There.* Just past the intersection on a side street—Pleasant Street—three New Order thugs were cornering an elderly man. One of them was pointing a pitchfork menacingly at his face. *What the...?* Meanwhile, a police officer was nearby, chatting and laughing on his phone and making zero effort to intervene. Were the authorities not even bothering to hide their anti-witch leanings?

Someone was going to have to put a stop to this nonsense. Shadow-Knight slowed his steps, closed his eyes, and murmured "*prohibere*" under his breath. *Nothing.* Perhaps he needed to be closer. He resumed walking toward the intersection—TV cameras were already gathering there, plus he spotted Greta and that witch who'd come to his house, Torrence, emerging from inside a bookstore, presumably to help the old man—and at the same time scrolled through his mental checklist for an alternative spell if necessary.

But before he could settle on one or reattempt *prohibere*, he saw a woman approaching the pitchfork-wielding thugs. Middle-aged, blond ponytail. The New Order shoulder patch was on her tweed Brooks Brothers blazer. She spoke to them quietly; they backed away from their victim and turned to listen. Curious, ShadowKnight cast *sentio* to try to hear their conversation.

"...on your side, however, we don't want to give our cause negative publicity," the woman was saying to the group.

They nodded and dispersed. *That* line of argument had done the trick? Avoiding negative publicity? He sensed, though, that there were more than persuasive words at work here.

"*Revelare*," he whispered.

Yes. That was it. That woman was a witch. And not just any witch, either, but an extremely advanced one. With *revelare*, he felt her power rippling from her like an energy wave. Who *was* she?

She was a New Order member...and she was also a witch? Like *him* in his witch-hunting days? Would Libertas be able to discriminate between a real witch hater and a witch posing as one... *if* she was posing? What if there were others like her?

Doubt seeped through his brain. He couldn't back out at this point, though. Maybe there would be a few casualties from Libertas, like the blond woman, but the cause was worth it. Hundreds of witch haters were here, now. And the president was due any minute.

No time like the present, right?

The woman, though. On an impulse, ShadowKnight cast a second *revelare* spell, to glean her identity.

Jessup. Dr. Jane Jessup.

Why did that name sound so familiar?

Oh, yeah. Binx and her friends were talking about the Jessups.

Dr. Jessup was checking her phone and peering around, so Shadow-Knight ducked into a bus shelter. On the glass panels, a dozen slick New Order posters partially covered homemade ads for garage sales and baby-sitters looking for work and Halloween pop-ups. When Dr. Jessup started in the direction of City Hall, he followed at a discreet distance. As they neared the main stage, the crowd became shoulder-to-shoulder, almost impassable.

Dr. Jessup went up to a roped-off area, where a barricade of police officers and a dozen men and women in black suits, likely the president's advance team or Secret Service detail, stood guard. ShadowKnight tried to remember if there had been Secret Service in his other life. Dr. Jessup spoke to one of the officers and was let through. On the other side were about a hundred New Order members, and beyond them, a dozen people rushing around on the main stage; they were setting up chairs, microphones, and American flags against a red-and-white backdrop that said HUMANS FIRST.

Humans first? Not for long.

ShadowKnight approached the same police officer Dr. Jessup had spoken to. "I'm with her," he said pleasantly, chin-nodding in her direction. "Dr. Jane Jessup. I'm her assistant."

The officer looked him up and down, then glanced at his sign. "Fine. Go on through."

"Thank you, sir." He hurried on before the officer could change his mind and resumed trailing after the doctor.

Where was President Ingraham, though? He was the *real* prey.

ShadowKnight closed his eyes briefly and willed himself to visualize the man's location. In his mind, he saw a line of armored black SUVs leaving the airport and heading for downtown.

Good. The president was likely a mere ten, fifteen minutes away. All ShadowKnight had to do was blend into the crowd—the VIP, close-to-the-main-stage crowd—and wait. He imagined Ingraham arriving, emerging from a black SUV, grinning and waving at his mindless, cheering fans...then ascending to the podium and launching into his bombastic speech before signing his terrible new law...

...or attempting to sign it, anyway. The second he lifted his pen in the air, with his Antima minions clapping and shouting and the TV cameras and cell phones rolling and recording, ShadowKnight would make his W-move and unleash Libertas. And liberate witches forever, fulfilling the prophecy.

Crowe was surely smiling down at him from wherever she was.

A familiar face. Two familiar faces. In the distance, Binx and her friend Ridley were heading in his direction, toward City Hall.

Ridley was carrying a HUMANS FIRST sign. Binx was carrying a sign with the New Order symbol.

ShadowKnight froze. The New Order symbol...that meant Libertas would target her, too.

Pokedragon, no!

25

WHAT'S PAST IS PROLOGUE

There are no spells for happy endings.
Not yet, anyway.

(FROM *THE GOOD BOOK OF MAGIC AND MENTALISM*
BY CALLIXTA CROWE)

\\ 'm burning this sign as soon as we're done here," Binx muttered as she and Ridley made their way toward City Hall. "I feel so gross carrying it, even if it is for super-important disguise purposes."

"I know exactly what you mean," Ridley replied. She cupped a hand over her eyes and scanned the crowd. Main Street was usually so chill—just teens and families strolling around and shopping and going to cafés—but at the moment, it felt more like a mosh pit under a gray October sky. A chilly breeze carried with it the deliciously salty-sweet smell of caramel corn from somewhere in the neighborhood—maybe the Candy Company, Harmony's favorite store? It was such a jarring disconnect against the backdrop of an Antima gathering.

"Do you see him?" she asked Binx.

"No. He's gotta be here *somewhere.* Seriously, we can't lose him again."

"I know. We won't."

The two girls continued in the direction of City Hall, pushing through the thickly packed rallygoers sporting their New Order patches and hate signs and pitchforks—were they protest symbols or weapons? She and Binx had been following ShadowKnight for the past half hour, losing him twice along the way but eventually finding him again. Now they'd lost him for a third time, and the rally was about to begin.

Last night, Binx had sent him a pretend-olive-branch message that Ridley helped her to compose, but he never responded. So at the moment, they were resorting to merely keeping tabs on him. Which they were doing only half-successfully.

They still didn't know what Libertas was, exactly. Was it benign, like an attitude-adjustment spell that would make everyone love one another? Or chaos-causing? Or something else altogether? Ridley was genuinely conflicted, and Binx didn't seem to have a clearer idea, either. On the one hand, she knew Binx wanted to believe Libertas was just a magical version of what she'd originally understood it to be—an activist group formed to protest peacefully and work for positive change. But on the other hand, they didn't trust ShadowKnight—perhaps he was out for blood?

Ridley's phone buzzed with a new text. It was from Iris:

Hello! It's Iris! FYI I'm with Aysha patrolling Church Street. I think Greta is still over on Pleasant Street. With Terrence or whatever his name is. How are you guys doing and have you heard from Div and Mira?

"It's Iris, with an update. Nothing urgent," Ridley explained to Binx. She then typed a reply to Iris, filling her in on everything and adding that Div and Mira were currently with Hunter and Colter and maybe their mom and Mira's dad, too, presumably near the main stage. She also reminded Iris that Div and Mira were totally incommunicado because they didn't want to blow their cover.

A few seconds, another text came in from Iris:

> Breaking news! Aysha heard someone say the president and his motorcade just arrived at City Hall.

Ohmigosh, it's starting. But before Ridley could relay Iris's message, Binx held up her phone, her eyes flashing excitedly. "Look!"

Ridley peered at the screen. It said:

> Ditch your sign ASAP. Dirrogh.

"Who sent this to you?" Ridley asked, confused.

"It's from ShadowKnight, finally! It just came through on our private server."

"O-kay. What does it mean, though? What's a 'dirrogh' or however you pronounce it?"

"You mean *where*. It's a location from a *Witchworld* mod. It's pronounced *deer-ogg*."

"O-kay," Ridley repeated. "Why is he texting 'Dirrogh' to you? And why does he want you to ditch your sign? Do you think this has anything to do with Libertas?"

Binx lifted her gaze and frowned at her sign, which bore the New Order logo with the letters *N* and *O* snaking through the flames. "I have noooo idea. He must realize the sign's just a prop to blend in, right? Plus, didn't we see him with a sign, too?"

"Well, technically I don't think he was carrying a New Order sign. I think he was carrying the 'humans first' one, like me."

"Same difference." Binx furrowed her brows. "Why did he write 'Dirrogh,' though? Obviously he's talking about the elf clans of Dirrogh. They were—lemme try to remember—yeah, they were the sworn enemies of the Kasorkya rebel witches. They had like a hundred-year war going on. In fact, that mod was called 'WitchWorldWar.'"

"Can you write him back and ask him to translate? Oh, but first, I was just about to tell you . . . Iris said the president's arrived."

"*What?* Oh, *hex!*" Binx exclaimed, pocketing her phone. "Okay, think, think, think. What should we do now?"

"*Calumnia,*" Ridley murmured. It was the third time she'd evoked it in the past ten minutes, and it was probably not even necessary, because Div had cast her advanced *calumnia* prototype on all of them. *Calm down, Stone.* "I think we should stick to Div's orders. She and Mira are covering the president angle and working on a way to keep him from signing the bill, right? Iris, Aysha, Greta, and Torrence are still patrolling and making sure no one's getting hurt. You and I need to focus on ShadowKnight. Can you trace his current location through your private server with your, you know, geolocating, um, *shortcut?* Or is that not a thing?"

"Yeah, of course it's a thing. Smart!"

As Binx went to work on the spell, Ridley slid her backpack off her shoulders and reached inside to make sure Paganini was still there. Named after the nineteenth-century violin virtuoso Niccolò Paganini, this was her wand, and she'd enchanted it to look like a bow. She'd been keeping it hidden away in her closet lately, per Greta's orders—and Div's, too—that the two covens leave their magical items at home.

Ridley had brought Paganini here today, though, in case she needed to draw on stronger powers. Or rather, in case she needed a tool to help intensify her own inner powers.

What was ShadowKnight up to?

Ridley knew they had to stop him if he was here to harm the anti-witch protesters and the president; they might be the enemy, but violence wasn't the answer. Still, they needed him to help bring Penelope back. If Ridley and Binx and their respective covens crossed him, would they be forever closing that door? Would Ridley lose Penelope to death twice?

A loud cheer. Past a heavily guarded rope barricade in front of City Hall, President David Ingraham was ascending the main stage and waving to the crowd. Even from a distance, Ridley could see his expression—smugness and superiority masked by fake humility and friendliness. He wore a navy suit, white shirt, and bright red tie.

Ridley elbowed Binx, who was poring over something on her phone. "There's the president!"

"I know, I know! I think I figured out ShadowKnight's location. He's"—Binx pointed to the far end of the roped-off area—"over there, I think, next to that family wearing those disgusting New Order T-shirts."

"Excellent! Let's go!"

Binx grabbed her arm. "Wait! I may have figured out something else, and it's not good."

"What?"

"I looked it up. The elves of Dirrogh. They were defeated—no, more like massacred—by the rebel witches of Kasorkya. The witches invented something called a W-move that delivered a deadly virus. This virus targeted the elves and only the elves."

Ridley didn't like where this was going. "Yes...*and*?"

"And I'm guessing that's what Libertas is. I think ShadowKnight came up with a W-move that will deliver a deadly virus, probably to all the New Order followers here. Or maybe even all the humans."

"Oh my god!"

"Exactly. We need to stop him, like, *now*. And we won't be able to do it alone."

"Reinforcements," Ridley agreed, and started texting.

"—and I'm pleased to announce that I will be signing the historic new law, Title 6, Section 129A, before you today," President Ingraham was saying to the crowd. "But first, let me tell you about some of its highlights...."

"We're running out of time," Ridley whispered to the others.

She was hiding in an alley between the public library and the bank, along with Binx and the eight other witches. She and Binx had summoned Iris, Greta, Torrence, and Aysha on an emergency ASAP basis. Div and Mira had joined them, too, along with Dr. Jessup; the three of them had managed to slip away from the rest of the Jessups and Mr. Jahani temporarily during the president's speech, saying that they had to take care of a possible media disaster that was unfolding nearby. The surprise tenth witch was Aunt Viola, who'd appeared suddenly by Ridley's side just minutes ago. "I had a vision you needed me," she had explained with a small smile.

After evoking *calumnia* again for no good reason, Ridley had made lightning-fast introductions, not mentioning to her aunt that Dr. Jessup was Callixta Crowe's famous descendant. There would be opportunities for that conversation later...assuming they all survived the rally.

Which was a big assumption.

"Listen up, everyone. I suggest we cast a group *prohibere tempus* spell to begin with," Dr. Jessup said, her voice steady and matter-of-fact as though she were talking her medical team through a surgery. "We can create a bubble of protection around ourselves with *obice*, then *prohibere tempus* will freeze time outside the bubble for about sixty seconds. During those sixty seconds, the president won't be able to sign his bill, and ShadowKnight won't be able to deploy Libertas. It'll buy us time."

"What happens after the sixty seconds, though?" Aysha pointed out. "The president's still gonna sign his bill, and ShadowKnight's still gonna set off his deadly video game weapon, and the haters, if any of them survive, are still gonna hate us."

"May I add my two cents to this discussion?" Aunt Viola spoke up. "Ridley's been keeping me updated over the past few days. She mentioned that Callixta Crowe sent Maximus Hobbes into our dimension through a portal, which means that the portal likely still exists. Which also means that we can send him back where he came from. Or I can, anyway... I specialize in interdimensional work."

Dr. Jessup quirked an eyebrow. "That's a fantastic idea! That still leaves the problem of the president's bill, though. Not to mention the anti-witch forces in general."

Iris turned to Binx. "Hey, fellow *Witchworld*er... didn't you say that ShadowKnight's using a W-move to distribute his virus? Like the rebel witches did in that nasty, ugly war between them and the elves of Dirrogh, although maybe the elves deserved it because of their campaign to permanently destroy the ecology of Kasorkya and make the witchdom a barren wasteland?"

Binx nodded. "Yes."

"Wellllll... if he's using a W-move, that means he's carrying around a W-stone, amiright? What if we steal the W-stone from him before he deploys it and before we time-blast him back to the nineteenth century?

We could then change up the stone by replacing the deadly virus with a spell or some other magical remedy that makes everyone stop hating witches. Including the president. Sorry, let me rephrase...that makes everyone, *including* the president, stop hating witches. And then, *bam!* We'll be like the rebel witches except instead of killing everyone, we'll be spreading love and harmony and world peace."

Silence.

"Hmm. That's not a terrible idea," Div said after a moment.

Iris beamed. "Wow, thank you! That's a huge compliment, coming from you!"

"I could use *mobilus* to steal the W-stone," Aysha offered. She was an expert at telekinesis.

Div nodded. "Excellent."

"What would we replace the virus with, though? Does anyone know a spell that would make everyone stop hating witches?" Greta asked.

"Actually, I've been working on something like that," Torrence volunteered. "It's a combination of a love potion"—he glanced briefly at Iris, blushing—"and a version of *praetereo* that might make people forget that witches and humans are enemies."

Why is Torrence blushing? Ridley wondered.

"*Blech.*" Iris crossed her arms over her chest and glared at Torrence. Then her expression softened slightly. "Fine, okay. Actually, that sounds kind of genius."

Torrence exhaled. "Oh, good."

"Thank you, Iris and Torrence and Aysha. Let's try it." Dr. Jessup craned her neck and glanced in the direction of the main stage. "The president is wrapping up his speech. If we're going to do *obice* and *prohibere tempus*, it's now or never. Everyone join hands, please."

The other witches obeyed.

"*Obice*," Dr. Jessup called out.

"*Obice*," the others echoed.

Ridley watched as an invisible barrier rose from the ground and encircled their small group, like an iridescent bubble. "Cool!"

"You can see that, Ridley?" Dr. Jessup said, surprised.

"Yes."

"Interesting. That's a rare power."

"My niece is very powerful," Aunt Viola said proudly.

"Apparently. Now, everyone . . . close your eyes and focus on the idea of freezing time. And repeat after me. *Prohibere tempus . . .*"

"*Prohibere tempus.*"

Ridley felt an almost seismic energy shudder through her and the other witches. She squeezed Aunt Viola's and Binx's hands a little harder.

"You can open your eyes now," she heard Dr. Jessup say.

Ridley did so, and practically fainted from shock and wonder at the sight that greeted her. Outside of the *obice* bubble, the world had become completely still. The president and the crowd had frozen in place. Nearby, a robin was suspended in air, midflight.

"We have sixty seconds before the time spell expires. . . . Aysha, please cast *mobilus* now," Dr. Jessup ordered her.

Aysha complied.

"We can't undo the bubble and take physical possession of the W-stone until the sixty seconds are up. Otherwise, we'll all be frozen in time, too," Dr. Jessup went on. "At exactly the sixty-second mark, Iris and Torrence? You'll need to grab the W-stone and make your magical alterations to it. Then, deploy the stone as fast as you can, or at least before ShadowKnight figures out what happened and resorts to a plan B."

"What about the virus, though? It's inside the W-stone, right? How do we get it out of there without having it make *us* sick?" Mira asked.

Binx gasped. "*That's* why he told me to ditch my New Order sign! The rebel witches designed their virus to target the Dirroghian elves' coat of arms. Guys, ShadowKnight must have designed his virus to target the New Order symbol!" She stopped and scanned the circle of faces. "Dr. Jessup, you need to get rid of your shoulder patch. I'm going to get rid of my sign. Anyone else have the symbol anywhere on their bodies?"

Everyone shook their heads. Binx and Dr. Jessup hastily dispensed with their symbols using *praetervolo*.

"I managed to locate ShadowKnight's W-stone and summon it. It should be here as soon as the time freeze ends," Aysha said.

"Well done, Aysha." Dr. Jessup peered at her watch, her expression hardening. "The sixty seconds are up in three…two…one…*obice converso!*"

The iridescent bubble protecting the ten of them vanished, just as a small, shiny purple object flew through the air toward them. Iris caught the W-stone, and she and Torrence began working on it immediately, their heads bent close together. Beyond, the robin resumed its flight. The president resumed his speech. The crowd resumed its clapping and cheering. And at the edge of the crowd, ShadowKnight was digging frantically through his pockets.

"Aunt Viola, is the portal ready?" Ridley asked nervously.

"I need another minute, darling girl," Aunt Viola replied. She waved her hands in the air and muttered under her breath.

Just then, ShadowKnight pivoted back and forth, scanning the crowd. Eventually, he turned, his gaze locked onto the alleyway where Ridley and the others stood. He dropped his HUMANS FIRST sign and began running toward them, his face radiating fury.

"Aunt Viola?" Ridley nudged.

"Let me help you," Dr. Jessup said to Viola. "The rest of you…can you slow him down, please?"

"I can do that," Div replied, stepping forward. *"Modero!"*

Her spell had its desired effect, and ShadowKnight's steps faltered to a walk. But then his lips moved, and he began running again. Obviously, he had some sort of counterspell.

"We think we've got it!" Torrence said, holding up the W-stone.

"It's my supreme honor to sign this bill before you today," the president was saying on the main stage. He picked up a pen and held it over a black binder.

"Deploy it . . . now!" Dr. Jessup commanded.

Torrence handed the stone to Iris. "You should do the honors."

"W-stone, *go!*" Iris shouted, flinging it toward the crowd.

The purple stone fell to the ground and burst into flames, or rather, a massive cloud of energy. Soon, the cloud broke into slender silver threads that flew, sizzling and sparking through the air. They sought out and landed on all the New Order symbols—on shoulder patches, on T-shirts, on signs.

And on the president's lapel.

Ridley held her breath. Would this crazy plan work? Or would it fail miserably, and they would all be arrested on the spot?

The president looked stunned for a moment. And then he gazed at the pen in his hand and at the black binder. He set down the pen and closed the binder.

"As I was saying, it's time for a change," he announced. "It's time to heal the divisions between humans and witches. We must learn to coexist."

There was cheering and clapping.

"*Yessss!*" someone screamed. Ridley realized it was her.

ShadowKnight stopped in his tracks and turned to listen to the president's words. He fell to his knees, shaking his head.

"The portal is open!" Aunt Viola exclaimed. "Let's send Mr. Hobbes back to his time."

An image of Penelope flashed through Ridley's head. Her sweet smile, her warm brown eyes. *We'll bring her back somehow, with or without ShadowKnight.*

"*Reditus?*" Dr. Jessup asked Viola.

"Yes. *Reditus.* Why don't we all cast it?"

The ten witches joined hands again and invoked the time-travel spell together. Ridley watched, fascinated and a little terrified, too, as a hole opened up in the sky and ShadowKnight's body began to glow.

He reached his arm out toward Binx, his eyes wide and frightened.

"Pokedragon, no! Please don't!"

Ridley felt her best friend's hand twitch and momentarily slip away.

Then slip back into Ridley's grasp again.

"*Reditus,*" Binx repeated, her voice steady.

"*Pokedragon!*"

With one last cry, ShadowKnight disappeared into the portal.

EPILOGUE

I t was strange being in ShadowKnight's house without him. As the other witches set up for the necromancy ritual, Binx walked slowly around the dimly lit room and trailed her fingers lightly across the equipment. Keyboards. Monitors. Consoles. VR headsets. All of it covered by an almost invisible layer of dust. How Maximus Hobbes had transported from the nineteenth century and morphed himself into a young twenty-first-century tech savant was beyond her comprehension. And it hadn't been an act, either. Binx knew a gaming addict when she saw one, and he'd definitely been a gaming addict.

Was he *still*, though? What happened to people when they time-traveled? Did ShadowKnight revert to his Hobbes identity when he landed in 1877...*if* he landed in 1877? Or was he still ShadowKnight, with all his newfound, circa 2017 knowledge and passions, trapped in an era without computers or video games or even access to electricity?

Was he even alive? His first journey through time had practically killed him, which was why the horrific heart-fire business had been necessary. Well, not "necessary," exactly, because was ShadowKnight's role in the prophecy ultimately essential to save witches from extinction? Was *everything* that had already happened by definition essential, since how can one unbake the cake of the present back into its original ingredients? Had C-Squared known in advance how all this would play out?

Binx chuckled and rolled her eyes. Now she was just being silly and random and philosophical, which wasn't like her. Although it was better than dwelling. Dwelling on recent events would only suck up all her physical, mental, emotional, and magical energy more than it already had.

You should have been honest with me, ShadowKnight.

She would eventually have come around to accepting his dark past. She could have handled the "I used to be a witch-hunter" detail. What she *couldn't* handle was the "I'm going to release a deadly virus to kill our enemies" part. Mass murder was fine in games, but definitely not IRL.

Luckily, Torrence and Iris's alteration of the W-stone, infused with the love potion and *praetereo* hybrid, seemed to have had the desired effect. At the rally, President Ingraham had pivoted from anti-magic to pro-tolerance, ripped up his proposed new law, and promised to draft yet another version that would ensure civil rights for witches. The rallygoers had looked momentarily confused, but the W-stone had affected them, too, because they'd listened to the president's words without protest. Some had even applauded. The work was just beginning, of course. The W-stone had touched only President Ingraham and a small number of his supporters. There were many, many others whose minds had yet to be changed. But having the president on the right side of the issue was huge progress. And already, footage from the rally had gone viral via the news and on social media. It would just be a matter of time before the New Order, and the rest of the Antima, fractured and folded for good.

Guess Div will have to settle for equality, not witch superiority. So will I. But for now, that seems like a good—no, great—outcome.

A photo caught Binx's attention. A headshot—was it a nondigital selfie? It was the size of a trading card, nestled in a metal bowl full of controllers and cables.

Binx picked up the photo and squinted...and gasped. Was that *her*? No, it was a young woman who resembled her, except that her hair was long and black and pulled back in a knot, not short and streaked with purple, and she wore a high-necked, old-fashioned-looking blouse, not a BLUE ANGEL PUPPY HEART T-shirt.

Who was this woman? Was she some sort of time-traveling version of herself? A nineteenth-century Binx Akari Kato?

"Binx? Over here, please. We're almost ready to get started."

Div was calling out to her. Binx slipped the photo into her pocket—she would solve this mystery later, maybe using her new magical facial-recognition app—and joined the others. They were standing solemnly in a large circle: Div, Aysha, Mira, Ridley, Greta, Iris, Torrence, Dr. Jessup, and Aunt Viola.

And in the center of the circle was Penelope, lying on the floor on a bed of pink rose petals. Next to her, thirteen candles flickered over a careful arrangement of bloodstone, black onyx, mugwort, and wolfsbane. ShadowKnight had promised to lead the necromancy ritual tonight at midnight during the fleeting dark moon phase with the help of the two covens. He was no longer available, obviously, and so Dr. Jessup and Ridley's aunt had stepped up with some of C-Squared's notes on the ritual. According to Dr. Jessup, C-Squared had explored necromancy and other dark arts in the years before her death. She hadn't been only about the love and light. Or rather, her concept of love and light had been very fluid and out of the box.

Fluid and out of the box...that was Binx's style of witchcraft, too. She had a newfound appreciation for C-Squared.

Dr. Jessup laid down a crystal vial of dark red liquid among the magical gems and plants. "This is Penelope's blood. We had a sample at the hospital from an old lab test," she explained.

"*Ew!* That is...I mean...*ew* thought of everything!" Iris said with a nervous laugh.

"Jane, what about Penelope's diary? Did you manage to find it?" Aunt Viola asked.

"Yes. With the help of Aysha's excellent *mobilus* skills."

"Thanks, Dr. Jessup!" Aysha reached into her backpack, pulled out a small leather-bound notebook, and placed it next to the other items.

"Oh, I almost forgot!" Binx reached into her own backpack and pulled out her Pokémon deck. She quickly found Xerneas, the black-and-blue stag with four pairs of antlers.

"Is it okay if I add this?" she asked the circle. "It's a powerful Gen Six Legendary that can help us with the ritual. It has the ability to extend eternal life—not that we're going for immortality here, but resurrection is *kind* of the same thing, right? Anyway, we'll know it's working when Xerneas's antlers turn seven different colors."

"Yes, of course, Binx," Dr. Jessup said, nodding. She turned to the others. "Before we begin, there's something very important that I need to share with you all. Viola and I discussed it on the way here, and it's the only solution we can come up with."

"The only solution to what?" Greta asked curiously.

"To our time-line conundrum. If our ritual is successful, we'll be bringing Penelope back to life when her family, her friends, her teachers, and others know her to be dead. Which would create an impossible situation. So Viola and I have decided to cast a series of spells that will make people forget what happened to Penelope on that fateful day... including Penelope herself. In her mind and in everyone else's minds, she spent the last month in the hospital with a bad head injury because she was thrown by a horse. She's now recovered and returning to her normal life."

"Wow, that's even more sci-fi and time-bendy than the portal thingama-whosit!" Iris burst out. "Well, maybe not. Maybe it's a tie."

"*We'll* know the truth, though, right? The ten of us in this room?" Mira said, sweeping her arm in a circle.

"Unfortunately, no," Dr. Jessup replied. "This amnesia, this rewriting of Penelope's history, will include all of us. These spells Viola and I will be using... they don't discriminate or make exceptions. It's all or nothing. After this is over, none of us will remember what happened to Penelope. In addition, all traces of her death, including her gravestone, the coroner's report, and so forth, will have disappeared."

Ridley stared at Dr. Jessup. "Does that mean..." Her voice trembled slightly. "Will I at least remember her from *before* she died? And will she remember me?"

Aunt Viola squeezed Ridley's arm. "We're not sure, darling girl. But this is the only way. And if the two of you are meant to remember each other, then you will remember each other. That, I'm sure of."

Ridley sniffed and brushed away a tear. "Yes. Okay. The most important thing is that she come back to us, right?"

Binx reached over and hugged Ridley. Her heart ached for her best friend.

Greta and Iris joined in on the hug, and so did everyone else. Even Div. *The ice queen* does *have a softer side, after all.*

After a long moment—*Are the two covens really hugging? The two covens are really hugging!*—Binx felt Ridley extract herself.

"I'm ready, guys. Let's do this," Ridley said, brushing away a few more tears.

The ten witches joined hands and began the ritual.

On the floor, Xerneas's many antlers shimmered with rainbow colors.

*   *   *

Iris's Krush date was a bust. As soon as they walked into the homecoming dance, Yasmine left Iris to fend for herself.

"Oh, there's my friend Taro! I'm gonna go talk to him. I'll see you later?"

"Um…" Iris stammered.

"Hey, Taro!" Yasmine fluttered her fingers and hurried away. *Argh.* Iris pulled her phone out of her vintage cat-shaped purse and pretend-scrolled furiously. *She's not my type, anyway. I don't really like girls who are cute and smart and funny and into gaming.*

The Sorrow Point High gymnasium had been transformed into a glamorous gold-and-pink party space with streamers, balloons, and silk flowers. The theme of the dance was "Moonlight and Magic," so there were paper moons and stars dangling from the ceiling, plus each table was decorated with craft wands, potion bottles filled with colored sand, and votive candles floating in crystal water bowls. It was all so romantic. Now, if only Iris had someone to be romantic *with.*

She didn't even have anyone to hang with in a not-romantic way. Binx, Div, Aysha, and Mira were present, but busily working the event as committee members. Which was surreal, in Iris's humble opinion. Aside from Mira, who was super-friendly and gregarious, that coven generally tended to avoid humanity and social interaction. At the moment, Mira and Div were at the refreshments table with a girl named Hannah, ladling lime-green punch into paper cups and handing out cupcakes. Aysha and Binx were out front with another girl named Hannah, overseeing the guest list and check-in process.

Where was Ridley, though? And Greta? *Especially* Greta?

"Hey, Iris!"

Torrence approached her, holding two cups of green punch. He offered her one.

✦ 267 ✦

"It's not a love potion, is it?" Iris said sarcastically.

"No. But it's not a *reverse* love potion, either."

"Ha."

"I still feel bad about that."

"Yeah. Me too."

The day after WitchWorldCon, when Iris had discovered that Torrence gave Greta a love-potion tea, she'd quickly concocted a successful counter potion to negate its effects. Then, a few days later, Iris had whipped up *another* love-potion tea, this time to make Greta like *her*, not Torrence. But before serving it to Greta, she'd changed her mind. She couldn't keep trying to win over her crush by using sneaky shortcuts and intrusive magical shenanigans; she wanted Greta to like her for real.

Last week, after a coven meeting, Iris and Torrence had spoken to Greta privately and confessed about giving her the love-potion tea and anti-love-potion tea. Greta, being the sweetest, kindest, most amazing person in the world, had forgiven them. She'd also indicated that as much as she liked them both as friends, she was still getting over someone...she hadn't said who.

Which meant that Iris was *not* doing so well in the "Greta liking her for real" department. Or in the Krush department. Maybe she was destined to be single forever.

"So are you having fun?" Torrence asked Iris as he leaned against a twinkle-light-covered column. "Are you a school-dance person?"

He looked kind of handsome in his retro black tux, but Iris wasn't about to tell him that. "No, times two. Are you?"

"Same. You're here with a date, though, right? I saw you walk in together."

"Technically, she's an *ex*-date. Our relationship lasted, like, twenty minutes."

"I'm sorry."

"Yeah, well . . . I'm not having a lot of luck lately with the dating thing."

"Same. I was doing just fine, but then this O.P. witch came along and foiled my plot."

"What a coincidence! The same thing happened to me!"

They grinned at each other.

"Iris! Torrence!"

Iris turned in the direction of the familiar voice. It was Ridley, hurrying toward them from the check-in area. She wore a rose-gold velvet dress and strappy red heels, and her hair and face shimmered with a subtle glitter effect.

"Ohmigosh, you look *a-mazing*!" Iris gushed.

"Thanks! My mom and Aunt Viola took me shopping. Can I hang out with the two of you? I just got here, and I'm already feeling kind of . . . I don't know . . . discombobulated. And my date, Binx, is busy at the moment."

"Of course. Here, let me get you some punch. Be back in a sec," Torrence said.

Once they were alone, Iris hooked her arm through Ridley's. "Is everything okay?"

"Well, yes. Except, remember that girl I told you all I liked? She's here with someone. I think he might even be her boyfriend. *Ugh.*" Ridley chin-nodded toward the center of the floor. A beautiful blond girl was slow-dancing with a cute blond guy.

Iris scrunched up her face, trying to remember their names. "She's Penelope something, right? And who's he? He looks familiar."

"She's Penelope Hart, and he's Colter Jessup. I think he used to date Mira in middle school?"

"Oh, wow. Yeah, I met him before. He helped me find my homeroom the first day of school because I got lost. Because that's what I do. Get lost. He's nice."

Ridley rolled her eyes. "Oh, great. He's hot *and* he's nice. I don't have a chance!"

The song came to a close. Penelope peeled away from Colter and started toward the restrooms. Colter joined a small group that was sitting at a nearby table. Then Penelope's gaze flicked in Ridley and Iris's direction. She smiled and wandered over.

"Ohmigosh, ohmigosh, ohmigosh," Ridley murmured under her breath.

"It's gonna be okay. Hello! Greetings!" Iris called out to Penelope.

"Hi! You're Iris, right? I love your kitty purse!" Penelope complimented her.

"Thanks! I bought it at this vintage store in New York City. Well, technically, my sister Kedren bought it, but I'm taking care of it while she's away at college."

"Cool." Penelope beamed at Ridley. "And you're in my history class. Ridley, right? Ridley Stone?"

Ridley rainbow-waved. "Hi! Yup, I'm Ridley. Soooo... how did you do on the quiz yesterday?"

"I'm not sure. I forgot to read that chapter, plus I didn't get much sleep the night before because I was up late rewatching *The Matrix* for the gazillionth time."

Ridley gasped. "You like *The Matrix*? That's my favorite movie."

"Really? Me too. What's your favorite scene?"

"Hmm, excellent question. Maybe the scene where Neo is mystically dodging all those bullets? No, actually, it's the scene where he meets Trinity."

"Ohmigosh, me too!"

"Also, there is no spoon."

"There is no spoon!"

The two girls giggled.

"So I'm just going to…and I'll be back in a…" Iris waved awkwardly and slipped away. Ridley and Penelope had an obvious connection. Maybe there was a chance for Ridley, after all? And maybe she, Iris, could help fate by distracting Colter for a bit? But as she headed toward his table, a startling—no, totally *shocking*—sight caught her attention.

Two girls were kissing behind a twinkle-light column, their slender arms wrapped around each other. Platinum-white hair mingling with long auburn curls.

Div and Greta.

Iris's jaw dropped practically to the floor. A moment later, Torrence appeared at her side.

"Did you know?" he whispered.

"Um…no? *Gah!* Did you?"

"No. Although…"

"Although what?"

"Greta and I had an interesting conversation recently. About how hard it can be to get over someone from your past. I thought she was speaking hypothetically, but…I guess not?"

"I guess not."

Iris stood there staring for a long moment, her heart hammering in her chest, wondering if there was a not-caring spell she could cast. Maybe that reverse-love-potion tea would be helpful right about now? On the other hand, things could always change. With time. If Ridley could feel hopeful about *her* crush, then Iris could feel hopeful about hers.

The song ended with a bittersweet-sounding chord. Greta broke away from Div and hurried away, looking flustered. Div shrugged and checked her phone. *Hmm, maybe things are already changing?*

"Hey, Torrence! Random idea. Let's make Greta jealous," Iris said suddenly.

Torrence blinked. "How?"

"We could dance together?"

"You...and me?"

"Yup. Unless you don't know how to dance? Actually, to be perfectly honest—what does that phrase mean, anyway? How do you be *imperfectly* honest? Anyhoo, I'm like the worst dancer in the world." Iris demonstrated a quick flossing move. "See?"

"I'm probably worse than you. Although I might have a spell to turn us into Fred Astaire and Ginger Rogers."

"Who?"

"You've never seen *Top Hat*? Or *Flying Down to Rio*? What is wrong with you?"

"What is wrong with *you*?"

The two witches continued joking and pretend-bickering as they strolled onto the dance floor. Homecoming was turning out to be not-horrible, after all. Sure, Iris had caught her soulmate making out with another girl. But it could be a one-off, and besides, there might be other soulmate candidates to consider. It was a big world.

In the meantime, life was definitely looking up. The New Order and Antima were pretty much history. Witchcraft was finally going to become legal. Any and all witches and suspected witches had been freed from jail, including Ms. O'Shea and her coven; in fact, the history sub was here at the dance, chaperoning.

And speaking of covens...*their* two covens had been talking about merging into one. Iris wasn't sure how she felt about that, especially given this new-old Greta-and-Div drama. But at least the seven of them—now eight, including Torrence—weren't mortal enemies anymore. Together, and with Dr. Jessup and Aunt Viola and lots of other wise witches to guide them, their powers would surely grow.

The next song started to play. "Spell or no spell?" Torrence asked Iris.

"No spell? I think I'm cool with making a total fool of myself," Iris said, flossing again.

LOVE-POTION TEA

From "The Tea with Torrence"

This is a love-potion tea for you to drink so you can invite love into your life.

INGREDIENTS:

* A small handful of fresh rose petals or rosebuds (or both!). Make sure the roses have not been sprayed with pesticides, and in any case, rinse them with cold water and dry on paper towels.

* A small handful of fresh mint leaves

* Two cinnamon sticks

* A slice of fresh ginger

* Honey or sugar to sweeten (optional)

* Bottled spring water (optional)

DIRECTIONS:

1. Boil water, preferably spring water. You can buy bottles of spring water at the grocery store.

2. Put rose petals and/or rosebuds in a teapot. Add mint leaves, cinnamon sticks, and ginger.

3. Pour boiling water into the teapot, cover, and let steep for ten to fifteen minutes.

4. While waiting for the tea to steep, infuse it with your intention. Close your eyes and think about a specific person, or type of person, your heart desires. Speak positive affirmations, like: "I deserve love" and "My heart is open to someone who will love me and treat me with kindness and respect."

5. When your tea is ready, pour into your favorite cup and sweeten with honey or sugar if you'd like.

6. Sit in your favorite spot and sip slowly. Chant the words:

I drink this fragrant tea
To bring my love to me.

ACKNOWLEDGMENTS

We want to thank all the people who helped bring this book into the world:

Alex Hightower, for her thoughtful editing, boundless energy, and support.

The rest of our amazing team at Little, Brown Books for Young Readers, including Megan Tingley, Angelie Yap, Annie McDonnell, Katie Boni, Christie Michel, Stefanie Hoffman, Shanese Mullins, and Savannah Kennelly.

Sweeney Boo, for her gorgeous, gorgeous cover art.

Mollie Glick, for always being there for us.

Vimbai Ushe, Lola Bellier, and Cesar Parreño, for their indispensable help.

★

Nancy would also like to thank:

Paige, my magical coauthor.

Clara Ohlin, my creative partner and inspiration.

My other young readers, Cecily Molnar, Vivian Molnar, and Anaya Truth Rickford.

Chris Reynolds, for answering my millions of literary Qs.

My cats, who sat on my lap (and on my keyboard) during long writing sprints and provided warmth, love, and endless amusing shenanigans.

My family. You are everything.

✶

Paige would also like to thank:

Nancy, the one person who I couldn't have done this book without.

My family of witches: Mum, Gamma, Greta, and Scout. Your magic inspires me every day.

All the magic makers out there. Thank you for sharing your gifts with the world!

✶

And last but not least, we want to thank our wonderful readers. You complete the circle of our storytelling, and for that, we are so honored and grateful.

PAIGE MCKENZIE is a millennial hyphenate: a *New York Times* bestselling author, YouTuber, actor, influencer, creator, artist, and producer. Her first book series, The Haunting of Sunshine Girl, was on the *New York Times* bestseller list for over a month. Paige is constantly creating. Her Etsy shop, the Homebody Guild, is full of her art and designs, and she is always updating it with new creations. Paige also interacts daily with her Sunshiners across a variety of media including YouTube (where she has over half a million subscribers), Facebook, Twitter, and Instagram. Paige is a founding member of Coat Tale Productions, with three projects in active development. Paige lives in Portland, Oregon, with the love of her life, a seven-pound Chihuahua named Pongo.

NANCY OHLIN was born in Tokyo and moved to the United States when she was nine. She has written, ghostwritten, or collaborated on over one hundred fiction and nonfiction books for children, teens, and adults, including her YA novels *Consent, Beauty,* and *Always, Forever.* Most recently, she collaborated with Paige on *The Sacrifice of Sunshine Girl,* Quvenzhané Wallis on the Shai and Emmie chapter book series, and Chloe Lukasiak on her memoir *Girl on Pointe: Chloe's Guide to Taking on the World.* Nancy lives in Ithaca, New York, with her family and many cats. She invites you to learn more at nancyohlin.com and on Twitter (@nancyohlin).